THE UNKNOWN EDGE

A Mystical Journey of Self-Discovery

Rajita Kulkarni Bagga

Sri Sri Publications Trust

The Unknown Edge

by Rajita Kulkarni Bagga

1st Edition 2020
2nd Reprint 2021

Published by:

THE ART OF LIVING

Sri Sri Publications Trust
The Art of Living International Centre, Gate No-7,
21st KM, Kanakapura Road, Udaypura, Bangalore – 560082
Email: info@srisripublications.com
Website: www.artoflivingshop.com
Toll Free 1800-258-8888

ISBN: 9788194293385

Layout by: Sri Sri Publications Trust

Printed in India by: Thomson Press India Ltd.

To

Mummy and Papa

for giving me

the gift of life

and

To

Gurudev

for teaching me

the art of living

Contents

Foreword

The inward journey leads you to a path Unknown,

Unknown to the limited mind,

Unexplored by those who do not seek to look beyond.

This is a path only for the brave-hearted,

Where concepts are shattered,

Only to reveal newer and higher dimensions of existence,

Where bonds are broken,

Only to reconnect at a level

Where there are no demands, only love.

Who knows what you may find

When you step beyond "The Unknown Edge",

In that secret place, the sacred cave.

The One who knows, will never tell you

But He will hold your hand and take you

To the goal

That is You.

***

The inward journey of a seeker is the most exciting ride where the Master reveals beauty after beauty, wisdom deeper than wisdom, love beyond love. It is a magical and mystical ride. I am sure you will enjoy going on this journey with Rajita. She is one of the best storytellers I have known. She takes you effortlessly to another world with her fluid and vibrant play of words. And as you move through the pages you are sure to get a glimpse of how the Master carries you through every stage of your life without you even knowing it. His ways are unknown but his Grace is the certainty in life.

Smt. Bhanumathi Narasimhan

Director,

Women Empowerment & Child Care Programmes,

The Art of Living Foundation

Acknowledgements

Writing this book has been a deeply transformative process for me. I have bared my soul in these pages. I would like to acknowledge the extraordinary debt I owe to all those who lent their wholehearted and encouraging support throughout this journey.

First and foremost, Pujya Gurudev Sri Sri Ravi Shankarji. For making my very existence an incredible celebration of wisdom, love and service. For moulding me into the person I am today, and for gently, yet surely, guiding and mentoring me to discover and know the right purpose of my life.

Bhanu Didi, the wind beneath my wings. My go-to person for inspiration, and for help in any crisis. You make me soar, and ground me too. You inspire me to be a better person. Lasting gratitude for your unconditional acceptance, joy and laughter. Narasimhan Anna, our Rock of Gibraltar, a stellar example of commitment to service, knowledge and relationships.

Ajay, my husband, beloved ally, my strong and most dependable pillar of support. My best friend, my kindest, most considerate life partner, force multiplier, toughest critic and biggest fan. The one person in the world who prioritises me over everything else. Because of you, I dream, I fly, I am free.

My parents, and my brother, Shantanu, the oldest and longest chords of my soul. My solid anchors. My heart. Shubhangi and little Ishaan, for flooding our beings with the joy of living.

My in-laws–Ma, Suman Bua, BP Bakshi Maamu, Sanjay Bhaiya, Priya Bhabhi, Suparna Didi, Susheel Bhaiya, Rupa, Benoit, Manu, Loveleen, and their families. The Baggas, Sharmas, Bakshis, Sawhneys, Raoulxs. All my amazing nephews and nieces living all over the world. Your love and warmth have nurtured me all through.

My maternal and paternal families–grandparents, aunts, uncles, first cousins, second cousins, sisters and brothers-in-law, my extended family–Kulkarnis, Ghatges, Deshpandes, Pant Balekundris, Kalkundris, Ghaligis, Khots, Inamdars, Deshmukhs and more. You have made me.

My school and college friends, Mukta, Medha, Krithika, Meena, Rajlakshmi, Marie Lou, Sujata, Sudha. We take off from where we leave. Four decades and counting. My MBA friends–all thirty of you. We learned the ropes of life together and that holds us as tightly today as three decades ago.

My cheer squad of Ajay Tejasvi, Arvind Varchaswi, Madhushri, Srividya, Mayank bhai, Zaver bhai, Kedar and Chinky. Always loving, always supportive. Indebted.

My wonderful Citibank family, and you are a thousand easily. My Citi bosses–Harit Talwar, Anjali Raina, the late Ashoke Dutt, and P S Jayakumar. You have had the most inspiring influence on my professional excellence.

My endearing Atlantis family, Surita, Sangita, Mridulla, Shalini, Meenal, Sujata Murali, Puja, Samya and Nandita. My support system and go-to friends.

My Sri Sri University family, Dr Singh, Dr Sharma, Lambaji, all Deans, Heads of Departments, faculty members, team members–every day, you achieve the impossible. The Global Board of Governors–your encouragement and support propel me ahead.

The incredible WFEB and TLEX global teams–you expand me and make the world my oyster, especially, Cristoph Glaser, Ewald Poeran, Lillian Nouwen, Madhu Rao, Dr Sanjay Pradhan, Jo Leinen, Alojz Peterle and Dr Herman De Croo.

My co-trustees in all the Art of Living Trusts. All the school Principals, teachers and teams of SSRVM and VVMVP schools. You are shaping the future of the world.

All Art of Living teachers in India, and around the world–for me you are the epitomes of living for a higher purpose and service to society.

All my friends in the Bangalore Ashram–your presence is an oasis of peace and tranquillity. It is the same for all Art of Living Ashrams in the world. You are my many homes. All the Art of Living Swamijis and Rishijis–thanks for the gift of being your friend and sister. You are the glowing light of knowledge for the world.

All my current and past Sri Sri University students, and all TLEX and Art of Living participants. Your joy is my happiness.

My home staff–you keep the ship sailing. Many many thanks.

Each one of you who helped me to pick myself up during moments of doubt and despair, while I was writing this book, I owe you. My thanks to the young team of designers, digital marketers, editors and film makers at Sri Sri Publications Trust, for all the hard work behind the scenes.

Nakul Dhawan, for being the glue from the beginning to the end. For spending hours and hours with me, being a brutal editor and the frank, true voice in my head.

Archana Pai Kulkarni, whose stellar talent smoothed the rough edges of the book, fixed its flaws, added zing to the words and made the book what it is now.

James Mathew, for going through the book with a fine-toothed comb.

My beta readers, for the time, reviews and inputs, especially, Nivedita, Bharathi, Mickey, Samhitha, Sunitha and Aman. Cirstin for spending time on the photographs. Thank you from the bottom of my heart.

Each one of you who said to me, 'We are waiting for your book,' and you, dear readers, who are reading it now.

My story is as good as the eyes that behold it.

Rajita Kulkarni Bagga
Mumbai,
December, 2020.

1
I Want To Live

We were at Masala Kraft, the Indian restaurant of the Taj Mahal Palace Hotel, in Mumbai. The occasion was a traditional Indian dinner to host our friend Erika Mann, a German Member of the European Parliament (MEP), visiting India with a delegation of twenty-one other MEPs. While poring over the ornate menu card to decide what to eat, thunderous sounds of a series of explosions jolted us. The unexpected ear-splitting boom quickened my breath, and I closed my eyes to collect myself. I assumed that guests at one of the weddings that I had seen listed at the reception were bursting crackers. But, my husband Ajay had already leapt from his seat, and was shutting the doors of the restaurant. I was shocked. What was happening? This was so uncharacteristic of Ajay. Even the hostess serving our table seemed taken aback by his behaviour. Just then, we heard another series of deafening blasts. These were definitely not crackers. I had never heard such terrifying sounds before. Erika looked panic-stricken. 'These are gunshots. From large guns,' she whispered, her face ashen.

How could it be? I was in complete disbelief. This was a five-star hotel. In Mumbai. Why would anyone bring guns here? In an instant, the restaurant burst into frenetic activity. The captains, the chefs, and the serving staff dashed frantically to push some tables against the door to hold it shut. The stunned silence that had descended after the boom, was now broken, as the guests regained their composure and began talking amongst themselves, and on their phones. Everyone wanted to know what was happening. My hands had gone cold and my body was shaking. I glanced at Erika. She looked distraught. What if she was right?

I heard someone say, 'Gang war.' Everybody was talking at the same time. A gang war in a hotel? This was unheard of. Not in this city! Then the Head Chef announced that all of us were to leave our tables and gather in the kitchen.

By then, Ajay had returned to the table. His phone rang. I could make out that it was from a close friend. He wanted to confirm that we were safe at home. When Ajay told him that we were at the Taj, he was incredulous. He confirmed what had begun to dawn on us. The Taj was under siege. Terrorists had attacked it! This was a nightmare unfolding. How could this be happening to us? How could this be happening at all?

Ajay began checking his BlackBerry for some more news updates when he saw an email from a Singaporean colleague staying at the Trident Hotel informing him that the hotel had been attacked by terrorists. She and their other colleagues staying there had received strict instructions to stay locked inside their rooms and not open the doors to anyone.

This was insane. How could both The Taj and the Trident be under attack? Someone shouted, 'The Oberoi has also been attacked.' What was happening, really? News was pouring in from all quarters. If I had an iota of hope that this was not true, that these were just ugly rumours, our friends' messages confirmed that deadly armed terrorists were indeed prowling right outside the door. I looked at Ajay. Our eyes reflected the same questions: Who was attacking us? From where had they come? Why?

Soon, the attacks intensified. We could hear sporadic explosions, while the loud gunshot sounds continued. It must have been around 11.30 pm when the staff asked us to vacate the restaurant. They were guiding people to use an internal staircase to go down to the basement which linked the old Taj building to the new wing. In spite of the mayhem, the staff lined the passage, their faces composed, as they bravely ushered us to the business club, The Chambers, on the first floor.

More news started coming in about indiscriminate shooting at Leopold Café, at Mumbai's train terminus (CST), and at The Oberoi too—the other places where the terrorists had struck. There was news of a bomb explosion near the airport. Someone sobbed, 'Everyone has been killed at Kandahar.' When I heard that, my heart went thud. Kandahar, our favourite Peshawari restaurant at The Oberoi, was where we had originally planned to dine with Erika that night! It was clear that the terrorists had attacked several important locations in Mumbai. We were at one of the major ones.

In no time, the sounds outside the door grew louder. The smell of smoke became stronger by the minute. We could all choke soon. Someone suggested that we jump out of the balcony. Someone else said we could slide down using the curtains. Everyone was on the phone, calling family or receiving calls. I was getting frantic. Emotions were running high, fear levels had peaked, anxiety was writ large on each face, and the atmosphere was thick with uncertainty. We had no idea about what lay ahead.

***

At 2 am, Sanjay Bhaiya (Ajay's elder brother) called from London. He was appalled that an Indian politician was giving an interview to a TV channel about being safe inside The Chambers along with many other CEOs and business leaders. This was outrageous! How could anyone be so foolish? To let out information of our whereabouts was nothing short of suicidal! The man was nixing all chances of us getting out alive, by literally leading the terrorists to us. What was the television channel thinking? How dare they broadcast such information and put so many lives at risk! Not only was it unethical, it was also downright mindless and dangerous. It could make things worse for us. And it did!

Soon, we heard the sounds of the guns very close. On the floor above us, we sensed what seemed like grenade explosions. Never had I foreseen this horrific time. Nothing had prepared me for this eventuality. Never had I imagined that I would find death staring me in the face in this bloodcurdling manner. One bullet, one bomb, and we would be gone!

Around the same time, the hotel staff announced that we would be evacuated from The Chambers. I was quite surprised because from all the sounds we were hearing, it appeared that the terrorists were close to our location. How would the staff keep us safe while we escaped?

No one had any information. We had no choice but to follow their instructions.

It is during calamities that the true face of our humanity comes to the fore. As soon as the staff made the announcement, some men scampered to get ahead. A few elderly ladies in wedding finery and high heels began rushing towards the exit. Everyone wanted out at once. Ajay held me back, signalling to me to let the elders go ahead. Just as we were reaching the main doorway, we heard thunderous sounds of gunshots. Thack thack thack thack!

It was as though the shots were being fired right next to us. The sounds made those scrambling to get out break into a mad stampede. No one knew where to go. Everybody started running helter-skelter. Some stumbled, some fell, and others dashed ahead. The crème de la crème of Mumbai were doing their best to hang on to their lives.

Somehow we dashed into one of the smaller meeting rooms. Someone pulled in one of the maintenance staff of the hotel. He had a couple of bullets in his stomach. The air was now thick with fear. The gunshots continued. Smoke started creeping in through the gap between the door and the floor, making breathing difficult. Every time a bomb went off, the building shuddered, and tremors ran up our bodies. Around twenty of us were huddled in the small room, hiding from the terrorists. Death was just a few metres away.

My heart was beating so fast I thought it would jump out. Ajay put his arms around me to console me. A zillion questions assailed me. Why were we stuck here?

What wrong had we done to go through this? When would we get out? Would we? What if we didn't? Is this it?

My stomach began growling. I was hungry and scared stiff. We were both bone tired. We hadn't rested in the last twenty-four hours. I wanted the horror to end that very moment. But, it was nowhere close to abating. Resigned to our fate, I slumped lower behind the table that was hiding us, when my phone screen began flashing.

It was Gurudev! I wanted to speak to him, but couldn't say a word. In a gentle, loving voice, he said, 'Jai Gurudev, Rajita.' My already racing heart leapt up to my mouth and a bolt of energy rushed up my spine. I sat upright from my crouching position, fumbling to hold the phone in a way so that Ajay too could hear. Though exhausted, I sensed my racing pulse, my quickened breath, and my beating heart—signs of life. In that instant, my whole being was uplifted. Tears started rolling down my cheeks. I wanted to live. How I wanted to live!

How had I come to this state? Here I was with Ajay, up against an unknown enemy. I would never have incorporated this ordeal into the script of my life, but the unexpected had occurred. This was real. Did I get mired in this carnage by myself or was I guided? When did it all begin? Was everything destined to be the way it turned out? How are we supposed to look at our lives? Is life a series of random events? Or does everything happen for a reason? And if there is a reason, are we supposed to look for it, and how? How much of our life is destined, and how much, free will?

When you ponder over such questions, you go back to where it all began and how. You live life as it unfolds, but when you reminisce, another perspective emerges. Retrospection makes you richer with the wisdom of age and more detached with the passage of time. Nuances that you missed start revealing themselves. You begin to connect the scattered dots in the big picture, like a jigsaw puzzle coming together effortlessly, each piece finding its perfect place. When you face death, life takes on new meaning.

2

Growing Up Overnight

I was born on August 9, in Mumbai. That day is commemorated as August Kranti Diwas, the day that the Quit India Movement was launched in 1942, also in Mumbai. Since it was a watershed moment in India's freedom movement (Kranti is the Hindi word for revolution), Papa wanted to name me Kranti! He often joked that I have lived up to that name in any case. Another suggestion was Rupa, but my Maushis (my mother's sisters) suggested Rajita. They were backed by Ajji, my paternal grandmother, a Sanskrit scholar, who was among the eldest in the family. She announced that Rajita meant 'one who is radiant, pure and brilliant' and hers was the last word on the matter.

Mummy, Shama, worked at the Reserve Bank of India and Papa, Dattatray, was an engineer with the Maharashtra State Electricity Board. As a young working couple starting their life in Mumbai, they were not too keen on leaving their first born in the care of a stranger. Those were not the days of sophisticated day-care facilities. Having no other choice, during the week, Mummy left me in the care of her parents, Auua and Ajja, who lived forty kilometres away from our home in Bandra's Kala Nagar area, a middle and upper middle-class neighbourhood of Mumbai. Ajja, my grandfather, was a veterinary surgeon who had retired as the Head of the prestigious Government Veterinary College, Mumbai. Auua was a homemaker.

Everyone fussed over me throughout the week. Usha Maushi, Shobha Maushi and Ashok Maama, Mummy's younger and unmarried siblings, doted on me. I was chubby, with a flock of thick and curly hair, a live doll. Every Friday, Mummy picked me up on her way back from office and I spent the weekend with my parents in our home.

When my parents dropped me off every week, I cried my lungs out. How agonising it must have been for Mummy to be away from her little baby as well. There was also the pressure of a demanding job, and of running the household that added to the pain of being separated from me in my most formative years. She was the only working woman from her generation in our extended family.

Papa stood by Mummy throughout. They had a remarkable relationship based on mutual trust and respect, and an unspoken understanding. What they were together was more important than what they were individually. It was a partnership of dignified equality. Theirs was a quieter world, with no noise of social and digital media, and more human connections. Yet it was a world where they had to work very hard to make their mark and start their new life.

After a few years, my parents moved to another home. I no longer had the comfort of spending the day with my grandparents. This added to my parents' stress. They found a day-care centre run by an elderly lady, where they dropped me off every morning and picked me up after work in the evening.

By then, I had begun talking. Every day, while handing over my little toy bag to me and my lunch box to the aunty at the day-care centre, Mummy told me she would arrive to pick me up at 6.30 pm. During the day, I had a set schedule—some colouring work, playing with the other kids, fixed meal and snack times, and a nap in the afternoon. By 5 pm, my eyes would start checking the clock. I couldn't read the time, but I knew instinctively that it was time for Mummy to arrive. If she was even a few minutes late, I burst out crying and wouldn't stop till I saw her. With the uncertainty of work pressure, the train delays and traffic, she could not always reach on time. But I was only four, and did not understand this. I felt abandoned and forgotten. I dreaded spending any more time in the day-care centre than I had to.

Aunty at the day-care centre, my Maushis, Auua-Ajja, Ashok Maama, the neighbouring aunties—a loving community of people nurtured me. It does take a village to raise a child.

***

I was five when my brother Shantanu was born. Ajji named him after King Shantanu, the mighty King of Hastinapura and the great grandfather of the Pandavas. It was also the name of my Atya (aunt) Shashi's father-in-law, who was well-respected in the country as a pioneer of industry, Shantanurao Kirloskar. Little Shantanu was adorable. His hair was thick and curly like mine. His cheeks dimpled deeply every time he smiled. We celebrated his birth in a big way. I could not pronounce Shantanu's name, so I called him Titu. Ajji and Ajoba, my father's parents, moved in to stay with us in Mumbai, which was a big support for Mummy and Papa.

Though I was a child myself, I cared for Shantanu like a grown-up. While Mummy was at work, I helped Ajji feed Titu, clean him, put him to bed, and do little things for him. He stuck to me all the time. His innocent infringement on my freedom irritated me a lot, because none of my other friends' siblings tagged along with them.

However different they may be from each other, the bond that siblings share is the first experience we have of friendship, partnership and teamwork. It either propels us towards a lifelong bond of love and security or becomes an in-house breeding ground for competition, one-upmanship and heartburn. A lot depends on the upbringing and the atmosphere at home. For me, Shantanu was a gift. As my constant playmate, he enriched my childhood while also maturing me into the older, responsible sister. I also experienced the joy of loving and learned important lessons in sharing and accountability.

Once, Shantanu and I were playing on the swing in the garden. Some children were playing in the sandpit. Intermittently, we were also playing a game of Frisbee, and as I was running after it to catch it, I heard a piercing scream. When I turned back, I saw a child lying on the ground near the swing, apparently hit by it. I looked around to check if Shantanu was safe but could not see him. In panic, the seven-year-old-me rushed to search for my brother in the crowd that had quickly gathered. To my horror, I discovered that the injured child was Shantanu! His little hands were cupping an injury on his forehead from which blood was oozing out like an open tap. I had never seen such an injury or so much blood, and had no idea what to do. I looked around for help but there were only children there. Shantanu was screaming in pain. Seeing him cry, some children also began crying. I felt guilty for not watching over him while he played. How could I have enjoyed my own game instead of keeping an eye on him? But, I had hardly been away. Things had changed in a fraction of a second. How could I have let this happen at all?

The blood kept gushing out of the wound. It was evening and I knew Mummy-Papa would be back from work soon. But Shantanu was in so much pain that I couldn't waste any time at all. Instinctively, I removed the floral shirt he was wearing and covered his injury with it. Picking him up in my arms, I ran as fast as I could to a friend's apartment in a nearby building, and banged on the door. I was too short to reach the doorbell. My friend's mother opened the door and immediately rushed out to take us to our common family doctor. Noticing that I was struggling to carry Shantanu, she offered to hold him but he refused to go to her and clung to me harder than before. As he lay on my lap in the autorickshaw, my green frock got completely soaked with his blood. Shantanu's injury was so deep it had to be sutured with five stitches. As the doctor treated him, his tiny fingers clutched my small hands. The sight of the doctor working on him, his shrieking cries, the smell of the blood and medicines, are still vivid in my memory.

Mummy-Papa returned from office just as we reached home. The moment I saw them, I burst into unstoppable tears. I could now go back to being a child. One look at us in that state and Mummy-Papa rushed forward and hugged us tight. Mummy broke down. This was any working mother's worst nightmare; something you can never predict or prepare for. The thought of whether she should continue working must have crossed her mind a thousand times. Later that night, as they put us to bed, I overheard her discuss this with Papa and Ajji. Both of them prevailed upon her to not let one incident make her give up her career. Their non-judgmental and unbiased encouragement and support ensured that she continued working.

***

Ajji stayed with us all through our growing-up years. She hailed from an illustrious family, the only sister of her four brothers, each of them as accomplished as the other. The Ghatge brothers are well known for their contributions to the fields of aviation, industry and academics. Ajji married into the household of the Kulkarnis, who had a big *sansthan* at Vantmur near Belgaum. Between Ajji and her four brothers, my father's generation had about thirty-five cousins. Ajoba's too was a large extended family, with many brothers and sisters. About forty-five people stayed in the big *Wada* (a traditional mansion house) on the banks of the Ghataprabha River. Every day was a celebration because it was either someone's birthday or anniversary or a festival. The atmosphere was one of abundance, and the relationships in our family are close-knit even now.

Ajji would tell us fascinating tales about that time. She carried the pain that their whole big Wada had got submerged when the Hidkal dam was built in the 1970s.

Almost every summer, Ajji would take me and Shantanu to Kolhapur. Her two brothers, Vasantrao Ghatge and Sakharamrao Ghatge lived there with their families. I loved listening to Ajji catching up with her sisters-in-law. These were normal conversations about the family. They would talk and I would listen and absorb. With every conversation, my knowledge about my family's roots increased. My uncles and aunts were over-achievers—engineers, scientists, architects, lawyers, barristers, doctors, politicians. Most of them had broken through geographical and cultural barriers, propounding ideas that were way ahead of their time. It was wonderful to be a part of such a large family. I too wanted to be somewhat of an achiever to live up to our family name. This pushed me to work really hard, and is probably why doing just enough has never been enough for me.

After Ajoba passed away, Ajji dedicated herself to the pursuit of knowledge. She never missed a day of reading the Bhagavad Gita. She taught Shantanu and me the fifteenth chapter and we would chant it every day. Ajji observed the Bhagavat Saptah (a seven-day continuous reading of the Srimad Bhagavatam) every year. During the *saptah*, the rules were strict. Ajji would sit down on her asana (a seat) in the morning at 10 am and get up only twice in the day before winding up at 5 pm, once for lunch, and once, to use the washroom. The rest of the time, she sat tall, and read the Srimad Bhagavatam aloud. One year, Mummy-Papa had invited all the members of our family and some friends and neighbours to participate in the saptah. Different people arrived at different times to listen to Ajji's reading. Ajji's recitation would carry the intonation and emotion of the story she was reading, with her voice rising and falling, and following the twists and turns in the story. One afternoon, I had invited all my school friends to listen to Ajji. No one else's grandmother performed this unusual feat. I felt quite special.

As we sat down in front of Ajji to listen to her, I got transported to the world of Krishna and his *gopis*, a world of devotion, faith, wisdom and love. My friends were getting restless, but I sat still, mesmerised by the stories. They charmed me more than the Enid Blytons and Nancy Drews. The profound message and depth of each story enchanted and anchored me. Ajji noticed my interest. That evening, Mummy had planned to cook a variety of snacks for the guests. She called me to help her in the kitchen, but I was more interested in listening to Ajji's recitation. I continued sitting beside her. Mummy called out to me again. Ajji motioned with her hand asking me to stay put. Mummy was exasperated by my behaviour but said nothing in front of the guests. That night Ajji told Mummy, 'Don't entangle her in mundane things. Her life is made for a bigger purpose. She is here for the world.' What did she mean?

My grandmothers, Ajji and Auua, were as different as chalk and cheese. Auua would cook all our special foods and pamper us. Ajji would tell us stories about gods and goddesses. Auua was very flexible and accommodating, tending to everyone's needs before her own. Ajji was disciplined and had a strict personal daily regimen. She abstained from eating onion and garlic, drank only hot water, and prayed before every meal. Auua was a city-bred woman, having lived in Mumbai from the time of her marriage. She knew her way around the city. Ajji moved to Mumbai in her late fifties, but had been on many pilgrimages around India. Auua wore a six-yard sari while Ajji wore a traditional nine-yard sari. They were unique personalities, and complete in their own special way. Both played a huge role in shaping me into who I am today.

Both my paternal and maternal families were spiritual. Ganesh Chaturthi was one of the festivals we celebrated with great fanfare. At Auua-Ajja's home, we installed Lord Ganesha for five days. Ajja was a rare combination of a scientific temperament and veneration for our ancient traditions and customs. I too felt like the host to the Lord, because He was visiting our home. Ajja took care of the main arrangements and I was his assistant, doing all the small chores. He was a stickler for perfection. The decoration had to be in accurate symmetry and our cleanliness in line with the prescribed tenets. There was a lot of activity in the kitchen, and we children played all day, unrestricted. The house reverberated with the anticipation of Ganpati Bappa's arrival. The air was imbued with the fragrance of flowers, incense, camphor—a sacred intermingling of divine scents. Even before the Ganesha idol was installed, I felt like He was already amidst us.

The first morning of the festival bathed the city with a flood of celebration. Delicious aromas filled up the house and I could smell my favourite steamed *modaks* getting ready. I loved watching Ajja perform the puja. Ganpati Bappa sat regal and resplendent watching the festivities.

He was God, but also a part of our family now, the much-loved guest.

The next five days were drenched in the sweet joy of the same festive routine. Gathering flowers in the morning, *aarti* three times a day, delicious *prasad*, the joy of being with uncles, aunts and cousins, and the cheerful, lively mood. All this while, God watched from close quarters.

On the fifth day, the thought of being separated from my God became unbearable. Saying goodbye to Ganesha, and watching Him get immersed in the sea cloaked me with sadness. I couldn't stop crying. When we returned home, the space which Ganesha had occupied was empty, and yet, there was His lingering presence, a feeling of fullness. Through all the rituals and ceremonies, I had experienced Him intimately. Though He had left us physically, we were constantly reminded that He was not just in the *murti*, but firmly entrenched in our hearts.

Sri Adi Shankaracharya has beautifully described Lord Ganesha as Ajam Nirvikalpam Nirakar Rupam—the one who is eternal, never born and formless. Yet in celebrating Him in His beautiful, lovable form, I found a way of expressing something that came from deep within me. That night when I slept, I could feel His benevolent eyes gazing at me and comforting me as though telling me, 'Even if you have immersed me, I am with you always.' My formative years laid the foundation of establishing a deeply personal bond with the Divine. This strengthened as I grew older. Even today, I cry inconsolably on Ganesh Visarjan days.

The richness of Indian culture allows us the flexibility to relate to the Divine in any form, in any manner, and as any relationship. Lord Ganesha always felt like a brother and friend, Bal Gopal as a little child, the Devi as a mother and sister, and Lord Shiva as a father. My family expanded effortlessly beyond the physical into the ethereal. Much later I realised that what we saw as different gods were only different manifestations of the same Divine energy, like different ornaments made out of the same bar of gold.

Our home was a hub for all our family members travelling to or from Mumbai. Despite their busy jobs, my parents were warm and wonderful hosts. We had a continuous stream of visitors—uncles, aunts, cousins. Ours was an open house. Mummy lovingly cooked the favourite foods of my cousins and Papa went out of his way to pick up or drop people to their destinations. They nurtured relationships, and were always available to our extended family in dire times.

When I was transitioning from grade five to six, during my summer vacation, my uncle, Brigadier Shashi Deshpande (*aka* Shashi Kaka) came to IIT Mumbai, for a two-and-a-half-month training stint. My aunt, Chabu Atya (Papa's youngest sister), and my cousins Shirin and Shubhangi too accompanied him. My parents insisted that all four of them stay with us. Along with Ajji, we were nine of us staying in our Mumbai apartment. We kids slept on mattresses spread out on the living room floor. Though it was quite crowded, no one fretted over 'their personal space'. All of us chipped in to do the household chores. We settled into a great rhythm of a daily routine with weekends filled with a visit to the Chowpatty beach or watching a movie. I loved that time. I learnt to share my cupboard, my books and my friends. Watching the five elders at home that summer taught me how to be accommodating and accepting. I understood that strong relationships need big hearts, not big homes or pockets.

As we grow, we learn from observation, absorbing what we see and hear in our surroundings, but there are some elements that come from deep within. Though my life was full in every way, in some ways, it felt empty. While filling me with all its splendour, it kept reminding me that this was not all there was to it.

All through my school days, we travelled in every summer and winter vacation. Mummy and Papa loved touring the length and breadth of India to visit temples, forts, palaces, parks, mountains and beaches. I loved to travel, explore interesting new places and learn new things. It was a dream for any child. But no matter where I went, I felt this strange churning sensation, an indication of something, as if I didn't belong there, as if I was supposed to be somewhere else.

Once, I was in the middle of the Kodaikanal Lake, with the cool breeze kissing my cheeks and the steady soothing sound of the water that was music to my ears. The setting sun had streaked the skies a pink-orange. It was a sight to behold. A perfect evening. Yet I had that same sinking sensation in the pit of my stomach. It was painful. This was not the first time it had happened. I was familiar with it. I wondered why it had returned at a time when I was in such a scenic place, in the lap of stunning nature, with my loved ones. This sensation welled up repeatedly when I was in large family gatherings too, whatever the occasion—weddings, birthday parties, exam result celebrations and other such events. It intrigued me, made me restless. There were times when

I looked around and wondered, 'Where am I?' 'Why am I here?' On some occasions when it was an intense pain in the stomach, I took medicine to ease it. All the check-ups and X-ray reports were normal. Yet, something was wrong. The sensation stayed.

***

I was in the tenth grade when a couple of my cousins got married. During the weddings, whoever met me had only one question, 'What are your plans for the future?' It left me confused and nervous. I wanted to become an architect. It wasn't a rational or well thought-out decision, just a feeling. My elder cousins were either studying at prestigious institutions like IIT or studying medicine or something equally awe-inspiring. That made me tense. What if I don't make it like them? What If I disgrace my parents? I was a good student, also very conscientious and sincere, but what if I didn't get enough marks? This weighed heavily on my head during my tenth grade, but ultimately, I scored a good eighty-six percent. In 1985, these were above average marks. I heaved a sigh of relief. I received an outpouring of congratulatory messages and gifts. Mummy and Papa were ecstatic. I had made it! I was now a member of the elite group of achievers in the family. But, I could not possibly subject myself to the tension again in the twelfth grade. To get admitted to a good architecture school, I would need exceptional marks in the twelfth board exams. This was too stressful. So, I decided to study Commerce. Mummy-Papa supported me wholeheartedly. What I didn't realise was that my decision would cause the whole family to descend on our home and try to convince me against opting for Commerce. 'Raju has scored such wonderful marks in the tenth board exams, why won't she do well in the twelfth grade?' my uncles and aunts chorused. Someone even told my parents that they were ruining my career prospects.

Despite this opposition, I enrolled for Commerce. I loved the subjects and the environment, and made great friends. But the pressure was now about proving that even in Commerce I could show my mettle. So I enrolled for a one-year Government Commercial Diploma at the same time. In grade twelve, I came first in the Maharashtra Board in Vocational Marketing, scoring the highest marks ever in the subject. It reinforced to my extended family that I was doing well.

Even in my senior college, I enrolled for ICWA along with the regular college, clearing Inter ICWA. This also meant working for twelve to thirteen hours a day. I had to compete with all the gold medals, patents, publications and achievements of my cousins.

During my MBA, when I became the only one of two students to get a summer internship at Hindustan Unilever, it was a huge relief for me. It was an indication that my life was starting on a good professional track. I looked back on the anxious sleepless nights with a sense of victory. My first significant achievement. It was also my first experience of working in a large corporation.

The towering Lever House at Backbay Reclamation in Mumbai was an iconic address in the FMCG business. My assignment was in the sales team. Just to get to work in that office was a milestone for me. It was a high-pressure, high-performance culture of towering excellence. To get an insight into the strategy and plans behind our everyday products made me feel more privileged than others at home. When Mummy bought Surf detergent powder, I knew its whole journey.

I worked really hard that summer. I would be on market beats, visiting shop after shop, recording stock levels, photographing shelf layouts, studying the impact of promotions on sales, surveying customer feedback and satisfaction. My days started at 9 am and did not end before 8 pm. I spent whole days in the markets in the taxing hot and humid Mumbai summer. That arduous and backbreaking training of two months gave me lessons to last a lifetime.

On the few days we were in office, all of us summer interns were allowed to eat lunch in the senior management dining area, where every meal was a seven-course feast.

Often we would spot Mr Keki Dadiseth, the then Chairman of Unilever in India, and other seniors too. I watched how they spoke, how they ate, their mannerisms, their confident self-assured body language and wondered what it felt like to be in such a senior position in an organisation. I was curious about what they thought, how they shouldered their large responsibilities and how they achieved their success. At twenty, the heights they had reached seemed way beyond my ambit. I was very lucky that my first brush with corporate India was with one of the most respected multinational brands of the world.

Twenty-five years later, at The World Forum for Ethics in Business, standing on the majestic stage of the European Parliament in Brussels, I watched as our annual award was handed over to Unilever for their global work in sustainability. While smiling at the photographers, a part of me was fondly reminiscing about my young twenty-year-old self taking her wide-eyed first steps at Lever House.

A year later, after my MBA, Citibank offered me a job through campus recruitment. Before I was born, Citibank (then called First National City Bank) had offered Mummy a job, but the family elders had advised her to join the Reserve Bank of India, considering it was India's Central bank. When I joined Citi, it was almost like life had taken a full circle. I was working in a world-class global organisation, a pioneer in consumer banking, with cutting-edge technology and some of the most talented professionals in India.

I started off in the Citibank Branch at the Sakhar Bhavan building, Nariman Point, in South Mumbai. Waking up to catch the 8.25 am train to VT station and taking the double-decker bus from there had its own excitement and intensity. I made many friends. A to-be-well-known beauty expert, India's first woman private equity head, bankers, journalists and a diverse variety of working women were my co-travellers on the train. Our first class ladies compartment had a life of its own. Women getting in and out at different stations, while making the most of the time on board—chatting, reading, listening to music, or just relaxing. A perfect analogy to the journey of life itself. With its start and finish pre-decided, it allows us to make the most of the limited time in between.

My days at work were long and the travel was taxing, but I felt very fortunate to have the job. I immersed myself in work. I was good at it too. Meeting clients, advising them, and building connections and relationships came naturally to me. Top industrialists, entrepreneurs, actors, film producers, music directors and singers were all part of my portfolio. One of the main reasons they may have felt comfortable with me was because I wasn't star-struck. The late celebrated film-maker Yash Chopraji would say that I was one of the very few people who could say a no to him. The late legendary actor Shammi Kapoorji had developed a great interest in the internet and whenever I visited him at his home in Blue Haven at Malabar Hill, he would take me to his study to show me his latest findings. He treated me like his own child and gave me big bear hugs. Having known me since childhood because of Ajja (his pets were Ajja's patients), he told me how proud he was of what I had grown up to be. I developed an unusually warm relationship with the late respected film music composer, O P Nayyarji. He had stopped music direction and had become a homoeopathy doctor. Tall and lean, he walked ramrod straight and was fit as a fiddle. He wore white safari suits with full sleeves, his face glowing with good health under his cowboy-style hat. He would visit us about once a month, making it a point to come to our Branch fifteen minutes before its closing time. After finishing his work, he often insisted on taking me to the Gaylord restaurant for coffee. There he would regale me with the most unbelievable tales of relationships, heartbreaks, successes and failures from the film industry. Once he said to me, 'You are of my granddaughter's age, but I don't know why I feel like sharing a lot with you. I feel lighter after talking to you!'

Around that time, the Citibank management decided to create model branches all over the world. The idea was to standardise customer experience no matter which city or country–the same look and feel, layout, interiors, colours, desks, even employee designations and roles. Our Mumbai Branch was going to be the first of this kind in India.

Citi brought in one of their most promising and dynamic leaders, Ajay Bagga, from Chennai to Mumbai, as our Branch Manager. He was a tough taskmaster with very high expectations from all of us. He infused us with intellectual stimulation and challenged us to face our professional fears, pushing us to achieve things we never thought possible. Yet, there was a softness about him. Originally from Delhi, he had great concern for the safety and security of all the women in the team. If we had to go for a late evening meeting to any client's office, he never sent us unaccompanied. This personal concern and attention from a boss towards his subordinates was a big leadership lesson early in my career. He also had a unique way to connect with customers, and they loved it. He could talk knowledgeably on a variety of subjects–history, politics, economy, world events, spirituality and scriptures. Everyone had deep respect for him, and often said, 'Bagga *saab*, you know everything about everything!' To add to this, his straight-faced sense of humour had us all in splits. With him heading our team, we became one of the star teams in the Asia Pacific region. Personally, he was someone who cared about me as a human being, not just an employee. The golden period of my life had indeed begun.

3

The Wrong Numbers

It was December 7, 1992. I had just completed six months of working at Citi and felt on top of the world. With this milestone, I was appointed one of the two custodians of the main vault of the bank. This meant that the two of us would have the keys and the combinations to open the locks of the vault in which all the cash boxes of the bank were kept. Opening and closing the vault was an extremely responsible and important daily activity. I felt the gravity of the task. That day, at about 2.30 pm, the customer rush in the Branch had started thinning and the tellers were tallying their books and cash. Everyone had started relaxing after the hectic Monday branch activity, when one of our clients came rushing in shouting that riots had broken out in the city. The Babri Masjid in Ayodhya had been demolished the previous day and this seemed to be the aftermath of that. The repercussions of what had happened far away had reached our doorsteps. Slowly, news trickled in that riots had indeed begun in different parts of the city. This was Mumbai, one of India's most cosmopolitan and safest cities. We did not know what to believe. Rumours abounded.

Taking cognisance of the situation, it was announced that everyone should wrap up work immediately and head home. I started gathering my things when I remembered my vault duty. I couldn't leave till every last box of cash from the consumer and corporate bank divisions was loaded back into the vault. I waited. It was 4 pm and the office was almost empty now, except for a few of us, and the other vault custodian. I was getting nervous with every passing minute. I didn't know how Mummy-Papa would get home. Shantanu was in college and would have to find his way back on his own. Being December, it would get dark soon.

By the time we left from the bank, it was almost 5 pm. Nariman Point wore a deserted look. There was not a single bus, car or taxi in sight. The few people we saw were all sprinting in the direction of Churchgate Station, presumably to catch a train. I started walking towards VT Station. I had worn a sari and high heels, certainly not the ideal gear for a long walk. It took me almost an hour to cover the distance. My feet developed blisters and started bleeding. By the time I reached the station, I was exhausted. To my shock, by then, even the local trains had stopped plying. I was stuck. I started crying in panic. There was no way I could walk home, thirty-five kilometres away. In desperation, I sat down by the road.

Huge crowds of people were walking in and out of the station, not knowing where to go. I could see the fear and anxiety on their faces. Everyone was trying to find some way to get back to the security of their homes. I looked around to locate a familiar face. There was none. After about half an hour, a goods truck arrived. It slowed down, and an elderly looking man leaned out of the passenger seat, yelling out to me, '*Aa jao* (Get in).' His tone was authoritative. Under normal circumstances, I would never have boarded a truck at the command of a stranger. But something in his eyes made me trust him implicitly. He helped me jump onto the back of the truck. He had picked up a few other stranded people like me on the way. Navigating through the city which now looked abandoned, we drove avoiding areas where violence had erupted. I sat quietly, watching my Mumbai look like I had never seen it before. The truck dropped me right at my doorstep. I only remember my saviour's face. I don't know his name and still have no idea who he was or where he had come from. There was no time to ask or exchange pleasantries. There were others who had to be dropped off. I could only thank him from the bottom of my heart.

It was a dark period for Mumbai. The riots continued for the next few days. They broke out again in January 1993. More than seven hundred people lost their lives in those two months. The carefree and secure spirit of Mumbai was broken. While we remember such incidents for all the horrific things that hatred makes people do, these are also the times that reveal magnanimous acts of kindness from the most unexpected quarters. That evening, none of us in the truck knew each other, or our religions or our professions. It did not matter. During that journey of ninety minutes, we were merely human beings connected by a crisis. For the first time in our lives, we Mumbaikars had to watch our backs. We heaved a sigh of relief when February passed quietly, with no untoward incident. It seemed that Mumbai was returning to normalcy. Unfortunately, it wasn't so.

***

It was March 12, a Friday. At about 2 pm, I was at my desk, when one of our clients, Mr Dilip Shah, rushed into our office looking stricken. 'BSE *mein* bomb blast *hua hai*,' he spluttered. We were aghast. This was preposterous. The Bombay Stock Exchange (BSE) was a secure, landmark building.

Why would anyone want to bomb it? But, there was no mistaking the urgency and terror in Mr Shah's voice. 'Wind up, go home. *Jaldi karo*,' he urged. Beads of sweat were trickling down from either side of his forehead.

One of our NRI (Non-Resident Indian) clients, Mr Singhvi, was at my desk. He was in his late seventies. After finishing the work in the Branch, he was supposed to visit our NRI service centre which was on the ground floor of the Air India building, a few hundred metres away from Sakhar Bhavan where my office was located. Panic started building up. Customers were scampering to finish their transactions and leave. Even my colleagues were hurrying to finish the business of the day, now that the news of the BSE bomb blast was confirmed. Mr Singhvi was unwell, and wanted me to accompany him to the Air India building.

I was torn. Should I go with him or wind up my work like my colleagues? But, I had already promised him that I would do so.

Just as I was leaving with him, the phone at my desk rang. It was a wrong number. Strangely, I received four consecutive wrong number calls on my intercom. Then one of my colleagues came to take my signature on some papers. All this took up a few minutes.

Not wanting to delay any further, we stepped out of the office. Mr Singhvi was walking slowly. We must have barely covered thirty metres, when we heard a deafening sound. Our ears went numb and all the buildings around us shook. The tunnel effect of that road made the sound reverberate so much that our bodies trembled. Mr Singhvi collapsed. I bent down to help him to his feet. Some passers-by came forward to assist me. We brought Mr Singhvi back to my office. People were running in all directions not knowing what had happened and where to go. A car bomb had exploded in the basement garage of the Air India building. Our office on the ground floor of the same building, which I was scheduled to visit with Mr Singhvi, was destroyed in a big way and many of our colleagues were injured.

Had I not been delayed by those wrong number calls, Mr Singhvi and I would have been in the Air India building office right at the time of the blast. Looking back, it is mysterious and uncanny how I received all those wrong number calls. Normally, I would get connected on the intercom only when the person calling in specifically asked the telephone operator for me by name. Neither before that day nor after, did I receive any wrong number calls on my desk phone.

Who or what was protecting me? Was it God? Who is God? How does He look? Or is God a She? How does the infinite, universal, intangible, all pervading, manifest itself? Air is everywhere but we feel it when we switch the fan on. How do we feel God then? It is said that God, Guru and our Self are one and the same. A Guru is a tangible manifestation of that intangible divine energy. Just like one wave embodies the entire ocean in itself, the Guru is an embodiment of that which is omnipotent, omniscient, omnipresent. If we say that God is always watching over us, and God and Guru are one and the same, then can we conclude that we are under the protection of our Guru even before we meet him physically? Our ancient texts say so. Just like the law of gravity existed even before Newton discovered it, the protective sheath of the Guru shields you even without you knowing it in an obvious way. Ajji used to say, 'Your Guru will find you when you are ready.' It is believed that the universe gives you signals when you are about to meet an illuminated soul. If the previous year was anything to go by, I had got enough and more signs.

Says Sri Adi Shankaracharya in his seminal text, Vivek Chudamani, 'There are three things which are rare indeed and are due to the Grace of God—a human birth, the burning desire and longing for liberation and the protecting care of the perfected sage.'

India has always been the seeker's paradise, the go-to place to learn the higher truths of life. It has been the cradle of four great religions of the world. It has attracted travellers and seekers from all over the world in all eras and even modern-day icons like the Beatles, Steve Jobs and many more have spent time here searching for the meaning of life.

Our country has an ancient tradition of Self-realised saints and seers. You feel comforted when you listen to Sant Kabir Dasji's poetry, soothed when you hear the Baani of Guru Nanak Dev ji, and awed by Sri Adi Shankaracharya's compositions and commentaries. The heritage that our saints have left behind is timeless and precious. The tradition of enlightened Masters like Sant

Tukaram, Sant Goswami Tulsidas, Sant Dnyaneshwar, Mira Bai, Akka Mahadevi, Ramakrishna Paramahamsa, Swami Vivekananda, Ramana Maharshi, Swami Brahmananda Saraswati and many other saints makes me feel fortunate to be born in a country where this spiritual quest has continued unbroken for millennia. We only know about Masters of yore, through what has been written about them, but I have always wondered how it must have been to have seen them and been in their physical presence. The expression of the knowledge imparted by the revered Masters has changed over the years to suit the times and needs of people, but what has not changed is the Guru Shishya Parampara. The Guru-disciple relationship is considered to be love in its supreme form. In the Narada Bhakti Sutra, it is said that a disciple relates to her Guru as a friend, as a beloved or as one who serves unconditionally. The Guru is a doorway to liberation; the disciple has to only walk through it. I did not fathom how close I was to this doorway on my own journey.

***

Circa 1993. Our family friends, Ranade Kaka and his wife, had invited us to Palamkote Hall, in Dadar, Central Mumbai, for a *satsang* (a programme featuring group singing, knowledge discussion and meditation) conducted by their Guru. I had just begun working, and getting away early from office seemed far-fetched. Mummy insisted that our entire family should attend the satsang. As it happened, I got held up at work, and we arrived at the venue much later than the appointed satsang time.

When we reached, a group of singers was leading the songs with the beats of the tabla and *dholak* reverberating in the whole vicinity. I had thought that since this was a spiritual satsang, the gathering would have mostly senior citizens. But I was surprised by what I saw. The hall was overflowing with people from all age groups, and many youngsters too. Some were in their working clothes, having come straight from office like me, some were wearing white kurta pyjamas, and many women were wearing their best festive clothes. Most of them were singing, a few were dancing, and others were sitting with their eyes closed in meditation. The energy, the joy, and the smiles! The atmosphere was electric.

Sitting on the stage was Pujya Gurudev Sri Sri Ravi Shankar ji, in pure white, his eyes closed and a beatific smile on his face, oblivious to the celebration around him. I had only seen his photograph at Ranade Kaka's home. His photograph did no justice to his real-life persona. He looked resplendent and majestic. There was a stunning beauty about him. His dark long hair rested abundantly against his shining white clothes. He sat in a regal posture, tall and yet at ease. His stillness was a stark contrast to all the sounds around him. He had an aura of peace around himself. The moment I saw him, I felt an inexplicable yearning to be near him.

Someone told us that the time for *darshan* was over and we had missed our chance. On hearing that we may not get to meet Gurudev up close, I was filled with sadness. To add to it, Mummy gave me a look that said, 'We missed the darshan because you were late.' In the meantime, the *bhajan* singing stopped and the people settled down for a few quiet moments. Everyone was sitting with their eyes closed, but I just couldn't close my eyes. I didn't want to miss seeing or taking in a single thing. Suddenly,

Gurudev opened his eyes and signalled to a man sitting on the stage. He whispered something in his ears, and the man took the microphone and announced, 'Jai Gurudev, if anyone is still left to take Gurudev's darshan, you can come up now!'

As we walked towards the stage, we realised that we were four of the very few people who hadn't received the darshan earlier. Papa went up first, offered his *pranam* and received a fruit from Gurudev. Then, it was Mummy, followed by Shantanu. When my turn came, I did *pranam*, and when I looked up at Gurudev, he said, 'You are late, but good you are here now!' He looked at me like he knew me. His eyes were deep like an ocean, loving and gentle. His smile was so charming, I felt enveloped by his presence in a way I cannot express in words. I thought how amazing this Guru is! He knows exactly when someone has entered the hall.

In the Bhagavad Gita, Lord Krishna tells Arjuna, (Chapter 4, Shloka 5), 'Both you and I have had many births; you have forgotten, but I remember them all.'

I have often wondered if Gurudev meant something more in what he said to me that evening. I have never asked him about it. But, I felt very strongly that this was not the first time I was meeting him.

Meanwhile, Mummy-Papa started looking for a suitable groom for me but nothing worked out to their satisfaction. That created a lot of tension at home. It affected me too, but my boss, Ajay, was a huge support, since each time an alliance came up, I had to leave early or take time off from work. He was also coaching and counselling me through the situation and I always thought of him with a lot of respect.

Ranade Kaka, who was also an astrologer, had told my parents, 'You can look for as many boys for her as you want, but she will get married to someone she already knows, someone who himself will propose marriage to her.'

So when Ajay asked for my hand in marriage, I was taken by surprise. Ajay was from a Punjabi family that had moved to India during Partition. Culturally, our families had little in common. I confided in Shantanu first, and then my parents and Ajji. Papa had a lot of questions, Mummy, fewer. Ajji supported me wholeheartedly. She told Papa, 'If Raju has to marry someone, it's this boy. He will liberate her.' Her prophetic conviction astonished me. On Ajay's side, the big support came from Ma. I had met her only once before when all of us as a team had been invited to Ajay's home, and she was visiting from Delhi. I had dropped a whole bottle of Coca-Cola on their carpet. So when Ajay told her that I was the one he wanted to marry, she said in Punjabi, 'Oh, that *kudi* who dropped Cola on our carpet? Very good. *Ohdi akkhan badi soniyan ne* (her eyes are very beautiful.)' God alone knows when she had noticed my eyes!

When our colleagues at Citi got wind of the development, there was a deluge of support from all of them. The news of our match made headlines in the office.

The late Yash Chopraji, was making *Dil To Pagal Hai* in those days. On a couple of occasions I had requested Ajay to accompany me to my meetings with Yashji. He would always be impressed with Ajay's knowledge. Thereafter, every time I met Yashji, he would ask me, 'Why don't you marry your boss? He is such a *changa munda* (good boy)?' As a film-maker, he had an eye for romantic stories and the thought of a traditional Marathi girl marrying her Punjabi boss must have excited him no end. So when I told him that Ajay and I were getting married, he was overjoyed and said, '*Maine to pehle hi kaha tha*!' (I had already suggested it!) Our extended families were amused and jubilant. From Ajay's family, no one had married anyone south of Delhi. In my family, I am still the only one married to a Punjabi.

Ajay's family had roots in Dera Ismail Khan and Peshawar. His paternal grandfather, Pandit Narain Dass, was the Solicitor General of the North West Frontier Province. He was a very pious, learned and respected man. The family were Zaildars and the women's prison for the province was in the compound of their *haveli*. Ajay's grandmother would tell us that the house was so huge, that she rode a pony to travel from one end to the other. They had a summer home in Dalhousie, now in Himachal Pradesh. Every year, the whole family accompanied by their retinue of staff and carriages, would go there to beat the Peshawar heat. In May 1947, like every year, they came for their summer break to Dalhousie. That was the last time they saw their home. Imagine going for a holiday and not being able to return home! A lifetime of savings, possessions, and relationships was lost. Life as they knew it was over. They were left with a few suitcases of clothes, no home, no vocation and no source of income to start anew. They were in their mid-forties, wealthy, prosperous, a family that enjoyed fame and stature. Overnight, everything was snatched away from them. Partition uprooted them. They were literally left with nothing and had to start afresh all over again. It was a trauma beyond comprehension.

Ajay's grandparents were offered land in Gulbarga in Karnataka. His grandfather was not keen to travel down south, because he wasn't sure his family could adjust to the language or the weather. So, he rewrote his law exam and re-qualified as an advocate. As he started picking up the threads of his life and earning an income, he also began settling all the members of his extended family who had got displaced by Partition. It was a mammoth task to rebuild life materially, emotionally and socially. He bought a 200-square yard plot in Central Delhi and built a home that became an open house for all members of his family.

I did not have the good fortune of meeting Ajay's father. He passed away two years before we got married. Ma, a strong, solid, and deeply spiritual woman, welcomed me into their family unconditionally, with an open heart. Ajay's family and mine were very different. His was a generous, large-hearted, gregarious Punjabi gene and ours was an understated, simplistic, self-effacing Marathi one. The food, dressing, festivals and the attitude to life were poles apart. So I had to make a fair bit of adjustment. There was one thing we had in common–our spiritual disposition and temperament. Ajay's entire family had taken Ram Naam Diksha from Shri Premji Maharaj of Shri Ram Sharanam. All siblings had started reciting the Ram Naam Japa (rosary) from the young age of fourteen.

4
The Gift of Happiness

Just a few months before Ajay and I got married, I had done the Art of Living programme. Ranade aunty insisted that I do the programme immediately after we had been to the satsang in Palamkote Hall. Thereafter, every time we met she would ask me, 'Have you learnt the Sudarshan Kriya?' From gently persuading me, she had now begun pestering me. I was so busy at work that I had no time for anything else. But Ranade aunty would not relent. Finally, I gave in, and enrolled myself and Shantanu for the Art of Living Part 1 programme, a good three years after we first met Gurudev! In hindsight, I feel I had lost precious time. Thank God, aunty had not given up on me.

I remember two things very vividly about that programme. How uncomfortable I was sitting on the floor and how phenomenal the Sudarshan Kriya was. During the Kriya, I felt transported to another world. My whole body was tingling with a scintillating sensation of energy, yet I felt so light, as though my body had no boundary. After the Kriya, when I looked at myself in the mirror, I felt that my face had become two shades lighter, as if a dense sheet had been peeled off it. It was luminous. From inside, I felt cleansed and purified.

On the last day of our programme, our teacher Hansaji beckoned me to sit on the sofa next to her. I was hesitant, wondering how I could occupy the teacher's seat. She called me again, 'Come. You have to sit here eventually anyway.' I didn't pay much heed to what she meant, happy just to be rid of my aches and pains.

After completing the course, I started practising the techniques I had learnt. I could sense subtle changes happening inside me. I felt light, bubbly, happy and more confident. My days were filled with positivity. My face glowed even more with every passing day. People around me started noticing the changes in me. Something had been lit inside me. While I am naturally a positive person, I was now full of enthusiasm every moment.

After marriage, I shifted to Cuffe Parade in Mumbai. There were no WhatsApp groups giving updates of upcoming programmes and follow-up centres then, and I lost touch with the people who had done the course with me. I was really keen for Ajay to experience the course and he wanted to as well, but we just did not know where to go.

One Sunday morning, a bright-looking boy stood outside our door. He said, 'Didi, what I am going to tell you will change your life!' I was impressed with his confidence and invited him in. This was Saket Kakkar from the Art of Living (now a teacher), who informed me about the next Art of Living course that was scheduled to be held in Cuffe Parade soon. What we needed had come home! Ajay enrolled for it immediately. In those days, the programme started on a Tuesday and ended on a Sunday. The Tuesday that Ajay's course was starting was my first Mangalagauri festival. For every newly-wed Maharashtrian girl, it's an important puja performed for Goddess Parvati.

Ajay would have to miss the puja and the celebration if he attended the programme. For some of the elders in the family, it was unthinkable, since the first Mangalagauri happens only once. Something inside kept tugging at both of us, indicating that Ajay must do the programme, which he did. Not only did he enjoy it hugely, it also had a very profound impact on him. This was the first of many times that we as a couple chose something higher than our immediate personal joy.

The organisers of the course told him about an upcoming Advanced Meditation Course in the Art of Living Bangalore Ashram the following month. The teacher insisted that if we were so happy learning the Sudarshan Kriya, the Advanced Course techniques would be an even deeper experience. Both Ajay and I had busy, high-pressure, banking jobs. My younger sister-in-law, Manu, was going to be married in November that year. We would have to take two weeks off then. Taking a week off in September was impossible. We agreed that we would go only if both of us could. Surprisingly, both our bosses sanctioned our leave!

We were a group of about forty who went to Bangalore from Mumbai by train. The twenty-four-hour journey passed in a jiffy. When we reached Bangalore, it was drizzling. There was a slight nip in the air.

I was not prepared for what I saw when we reached the Ashram by mid-morning. It was like entering another world—cool breeze kissed our moist cheeks, birds were chirping merrily, the air was thick with the fragrances of flowers, incense, and also the aromas of spices that wafted from a kitchen nearby. The sky was overcast, a stark contrast to the burning Mumbai sun. Prashant Rajore, the Ashram Administrator, was standing at the end of a flight of steps descending from a large hall. He assigned us our accommodation.

The course was special because Gurudev himself was to conduct a few meditation sessions. It was the first time we were going to spend a few days at a stretch with multiple opportunities to meet Gurudev. We spent the first day exploring the Ashram, going up to Sumeru Mantap, a gorgeous coliseum on a hill, and sitting by a lake. Our teacher, Raghu Raj Raja, now known as Swami Sadyojatha, had a dignified presence. Hailing from one of Kerala's royal families, he had been in service with Gurudev since the early 1990s. He continues to be a huge inspiration to people around the world.

All of us would also wait eagerly for the sessions with Gurudev. This was my first experience of hollow and empty meditation. I felt quiet, serene and settled. Though my body ached, having to sit on the floor for hours, my mind felt clearer and expanded. In the meditations, I experienced complete emptiness and fullness at the same time, my first encounter of Samadhi.

I got access to an inner dimension of myself, which I never knew existed. The satsangs were melodious, the Ashram food, *prasadam*, was simple and delicious. We planted trees outside the Shanmukha Block, which stand tall now. As the days passed, I felt a sense of déjà-vu, of familiarity with the Ashram, an unexplainable sense of belonging. I noticed that the knotty feeling in my stomach, which was a constant presence since my childhood, had left me! All my life, despite being cocooned by the love of my family and friends, I had felt incomplete. Here, I knew no one, but I was completely at home.

The knowledge that Gurudev shared was very simple and practical, yet very profound. His joyful interactions with everyone in the satsangs were a pleasant surprise to me. I didn't know what to expect and had my own assumptions of how a spiritual master behaves or is. Gurudev was easygoing and relaxed; he interacted freely with everyone and there was no strict protocol for interaction with him. The Ashram residents related to him like one would to the head of the family-affectionately respectful.

A day before the course ended, we were taken in small groups to meet Gurudev personally. It was after satsang and Gurudev was seated on a low chair outside a round *Kutir*. It was called Shakti Kutir. There was a small porch where some of us huddled in front of Gurudev. Some others stood on the side. The air was cool and Gurudev sat there happily letting the breeze blow his hair gently. He was smiling at us or was it just to himself? Everyone was quiet. There was an air of contentment, the joy of just being there. The *raat rani* creepers were in their intoxicatingly fragrant bloom, the lighting was dim and the buzzing sounds of crickets and night insects added to the surreal atmosphere.

Gurudev met all of us individually. His one common question to everyone was, 'Are you happy?' Some people shared their problems, others asked for his advice on personal matters. It didn't matter who was around, people felt comfortable sharing what they felt. Ajay and I did pranams together. Gurudev gave us a big smile. It was the second time I was so close to Gurudev physically. For Ajay it was the first time. Just being in his physical presence evoked in us an effervescent, ebullient vibration. That night we literally floated back to our rooms!

At the end of the course, I couldn't get myself to leave. Normally, I don't let emotions cloud my judgement, but that day I just wanted to stay back. It was a Saturday; our train would reach Mumbai on Sunday and I had to resume work on Monday. I was clear about it, and yet, I could not bring myself to move. Ajay cajoled me patiently, and our group was getting impatient, as we would be late to catch our train. I was crying like a child. My head hurt with all the weeping. Just then our teacher, Raghu Bhaiya, came looking for us and asked, 'Who is Rajita?' I raised my hand. I worried that I had broken some Ashram rule by crying and making a scene. 'Gurudev has sent a message for you. He has asked you to leave for Mumbai now. He has said that you will return here soon,' he said, smiling.

What else do you tell someone who refuses to leave your premises? With a heavy heart, I left and cried throughout the journey. When we reached home late Sunday evening, surprisingly, I was refreshed and light, but the sadness stayed. The physical tiredness of the journey was nothing compared to the longing that tugged at my heart.

I went to bed and was woken up by the phone ringing. It was 7.38 am and Ajay was talking on the phone. Hanging up, he turned to me in disbelief. The call was from Nandan Mer, a senior Vice President at Citi, who informed Ajay that Citibank was going to start an international project based on a disruptive, new concept of remote banking, where a customer wouldn't need to visit the bank at all. It was going to be piloted in Bangalore and Nandan was asking Ajay to move to the city to head Sales and Distribution.

Gurudev had assured me that I would return to the Ashram soon. A Guru's *vaak* (speech) is Brahma's *vaak*. It has to come true. Only, in our case, it would be the very next day!

5
Bangalore Calling

I had lived only in Mumbai since birth. In comparison, Bangalore was quieter, greener and smaller. I was overjoyed that home to office was just a ten-minute drive, a luxury impossible to imagine in Mumbai. I became the Head of the Citibank Phone Banking Unit in Bangalore. This team was pivotal to the success of the global remote banking project. All customers acquired by Ajay and his team would be calling our 24/7 platform to service their banking needs. I inherited a team of twenty-four people which soon grew to seventy-five in a period of six months. This meant continuous recruitment, training and expanding the premises rapidly. Ajay's team was also new and had moved to Bangalore from different parts of India. We were all settling into a new rhythm of home and work.

Moving to Bangalore also meant being able to drive to the Ashram whenever we wanted to. Almost every weekend, we went to the Ashram for satsang, where we made friends with the teachers and *sevaks*. They were kind, had big smiles on their faces and seemed to live life lightly–a sharp contrast to the somewhat aggressive behaviour I was used to at work. We had a big circle of colleagues in the office, and at the Ashram too, I was slowly finding a new family.

One weekday, I got a call from the Ashram that Gurudev was landing in Bangalore from his international trip by 5 pm. Ajay and I decided to drive to the airport to receive him. Dr Nisha and Umesh Bhaiya from the Ashram were already there. Also waiting was an elderly dignified gentleman wearing a traditional *veshti* and kurta. He was tall and aristocratic, and had a kind, smiling face. He looked at me lovingly and motioned me to stand near him. That spot gave me the perfect view of the gate that Gurudev would come out of.

In a few minutes, Gurudev walked out regally, smiling broadly. People rushed to meet him and crowded all around him. Despite the long journey, there was no sign of tiredness on his face. His smile permeated the whole area. I too broke out into a spontaneous smile. Gurudev's presence radiated joy and light. Just being there filled me with happiness.

At that time, there were only a handful of us, but now, a few hundred if not thousand, wait to receive him, at any city he travels to. Even if his flight arrives late in the night or gets delayed by a few hours, they keep waiting. No matter how long or tiring the journey, Gurudev greets his devotees with a freshness that matches that of the bouquets and garlands with which they greet him. Gliding effulgently through the crowds, and blessing them, he collects every flower, letter, sweet, chocolate, or any other offering the devotees bring.

Right behind Gurudev was Bhanu Didi. I recognised her from the photographs I had seen. A white Zen car pulled up almost instantly, driven by a young bright-looking boy. Gurudev sat on the front seat, Bhanu Didi on the rear seat, and the elderly gentleman next to her. He invited me to travel with them. It was unthinkable. Could I drive in the same car as Gurudev? What about Ajay? What is the protocol of behaviour when you are physically in such close proximity to Gurudev? Many such questions raced through my head. That moment Gurudev turned back and said, 'Rajita, *aa jao* (get in).' How did he remember my name? Ajay signalled that I go ahead and he would follow. On the ride, the young boy kept sharing many tidbits of news with Gurudev, about the new buildings on our route, happenings in the city and some events in his college. He spoke in English, Kannada and Tamil. It was like a family conversation–intimate and easygoing. I was impressed that he was able to talk so freely with Gurudev.

Bhanu Didi smiled at me a couple of times. She spoke to the elderly person in Tamil in a low tone so as to not disturb the conversation Gurudev was having. He asked me if I was comfortable. I felt I was intruding into a very personal space, but I was also at ease and a part of it. I was getting an important lesson in how to embrace people and make them comfortable. I was being taught by action, not words.

We arrived at a traditional house in a quiet leafy lane of Jayanagar, where more people were waiting to greet Gurudev. We had reached Gurudev's home–Manjula. It turned out that the elderly gentleman I was sitting next to was Pitaji, Gurudev's father, and the young boy was Ajay Tejasvi, Bhanu Didi's son.

A distinguished looking woman in a beautiful traditional Kanjeevaram sari, and jasmine flowers in her hair, came out to greet Gurudev. It was Gurudev's mother, Visalakshi Amma. She welcomed both him and Bhanu Didi with a garland and a gentle hug. I waited outside for Ajay. We were not familiar with the Bangalore roads and I was hoping that he would find his way easily.

The overall mood was so joyful that I found myself relaxing. Amma came out with many cups of filter coffee. I was stunned that Gurudev's mother was serving us. Shyly, I took a cup. Then, a tray filled with apples and bananas arrived. I felt special eating in Gurudev's home. Soon, Ajay reached. With everybody dressed in saris and kurta pyjamas, we stood out in our formal Western office attire. Gurudev was still inside the house. We sat on the wrought-iron swing in the porch, unable to leave. No one asked us to leave either. The house seemed to have an infinite capacity to accommodate endless guests. We got chatting with Ajay Tejasvi, and his younger brother Arvind Varchaswi, who spoke to us with a naturalness that generally comes from years of knowing each other. It was almost 7 pm now. Gurudev came out and, as he took leave of the guests, told Ajay that he would drive to the Ashram in our car. I couldn't believe my ears. I rushed to the car to tidy it.

On the ride from the airport, Ajay Tejasvi had played melodious Carnatic instrumental music in the car, but we had no such music, only Hindi film songs. I felt nervous. We loaded Gurudev's luggage in the boot and spread his yellow asana carefully on the front seat. Arvind gave me a black-coloured bag to hold on my lap. It was just the three of us in the car. Gurudev, Ajay and I. The air inside acquired a fragrance. Ajay's eyes were fixed on the road and I was silent. As we navigated through the evening traffic, Gurudev himself gave directions to Ajay, and asked him to turn on the music. Embarrassed, Ajay told Gurudev that we had only Bollywood music. Gurudev smiled and asked him to play it. Concepts of propriety and inappropriateness are only in our minds. Gurudev was relaxed. As old Hindi songs played, he looked out of the window, asking us questions about our work. He shared details about his recently concluded trip, and his soft, loving demeanour enveloped us. I was capturing every moment in my heart. I didn't want the ride to get over.

Gurudev has the most endearing conversations during commutes. It could be about work, or giving advice, reading the news, or imparting an insightful life lesson out of something mundane. There is a lot of light-hearted banter and laughter. The range of possibilities on a car ride with Gurudev is wide. The world over, people yearn for this moment. Wherever Gurudev travels, he makes the people who accompany him on commutes feel very special, giving each one attention, and inquiring about their lives. He has a penchant for saying or doing something life-changing. For devotees, such a moment may come once in a while. For Gurudev, it can be many times a day!

When we reached the Ashram, a big crowd of ashramites was waiting at the main gate to welcome Gurudev. A group of Veda boys was chanting Vedic mantras. Even the birds and trees joined in the reception. Gurudev walked to his Kutir, followed by the ashramites, their white clothes glowing bright in the dark night. The Master was home.

That evening with Gurudev filled us with light. Our trips to the Ashram became more frequent and our relationships with the ashramites started deepening. Pitaji and Amma became Tatha and Paati, Bhanu Didi became Didi, and Narsimhan Anna, just Anna. We loved the bright and obedient Ajay Tejasvi and Arvind.

I learnt a lot just by watching Paati and Tatha. A regal woman, open-minded, small-framed yet strong-willed, Paati stood tall, an embodiment of integrity, humility and dignity. Manjula was an open house. Everyone received a warm, gracious welcome and was fed generously. Hot filter coffee was always available. People from all parts of the world called it home. Sometimes, Paati didn't even speak the language of the visitors–German, French or Russian. Yet, she greeted them with the warmth of a mother. True to her name, she had a broad vision which effortlessly embraced the whole world as her family. She watched the happenings at the Ashram with an astute eye. She often questioned the Ashram cooks, Ramesh and Girish, about the prices of the vegetables. If she happened to know a place with cheaper rates, she made sure they bought them from there and saved money. She herself lived very simply. Everyone loved and respected her deeply.

Whenever Gurudev was in the Ashram, she would cook for him and carry the food herself from Jayanagar to the Ashram. If by chance, a meeting delayed his lunch, she admonished everybody. Gurudev would mischievously say, 'All of you leave now, or Amma will scold me.' I would cherish these moments and lock them in my memory.

Amma loved Ajay and me. She would rarely drive with anyone other than Ajay Tejasvi, but she made an exception with Ajay, who drove her to the Ashram often. She would sit on the back seat listening to the chants played on the music system. She seemed amused by me. She saw me dressed in Western formals, going to work during the day, and singing *bhajans* in the evening, wearing my growing stock of silk saris. She noticed that I wasn't too interested in doing kitchen work and would prod me to do some. 'Bend, bend,' she would say to me, exhorting me to reach out to pick up the utensils kept on the lower shelves of the kitchen at Manjula.

Office would be so hectic that on the drives to and from the Ashram I would often catch a wink. On one such drive, I overheard her telling Ajay, 'What is this, your wife keeps sleeping always. Give her some vitamins.' For a woman who was on her toes for fifteen to sixteen hours a day, it must have been a cause for concern. Her life was an epitome of knowledge and service. Every Thursday she would eagerly wait for Gurudev's Knowledge Sheet. In those days, wherever he was, Gurudev used to share his wisdom on a topic that came up spontaneously with the group of people around him. This weekly 'Knowledge Sheet', which included a newsflash that covered the highlights of Gurudev's activities that week, would get faxed to all Art of Living *satsang* groups around the world every Thursday. Compiled as, 'Intimate Notes To The Sincere Seeker,' these Knowledge Sheets are a source of solace and upliftment. For Paati, this was one of the biggest highlights of her week.

Tatha was cheerful, optimistic, extremely learned and hardworking. He had dedicated himself to service and spent every waking moment productively. An expert in astrology and healing, if you asked him, 'How are you Tatha?' he joyfully replied, 'Nothing to complain.' He had played a very important role in building and starting the Ashram in Bangalore from scratch. He started VISTA India (a service initiative) where hundreds of young girls got trained in tailoring, embroidery and other vocational skills. Often, he stayed on the campus of VISTA on the outskirts of Bangalore, in a simple room, with bare minimum belongings. Whenever we visited the place, we urged him to make his living quarters more comfortable, but he insisted that simple living and high thinking was the right policy. The Colombian coffee that he treated us to is easily the best I have had.

Paati's polite and gentle interactions with Tatha were endearing. They treated each other with the kind of mutual respect and love that was aspirational for a young couple like us.

In a world that had begun to move at a fast pace with advancing technologies, their relationship provided the moorings of traditional values and marital harmony. They were living to serve a higher purpose and it reflected in their compatibility and camaraderie. They were role models of how a couple could have both a happy marriage and an unwavering commitment to serving humanity.

They propelled us to do more *seva* and we looked for opportunities to be of use. On one such visit to the Ashram, the Administration sevak asked us whether we could host a teacher, Pallavi Wagh, from Mumbai, for a couple of nights. She was helping organise a CEOs' gathering at Windsor Manor Hotel, at which Gurudev was going to give the keynote address. We agreed readily.

By now, our home had become quite a hub for visitors moving to and from the Ashram.

When Pallavi reached our home, she exclaimed how nice she felt instantly. We lived in Richmond Town in a beautiful building, overlooking a huge park. Pallavi prodded us to invite Gurudev home. It would be such an honour, but we did not know how to go about it.

The CEOs' programme was going to be held the following morning. We were also supposed to be a part of it. Over early breakfast that day, Pallavi asked us again if we had invited Gurudev home. She said that she had a dream, where Gurudev had already come to our home. Encouraged by her conviction, we called the Ashram landline, and a senior Art of Living teacher, Kishore Da, answered. He promised to get back. We were now in a quandary. Would Gurudev come? Should we start preparing for his arrival? What was the right way to welcome him? It was about 9.30 am when we got a call informing us that Gurudev would indeed come home after the programme. We were overjoyed.

I didn't know where to begin. My housekeeper offered to mop the house with rose water. Ajay headed out to buy flowers, garlands and sweets. I decided to make masala milk. I kept the milk to boil, and got busy with organising things and tidying the home. In this flurry of activities, I forgot all about the milk. When I rushed to check, I was greeted by the odour of burnt milk. I was devastated. This was all the milk we had at home. There were no Tetra Paks in those days. Nevertheless, I added the dried fruit masala to the milk and left it to cool. I prayed hard for it to become okay, knowing well that it was impossible. Ajay returned with bagfuls of sweets and flowers. We organised everything in just an hour and a half. It was as though time had stopped. When Gurudev arrived, he asked us why we hadn't attended his talk. How could that have been possible? We could either have prepared the house or attended the talk. Over the years I have learnt that in Gurudev's scheme of things, it is always 'and', not 'or'.

We offered Gurudev the sweets and savouries, but I did not dare to bring out the masala milk. Suddenly, out of the blue, Gurudev announced, 'I will have masala milk.' Nonplussed, I wondered how he knew. I hadn't told anyone about it. I was left with no choice but to serve it. Uneasy, I watched in disbelief as Gurudev drank it with great relish. He took a tour of our house, including the messy areas, as though blessing every nook and corner of it. We followed, showing him the family pictures, the artefacts, our certificates and awards–memories and milestones of our young lives. Gurudev took keen interest in every little thing. It was humbling and encouraging. After an hour, we saw him off with a full and heavy heart. I rushed to the kitchen to check the masala milk. The bottom of the vessel was charred. Anxiously, I drank a sip. It tasted perfect. Not a trace of the burning!

Our home became an even busier city hub for the Ashram. Many a time, devotees travelling from USA and Europe stayed over at our place for a night or two before moving to the Ashram. Ashramites used it as a transit place when out in the city. It became a full and open house, and it didn't matter whether we were home or not. Anyone could come for a meal, a cup of tea or just to relax in between meetings. Everyone would always say how they felt welcome and at home. Travelling Swamijis left behind their spare clothes in our cupboards.

We began to stock flavours of their favourite juices in our pantry. We also welcomed with great joy and grandeur newly married couples who would wed in the Ashram. The couples stayed at our place for the first few days of their new life. Couples from all over the world will have memories of the time they spent at our home. Our neighbours wondered how we had relatives of so many different nationalities.

Ajay and I were getting busier. My team had grown to over a hundred and fifty people, and Ajay was gaining global recognition for the rapid execution of the expansion plans. One afternoon, I got a call that we could join the Sahaj Samadhi Meditation course starting that evening at the Ashram. On reaching the Ashram, we realised that there had been some miscommunication, and the course was to begin the following week. Disappointed, we decided to get back to office and catch up on work. On our way out, we met Didi. On hearing what had happened, she asked us to follow her back in. We waited at the administration block, while she seemed to organise something. Soon, a volunteer took us to Shakti Kutir, Gurudev's *Kutir*, where Didi was waiting for us. She explained that she would initiate us in our Sahaj Mantra—only the two of us. And since no other venue was free, she was doing it in the meeting room of Gurudev's Shakti Kutir. It was the most sought-after place in the Ashram. People waited for days and months to get access to Gurudev's *Kutir*. We would now see it from inside!

The *Kutir* comprised a meeting room and a small bedroom with an attached bathroom. Gurudev stayed here and conducted most of his meetings here too. We entered the *Kutir* with great anticipation.

The meeting room was circular and lined with idols of different deities, crowns and head gear, even soft toys and other children's toys. There were piles of papers and letters, some CDs, books and tapes in an open cupboard. Garlands, flowers, fruits, nuts, boxes of sweets, packets of savouries, and bottles occupied both sides of a big chair, which appeared to be Gurudev's seat. It felt like a wonderland.

Sensing my surprise, Didi explained to me that these were loving offerings of devotees, and Gurudev accepted everything to make them feel happy.

There was a distinct, sublime presence in the room. The intermingled sweet scents of sandalwood, jasmine, saffron and rose permeated the room, enveloping me. Didi signalled to us to sit down on the floor in the centre of the room. I knew I had to close my eyes to learn meditation, but all I wanted to do was soak in every detail around me. That hour was one of many firsts. The first time we stepped into Shakti Kutir, the first time we participated in the Guru Puja up close, and our first experience of deep and blissful meditation with a mantra. The next two days of the course were held at Manjula. Sitting in front of Divine Mother Bhuvaneshwari on the first floor of their home, Didi guided us into meditation, teaching us how to use our personal mantra. I had already experienced the marvellous hollow and empty meditations of the advanced course. But for experiencing them we needed to be in a programme with a teacher guiding it. This was different. The mantra was our own. Invoking the mantra in the mind felt like taking a cool internal shower, with the mantra cleansing us of all the unwanted baggage. I felt lighter and brighter. Our initiation was complete.

The journey to the source had begun at the source. Bangalore, the Information Technology city, now became the city of Inner Transformation for us.

Life kept bringing along a variety of experiences, both professionally and personally. The tough ones added depth and the good ones made us expand with joy. For both of us, it was a hectic time. We had important responsibilities, quite interrelated to each other's work which brought about their own complexities. Sometimes the stress of the global expectations, and being under the spotlight, would get to us. Our morning *sadhana* became our armour to prepare and protect us through the day and the evening meditation became a cleansing shower to wash away the day's tiredness.

People had started urging me to enrol in the Teachers Training Programme (TTP) and become an Art of Living teacher. That was a major step for me. Additionally, getting so much leave from work at such a busy time of our global rollout was almost impossible. In those days, the TTP was in two phases of fifteen days each. Surprisingly, I got leave quite easily. Vinod Menon was our teacher for TTP Phase 1. He regaled us with story after story of Gurudev. He was a stickler for discipline, and those fifteen days were like a roller-coaster ride. Anything could happen anytime. Of all the trainings I had attended in my life, this was the most mind-blowing yet. For the first time, I was thrown into such a diverse group of people. There were tough moments when I felt challenged and confused.

I was lodged in a dorm with twenty other women. I would wake up at 3.30 am to get a dry bathroom in the common toilet facility. I was used to a certain lifestyle which was brought down to the bare basics here. At work, I was the boss, with more than two hundred and fifty people ready to follow my lead. Here I was just one amongst the two hundred and fifty who had to follow the lead of the teacher. It was not easy. My innermost insecurities and fears surfaced. Being an Assistant Vice President in a multinational bank was a big deal for me in the world I belonged to. It did not matter here. The CEO and the homemaker, the professor and the student, man and woman, young and old—everyone was equal here. All labels, positions, name and fame had to be dropped at the door. I persevered, stayed the course and completed Phase 1.

The next TTP Phase 2 was scheduled to happen in two months. Gurudev encouraged me to enrol in it. Normally, there would be a gap of at least six months between the two TTP phases, so you got enough time to complete your allotted service projects and file your report for selection. The TTP coordinator told me that I was selected for Phase 2. How was I going to get leave from work? To my utter surprise, my boss agreed. This was unheard of. I had to work very hard those two months to catch up on all the work that I would miss because of my leave.

During the TTPs, our schedule was gruelling, allowing us barely a few hours of sleep. For almost three months, I ended up working for almost fourteen to sixteen hours a day. TTP 2 tested me further. I was in a cohort with a few people whose behaviour challenged and agitated me. Situations were created that made us push our boundaries and come out of our comfort zones. The unique processes, techniques and wisdom of the course were chiselling and polishing us in ways that were visible and invisible. The three-hour daily yoga and *sadhana* practice, made most of us lose weight. The reflections and out of the box exercises were making us shed the load within. I found myself dropping some more judgements, and accepting some more people. The snores of some of the women in the dorm bothered me less, and a wet bathroom became okay to use. I realised that gently I was being made capable of better handling my own emotions and responses without the trappings of designations and descriptions. The two TTPs recalibrated my whole being in a manner no other training programme had done before. Externally and internally, I was a changed person.

It was a great joy and honour to become an Art of Living teacher. Receiving the course manual from Gurudev himself felt like a new phase of my life had begun. At Citi, I had conducted many 'Train the Trainer' sessions, and was a certified trainer for several prestigious in-house trainings, and also a trainer for many external programmes . But this was totally something else. It was sacred. It was the knowledge of life. The quintessence of it distilled and simplified. Many years later, Gurudev had said at a Teachers Refresher Meet at Bad Antogast, our Ashram in Germany, that the Part 1 course of the Art of Living is not just any course; it is the essence of the Vedas brought to the world in a way convenient for today's times. It is a part of a grand cosmic design. That I could be a part of it was undeniably the biggest honour of my life.

6

Rajita Will Do It

I love festivals. After meeting Gurudev, the Guru Purnima festival took on a new meaning and gravity. I look forward to celebrating Guru Purnima every year.

Gurudev says, 'Guru Purnima is the day for reflection. It is the New Year for a spiritual seeker, for one on the path. Just like you have the calendar New Year on the first of January every year, for a spiritual seeker, the New Year is on Guru Purnima. It is a day to review one's credits and debits, look at the balance sheet of life, be grateful for the achievements, and make resolutions for the coming year.'

Every Art of Living chapter and Ashram all over the world celebrates Guru Purnima with great reverence and devotion. Normally, Gurudev is in North America during this time. In 2000, The Art of Living Guru Purnima celebrations were going to be held at the beautiful Lake Tahoe, California, in Gurudev's presence.

For a devotee, to spend this day in the presence of their Master is the greatest blessing. I too had a deep desire to be a part of this celebration, but it didn't seem feasible. As the local Head of CitiPhone Banking I was in charge of an intensely operational job. Joining the Guru Purnima tour with Gurudev meant three weeks away from office. I knew it was impractical.

One evening, Ajay asked me, 'Why don't you go to Lake Tahoe?' We spoke about it for some time, and suddenly, it seemed possible. It boiled down to meeting two conditions. One, permission from Gurudev, and two, leave from work.

When we went to the Ashram that weekend, we asked Gurudev whether I could travel to Lake Tahoe. He replied with a very happy and emphatic Yes! He said, 'Bhanu is also coming; you come with her.' I rushed to Didi to share the news. Now, I had to get leave from work.

When my boss agreed, my joy knew no bounds. Immediately, we started the visa process. This was my first round-the-world trip. Bangalore-Chennai-Singapore-Tokyo-San Francisco-Lake Tahoe- Germany-Bangalore.

I began shopping, packing, planning at top speed. I was extremely busy at work, wanting to ensure that everything ran smoothly in my absence. I didn't want anything to fall apart during my time away.

Finally, the day arrived. Sharmila Murarkaji, a senior Art of Living teacher, was also travelling with us. It was lovely sitting next to Didi on the flight to Chennai and having normal, everyday conversations.

At Chennai, we had a satsang at another senior Art of Living teacher, Ganeshji's house, with Didi singing a few bhajans in her melodious voice and guiding us in meditation, before we flew off to Singapore.

Shailajaji, one of the first Art of Living teachers of Singapore, and her daughter Radha, picked us up at Changi airport. Shailajaji hosted most Art of Living teachers travelling to Singapore. Gurudev often says, 'Make your home an Ashram.'

What is an Ashram? A place where people come, rest, eat and gain some knowledge. Shailajaji's home in the Upper Thompson area was a veritable ashram. It opened its arms out to everyone. The food served was delicious and joy abounded in her home through satsang and knowledge.

Staying at Shailajaji's place gave me important insights into how to be a good host to visiting devotees and teachers. My time with her made me realise that without planning or consciously knowing, our home in Bangalore which hosted global family members of the Art of Living, had become an ashram too.

The next day, another Art of Living teacher invited us and about forty other women to meet Didi. Some of them had just returned from a trip to Mount Kailash and Manasarovar Lake. We reached the teacher's home around noon, where women dressed in stunning multi-coloured Kanjeevaram saris and wearing jasmine flowers in their hair, gave Didi a traditional Indian welcome. After the initial greetings, the host requested Didi to sing a few bhajans and share some knowledge, after which the women shared the experiences of their trip to Mount Kailash. For almost half an hour, a tall lady, with long curly hair, regaled us with their adventurous experiences, insisting every so often, 'You must all make a trip to Mount Kailash. It's a once in a lifetime experience.' Her sharing buoyed me up. All I could think of from that moment was how wonderful it would be to make the pilgrimage to Mount Kailash and walk on the sacred ground. I made a mental note to talk to Didi about planning this and wondered if it would ever be possible.

Soon it was time for lunch and someone played bhajans on a cassette player. There was an instrumental interlude after which Chitra Roy's mellifluous voice wafted out, '*Aaye hai Satguru Kailash uthaye, laaye hai saare teerath yahan. Mere to man main behti hai Ganga, Yamuna yahan, Kaveri yahan.* (The Satguru has arrived, carrying Mount Kailash, bringing all sacred pilgrimage places right here. Ganga, Yamuna and Kaveri are flowing right now, right here in my heart.)'

In the Guru Gita, Lord Shiva tells Devi Parvati, 'Just the toe of the Master holds all the places of pilgrimage'.

As realisation dawned, my gaze met Didi's. A silent vibe of understanding passed between us. Didi smiled at me and continued eating her rasam rice.

That afternoon, we drove around the busy streets of Singapore. Having travelled there several times for work, I loved the familiar vibe of the city. The time with Didi and the Art of Living teachers and volunteers was full of laughter, sharing devotional stories, and evoking deep wisdom. It was like spending the most intimate time with my family. Didi looked after me like I was her own child, ensuring that I was comfortable, had eaten properly, and my room was well organised. She checked every minute detail.

Though I had been a host many times, this was the first time I was staying at a devotee's home. Watching

Didi, I learnt many nuances that would help me in the years to come—how to be at home yet not intrusive, how to be personal yet not too familiar, and how to be grateful without sounding obligated. The skill of staying with your hosts is a fine balance between formality and naturalness. Didi did it with dignity and Grace.

From Singapore, we went to Tokyo, where Didi was to conduct a Sahaj Samadhi Meditation course. We were staying at the home of Mohan and Meena, a lovely couple who had moved there from India a few years ago. Their traditional Japanese home too had the warmth and vibrancy of a mini Ashram.

I heard Meena tell Didi that though she and Mohan had put in a lot of effort to gather a big group for her course, she was disappointed that not many people had registered yet. That night, I asked Didi, 'You have come all the way for this course and if there are not enough people, won't you feel bad?' Didi replied, her voice calm and confident, 'There will be a lot of people. Our sattva will pull them to us.'

True to Didi's conviction, the hall started overflowing with people eager to learn meditation from her. Years later, during one of the Teachers Refresher Meets, Gurudev revealed, 'Knowledge has organising power.' I had got my first practical tutorial in this from Didi in Tokyo.

After a memorable few days in Japan, we boarded our flight to San Francisco. We were in the economy class, sitting almost at the rear end of the plane. When the lunch service started, I told Didi that I felt like eating ragda patties (a tangy delicious snack, popular in Mumbai).

Both of us laughed out loud, as the chances of getting this local Indian snack on a flight from Japan to US were nil. Soon, the air hostess was handing us our special vegetarian meals. I requested Didi and Sharmilaji to start their lunch. When I looked expectantly at the air hostess for my tray, I noticed her communicating in some sign language with her colleague in the next aisle. She looked flustered. Something was amiss. Next, I saw her approach me. 'I'm so sorry, we have run out of vegetarian meals,' she said, apologising profusely.

She promised to check if there was a spare meal in the business class section. Luckily, I wasn't too hungry. About forty minutes later, she returned with a smile on her face and a meal in her hand, looking triumphant. 'I have found one vegetarian meal for you,' she said. She had no idea how it had appeared as it was not from the menu of their flight. By now, I was quite hungry and decided to have the meal. As I opened the foil, a familiar aroma hit my nostrils. Ragda patties!

'Ask and you shall get,' I had read. I was both wonderstruck and overjoyed. At that moment, I felt that I could have asked for anything in the world and I would have got it. For now, ragda patties would do. I dug into a patty, and closed my eyes. Pure bliss.

When we reached San Francisco, we were exhausted. It had been a long flight and we were jet-lagged. The Shahs, old-time devotees of Gurudev, picked us up. They had thoughtfully brought a car with a huge trailer to accommodate our suitcases. The four-hour drive to Lake Tahoe was stunning. Nature's bounty, the little towns we drove by, the pine trees, the clear blue skies, the crisp fresh breeze, everything was pristinely beautiful. I was struggling to keep my eyes open so that I could take in all the sights. This was my first trip to America. I didn't want to miss anything.

It was also the first time I would be spending Guru Purnima with Gurudev. It was as though nature had come alive and was escorting me personally to my destination. The trees, the mountains, the lakes, the flowers and the wind were all welcoming me and whispering sweet songs of devotion. The Yoga Vashista says, 'The mountains, the forests, the earth and the sky—all these are but Infinite Consciousness.' This journey was delivering me through the Infinite Consciousness to the One who Himself embodies it.

There is something exceptional about the journey to meet your Guru, whether it means travelling a thousand miles or walking a hundred steps. The anticipation, the joy and the exhilaration are the same. It is as though the energy of the Master beckons you with its exuberance and vitality. As we neared the lake, the landscape became breathtakingly beautiful. The water was crystal clear and turquoise blue. I clicked away on my Kodak camera to capture the panoramic view.

By the time we reached our final destination, the sun was about to set. It was a sprawling resort of holiday homes and hotels surrounded by majestic mountains. It had a convention hall and banquet rooms too, where all the Guru Purnima special Art of Living courses had already begun a day before. We drove straight to the hall where Gurudev was in a meeting with some of the local teachers. He greeted us with a big smile and Didi began telling him about our journey, her words interspersed with peals of laughter. I sat behind her, happy to just soak in the moment. The place felt familiar. The fragrance, the spirit, the smiles and the joy were a confirmation that Gurudev's presence had turned this resort into an Ashram.

Guru Purnima is the most important time of the year for a devotee. Gurudev has said, 'A Guru does not simply stuff you with knowledge but kindles the life force in you. What happens in the presence of a Guru? Every cell in your body becomes alive. This is called Diksha, which means the height of intelligence, not information. An Acharya gives you information, but a Guru invokes intelligence in you. The pinnacle of the intellect is an awakened intelligence, and the Guru awakens that intelligence. The mind is connected with the moon, and the full moon is a symbol of completion, celebration, and a pinnacle. Guru Purnima is the day when the disciple wakes up in his fullness, and in that wakefulness, he can't but be grateful. This gratitude is not the gratitude of you and me, or of Dvaita (duality), but it is the gratitude of Advaita (non-duality). It is not a river moving from one point to another point, but an ocean moving within itself.'

The time during Guru Purnima celebrations is drenched with devotion and gratitude to the Guru.

All the different courses planned that week were culminating in the Guru Purnima celebrations. The long summer days were filled with deep meditations, knowledge sessions, soul-stirring satsangs and joyful time with Gurudev. Knowing that for some of us it was the first time in the US, Gurudev took us out for a sightseeing tour. Cecilia, one of our teachers from South Korea, took some magnificent pictures of Gurudev by the lake. The azure waters were a perfect setting to Gurudev's silhouette, with his hair and his shawl flying in the wind. This lovely picture still sits on our mantelpiece.

The local organisers had planned a short boat cruise after the Guru Purnima celebrations. On the boat there were at least five hundred people. I was on the upper deck with a few of our local US teachers, meeting and greeting people. We could buy snacks and hot beverages on the boat. There was a nip in the air, and I felt like having a hot cup of tea but had forgotten to carry my wallet. Just then, as if he had read my mind, a volunteer came with a cup of tea and said, 'Gurudev told me to give this to you.'

We often joke that when you have a Guru, you have no privacy. You cannot hide your thoughts, feelings or desires from him. You can hide nothing at all!

Once, Gurudev shared that Masters of yore made it a point to ensure that their disciples' wishes were never granted. They did this to ensure that by killing every desire, big or small, the disciples would become more and more dispassionate, taking them closer to liberation. Gurudev said that he had chosen the opposite approach. He had decided to let every desire of his disciples get fulfilled, so that they could rise higher to seeking wisdom and serving, rather than hankering for small things.

While speaking on the benefits of having a Guru, Gurudev had said, 'When you have a desire for something, in order to get it, you need guidance. You need someone to give you what you want. But then there is no end to desires, and sometimes, you are not even sure of your own desires. That is where the Guru comes into play. The Guru principle or Guru-tattva will give you that which is good for you and not everything that you want.'

From Lake Tahoe, our next destination was Germany. We were to spend five days in our European Ashram in Bad Antogast, a two-hour drive from Frankfurt airport. It was the first time I was flying with Gurudev. A huge group of devotees came to see off Gurudev at San Francisco airport. There was laughter, tears, smiles and hugs. Everyone was trying to snatch a last word with him, ask him one quick question, share just one bit more of information, and offer a flower or some sweets or chocolates. We had already checked in. A few teachers from the USA joined us. As he walked towards the security check, a large group of devotees followed him. Gurudev turned around and waved to all. There was a roar of 'Bye, Gurudev', 'Jai Gurudev', 'See you soon, Gurudev', 'Come back soon, Gurudev'.

We had a few minutes before boarding the flight. Sitting in the lounge, Gurudev carefully put away in his bag all the letters and chits (of messages) he had received from people at the airport. He would read those on the flight. He lovingly offered the big bunch of flowers he had got, to the lounge staff to place in a vase there. He gave us all the sealed boxes of chocolates or sweets to keep in our hand baggage to be given as prasad to the people who would come to Frankfurt airport. Someone had given a box of idli and chutney. Gurudev had a bite and distributed the rest to us. I was amazed to see his personal and precise attention to each thing! Everything was important and nothing was wasted. My seat was right at the back in the economy section, so when we landed in Frankfurt, it took some time for us to disembark. To my surprise, Gurudev was waiting for us at the gate. Only after our whole group had got out, did we start walking to the immigration counter.

The drive to Bad Antogast was stunning. It was my first trip to Germany. Driving at the speed of 200-220 kms an hour on the German autobahns was my first introduction to the country. This drive was stunning too with small towns, large fields and forests on both sides of the road. As we neared our Ashram, the forest got denser, the air became crisper and sweeter. A large group of devotees was waiting to welcome Gurudev. He got out of the car. More laughter and tears, smiles and hugs. Cheers and sounds of 'Welcome Home, Gurudev', 'Jai Gurudev', 'Love you, Gurudev' rang in the air. Our Ashram was a centuries-old, large, intimate and cosy building, now reconfigured for our needs. The coming days were marvellous. I felt instantly at home. Like, I belonged. I met more new people and forged many new friendships.

On a couple of days, Gurudev made me go for short excursions to the nearby towns and attractions. I soaked in every minute detail. We went to the ancient city of Strasbourg. Just a forty-minute drive from the Ashram, across the French border, it was home to the European Parliament, The Council of Europe and many other important institutions. The evening satsangs in the Ashram were just heavenly. Devotees had come from all over Europe, Middle East, Russia and Africa. Bhajans and songs were sung in many different languages every day to the beats of a variety of drums. Guitars, flutes, bells, and a number of other musical instruments added to the energy and tempo. In contrast to this, the stillness of the forest reflected in the stillness of our meditations. Or was it the other way around?

Gurudev spent his days meeting people from all the countries, discussing organisational matters, answering personal questions and giving guidance. Never mind that some words were lost in translation, the connection between the Master and his devotees was direct: soul to soul. Whenever I was allowed, I would just love to sit at the rear end of the meeting room and watch Gurudev's conversations. It was like getting invaluable lessons in life and leadership, institution and relationship building.

One of the highlights of Gurudev's stay in Bad Antogast is his daily walk in the forest. No matter what time of the day he decides to walk, whenever he leaves his room, word gets around the 'house' (as the Ashram is called) and people rush out to join him. Sometimes, a hundred people can accompany him on such walks. They use this time to get by his side to have a short conversation, ask a question or just revel in the joy of being in his close proximity.

Gurudev also uses this time to chat up everyone, and have some light-hearted banter and fun. On one such walk that week, I found myself walking next to Gurudev and remarked to him how I had noticed that the pine trees in Black Forest had their branches turned upwards, whereas the ones in Lake Tahoe had them turned downwards. Both looked so beautiful. Smiling at me indulgently, he replied, 'When you have beauty in your eyes, no matter what the differences, everything looks beautiful.' And just like that, he continued his brisk walk. As I bid goodbye to my new friends, I did not know that this was just the first of the countless more visits I would make to our German Ashram, and it would become my European home over the years. Back in Bangalore, Ajay was waiting at the airport to receive us. I was home after discovering many homes around the world.

***

In August 2002, the Visalakshi Mantap (a meditation hall) was under construction at the Ashram. It was going to be a unique, five-storeyed, 108-feet high, lotus-shaped structure, an architectural marvel. Gurudev had announced that it would be inaugurated in mid-January. Ajay's new role in General Electric needed him to be based in New Delhi. I had not yet got a transfer to Delhi from Citibank. With the inauguration just a few months away, there was a lot of work to do. We decided that I would continue living in Bangalore till I got the transfer, while Ajay moved to Delhi. I was young, and it was not an easy decision. Our once full and busy home felt empty without Ajay's larger-than-life presence. While the days were hectic in office, the time outside work would have been unbearable had it not been for Didi and her family. They ensured that this time did not feel like an ordeal for me. Though Ajay Tejasvi had moved to Los Angeles to continue his Masters (studies), he would be in touch with me regularly. With wisdom beyond his years, he always had a kind ear to hear me out.

Anna too was a tower of strength. Running a household alone involves taking care of so many matters. Whenever I was at a loss about what to do, I relied on his counsel. He got a beautiful idol of Raja Rajeshwari Devi made for me, advising me that praying to her would give me strength and confidence. She still continues to have the pride of place in my puja room.

Arvind was a bundle of enthusiasm. Whether it was to go shopping for regular home stuff or to accompany me for my driving lessons at 6 am, he came along lovingly. All of them embraced me like I belonged to them. I had hundreds of meals, celebrated all the festivals, participated in many pujas with them. It was a joyful time brimming with positivity and goodness.

I practically lived in Manjula. I learnt a lot about our rich heritage, ancient texts, saints of India, music and art. In this home, computers effortlessly intermingled with tablas, sambhar with parathas and pujas with world news. I settled into a rhythm of life which was also a paradoxical combination of cutting-edge banking at work and a deep dive into culture, tradition and spirituality off work.

Didi took me under her wing. Apart from the hours in office, I spent almost every waking moment with her. She was a marvel. Her enthusiasm, joy for life, laughter and beauty were just the outer expression of her deep devotion, profound wisdom and spirituality. Her generous heart, infinite patience, ability to accept everyone for what they were, and love everyone unconditionally, was a first of its kind experience for me. Her implicit faith and unbounded capacity to serve was deeply inspiring. I had never met anyone quite like her. I learnt the delight of dressing up and appreciating the fine things of life, developed the love for chanting mantras, and was tutored effortlessly in the meaning of living a purposeful life.

The Art of Living family and the Ashram were my extended anchors. I was cared for without anyone making a big deal of it.

Meanwhile, work at the Visalakshi Mantap was in full swing. Almost seven thousand workers had been working for over three years to complete this magnificent masterpiece. Hundreds of traditional craftsmen were engaged to carve out the intricate statues of the Ashtalakshmi (eight manifestations of Devi Lakshmi, the Goddess of Wealth) and the 1008 lotus petals across the five storeys. Visalakshi Mantap has a fifteen-foot high Kalasha, among Asia's largest. One would assume that building a structure like this would need professional architects, agencies, technicians, and the like. But, Gurudev's approach was unique. Most of the team comprised volunteers, and not more than five percent professionals. Gurudev personally supervised the progress of the construction. He visited the site every day that he was in the Bangalore Ashram, walking through the scaffoldings, cement bags, bricks, rocks and stones, pointing out the tiniest of corrections. Nothing missed his sharp gaze. He allowed no shortcuts and settled only for the best. Gurudev often said that millions of people from around the world would come and meditate in these halls.

The inauguration date was fast approaching and completing the building was topmost priority. Everyone involved in the project had a sense that they were part of a historic effort, but I doubt we grasped the scale fully. For the eighty-one pillars in Visalakshi Mantap, we built eighty-one homes to gift to homeless women.

As the preparations for the inauguration ceremony began, I drove to the Ashram every evening after work, to be a part of meetings and discussions.

Gurudev had chalked out the programme. The first day of the event was going to be a congregation of renowned and revered religious pontiffs and saints. The second day would be a full-morning function presided over by the then Vice President of India, H E Shri Bhairon Singh Shekhawat. Shri L K Advani, Deputy Prime Minister of India, the First Ladies of Poland and Botswana, Chief Ministers, industrialists, business leaders and other international dignitaries were also scheduled to attend.

I was getting deeply involved in the preparations of the inauguration. Nikhil Sen (who was then the head of Britannia and whom we called Nikhil Bhaiya), and I made checklists, flow charts, role descriptions and so on. There were forty-nine work areas—design and printing of collateral, hospitality, travel, transport, guest relations, international coordination, and more. One such primary work header was the 'Master of Ceremonies', the team that would be the host/hostess for the functions on both the days. I had identified names of a few of our senior Art of Living teachers as possible MCs, and put them down on our lists.

One day, Gurudev called us to review and discuss all the arrangements. I gave him a copy of my detailed checklist. He went through the primary sheet carefully. When he came to the category, 'Master of Ceremonies', he looked at me and said, 'These people can do something else. You be the MC.' I was certainly not prepared for this. Considering that I would be terribly busy coordinating the whole programme, there was no way I could be the MC. I thought of it as a casual remark and was sure that he would eventually be fine with the names I had chosen.

The mind is a trickster. To prove itself right, it was willing to think that the Guru could be wrong. I was also wary as I had no previous experience whatsoever of being a Master of Ceremonies. As an MBA graduate and working with Citi for over a decade, I had enough experience in making presentations, facilitating training programmes, debating and public speaking, but I had never been an MC before. I returned home without giving much thought to Gurudev's suggestion.

Over the next few weeks, the frequency of our meetings with Gurudev increased, with discussions going into detailed planning. Didi, Chinky Sen, a dear friend and an Art of Living teacher, and I, would go on the weekends to buy extra furniture for the guest lounges and Kutirs. The three to four times that we met Gurudev, he pointed out that I had not changed the name of the MC to my name on the master spreadsheet. Though Gurudev mentioned this repeatedly, I continued thinking that he did not really mean it. The possibility of seeing myself in this role was far-fetched.

As the pace of work became more frenzied, Art of Living teachers and volunteers from around the world started arriving in Bangalore. I had decided to take two weeks leave from the first of January to be available for the last lap of preparations. Ajay also arrived from Delhi, and we flung ourselves into the flurry of activities.

We left every morning after breakfast and returned home late at night. Everyone was enthusiastically working round the clock.

The construction of the Visalakshi Mantap went on till the very last minute, and there was barely any time left for decorations. The guests had started arriving, the state security protocol started paying visits to the Ashram to check the venue and facilities, the decorators were demanding time to decorate the venue, the pundits were planning the yagna, and the protocol offices of all international and Indian dignitaries were writing hundreds of emails for logistic coordination. Everything was happening simultaneously at mindboggling speed.

A congregation of all saints was held on January 16, the very first day of the event. We left the Ashram on the fifteenth, late in the evening, at 10.30 pm, after Gurudev insisted that we call it a day and rest. We left quite reluctantly. By the time Ajay and I reached home and got to bed, it was well past 1 am. We were so excited that everything we had worked for the last few months would now come to fruition that we did not feel tired at all.

The next morning, after completing our Sadhana (daily kriya practice and meditation), we rushed to the Ashram. When we had left the previous night, we had left the 'site', but the next morning, we were greeted by a magnificent, resplendent Visalakshi Mantap. It had been miraculously scrubbed clean of every last piece of gravel, stains, polish marks and wooden shavings. Every inch of it was shining bright in the fresh sunshine of the dewy January morning! That this incredible transformation had happened overnight was beyond belief. It was as though a fairy had flown over the edifice, waving her magic wand. The morning function was awe-inspiring, with all the saints blessing us with their words of wisdom. Each of them espoused the importance of spirituality in uniting the world and making it a happier, more peaceful place. Gurudev emphasised that we are a One World

Family–Vasudhaiva Kutumbakam. He had made it a living reality for us. Right there in that magnificent hall were men and women from around the world, united by knowledge, love, and a quest for the higher truth.

I had worried that the hall would reek of fresh paint. I needn't have. The air was suffused with a divine scent—an extravagant bouquet of fragrances–jasmine, sandalwood, rose and incense. It was mysterious, how it had all worked out. My practical mind was in a quandary.

After lunch, we got busy with the preparations for the next day's functions. Checking last-minute details, stitching up the programme, and other related activities. Gurudev was to meet us after 5 pm, if we needed his advice on something. It was 3.20 pm, when a volunteer arrived with a message that Gurudev wanted to meet me. I ran up the stairs to Gurudev's Kutir and was still panting, when I gingerly knocked on the door. Gurudev was talking to the late Shri Manu Makhijaji, a highly respected businessman and devotee from Hong Kong. 'Come in,' Gurudev said. 'Haan, Rajita, show me your speech.' 'What speech?' I asked, stupefied. 'Show me what you have written as the MC for tomorrow,' he said again.

My chin dropped. The colour drained away from my face. It hit me that Gurudev had really meant it when he had said that I should be the MC for the programme. Why had I not taken him seriously? How could I have been so flippant about it? What would I do now? I had nothing ready. A wave of panic swept over me. I couldn't possibly do it. I didn't even know how it was to be done. The exhaustion of the last few weeks, fear, the nervousness due to the lack of time, and a multitude of unclassifiable emotions shook me, and I started to cry.

Soon, I was sobbing uncontrollably. Manuji was watching me, bewildered. I was quite a spectacle indeed: squatted on the floor and bawling away. Gurudev too was amused. He let me cry for a few minutes, and when I calmed down, he handed me a tissue. Wiping my face, I started spelling out why I couldn't be the MC. 'I will be busy coordinating the dignitaries,' 'I don't have time to write anything,' 'The person who has prepared to be MC will now feel bad,' 'I have been standing in the sun so much, my face looks tanned and dull,' 'My hair doesn't look good . . .' I blurted out every possible reason. For every excuse, Gurudev had a valid counter argument, 'We will ask the photographers not to click you,' he assured me, calmly. As he called out the evasion for what it was, I became aware of the real reason that scared me. 'Gurudev, I have done a lot of public speaking in my life, but here I will be representing you. I don't want to say something stupid and let you down.' Gurudev looked straight into my eyes and said, 'How can you think that I will let you let me down?' His look was intense and kind, his words, both an order and a blessing.

That was it. I had no choice. I left the Kutir and got ready to rush home to write my script for the next day. I reassigned some of the tasks I was handling, but by the time we finally reached home, it was 10 pm. I made a weak attempt to pen down some points. Nothing met my satisfaction. Ajay kept reassuring me that I would do a great job. By the time we went to sleep it was past midnight. Within just a few minutes, our phone rang! On the line was the administrator of the Ashram, inquiring whether I had got police clearance to be present on the stage. Apparently, since the Vice President and Deputy Prime Minister of India were our guests, the clearance was mandatory. The MC on our master list had the clearance, but I did not. This was a new twist to the tale. Though it was very late, I decided to call up Gurudev. When he answered, I told him once again why I couldn't be the MC. Very calmly, he replied, 'Don't worry, come early to the Ashram with your ID, and the police can do the check and give you the clearance. Reach the Ashram by 7 am'. It was my last futile attempt to wriggle out of the MC role.

We reached the Ashram by 7 am, got the verification done, and the programme began on time. The programme schedule was planned in a certain order, but Gurudev kept calling me and making changes on the spot. It happened so many times that my papers got jumbled up, but the programme was going well and the energy was incredible. I was actually enjoying myself.

Just then, Gurudev signalled me to come nearer and whispered that I should sing the Art of Living birthday song for the then Governor of Karnataka, H E Shri T N Chaturvediji. I am no singer, but by then I had become almost immunised to unexpected changes, twists and turns, and had run out of expressions to convey my shock. I rearranged my facial muscles into an air of composure, and began singing. To my surprise, my voice sounded melodious to my own ears.

We were almost at the end of the programme, and only one Swamiji was yet to speak, before we closed the inauguration function. I started to introduce him, but could not recall his name. I was blank. Without making it obvious, I shuffled my papers, running my eyes over my notes frantically, but with the number of changes that had taken place, I had no clue which paper had his name. I racked my brain to remember, closed my eyes for a moment, scanned the papers yet again, with no success.

My podium was to the right of Gurudev's seat on the stage. There was a distance of about fifteen feet between us and where the other dignitaries were seated. I started, 'It is my great honour now to invite Sri . . .' No name came to my mind. After what seemed like an eternity, feeling totally helpless, I turned left to see Gurudev leaning forward in his seat and mouthing Swamiji's name silently. Surprisingly, I got what Gurudev was saying, I completed my introduction of the Swamiji, and to my relief, no one seemed to have caught on to what had happened.

A lot of people complimented me, saying I had done a great job. I was elated. I didn't get a chance to meet Gurudev that afternoon. In the evening, we had satsang in the amphitheatre opposite Visalakshi Mantap. I was standing by the steps when Gurudev arrived for satsang. I bowed down to do pranam to him and he said, 'You were so good today. You did a great job!' He walked a few steps ahead, turned back and said to me, 'See, I didn't let you let me down.'

From that day, I have learnt to accept and surrender to the Master's intention, because it has an intelligence of its own. After this event, because of Gurudev's sankalpa, I have been the MC for hundreds of events of the Art of Living, including the Silver Jubilee Festival in Bangalore, The World Culture Festivals in Berlin and New Delhi, and many more. I have had the chance to speak on many global platforms like The United Nations, The World Bank, The European Parliament, the Pre G-20 Summit. I have addressed more than 500 global conferences, and several prestigious platforms at sought-after events by the global leadership community. In my training and talent development career alone, my team and I have facilitated over a million man-hours of training–all of which meant standing in front of an audience for hours together. The largest gathering I have addressed is of 3.75 million people at the World Culture Festival in Delhi, an opportunity that even important political leaders seldom get.

I have also got completely comfortable with being told to speak or host an event at the last moment. Once, Gurudev called me to host a Guinness award-winning cultural event in Marathi, at a few hours notice. Though my mother tongue is Marathi, I was not proficient in the ornamental Marathi required to host a programme of that scale. The event, Antarnaad, was going to feature 2,750 singers on one stage in Pune, while I was in Mumbai. I worked on the script on the drive to Pune. It turned out to be another spectacular record-breaking Art of Living event.

At another event in Mumbai, the ground was packed with about two hundred thousand people, and Gurudev was about to go on stage in ten minutes. There was already an English MC and a Marathi one. Gurudev pointed out that someone was required to speak in Hindi as well. This was worrying for everyone–how do you get a Hindi MC at the very last minute? Seeing this, Gurudev said, 'No problem, Rajita will speak.' He turned to me, 'Rajita, go start the programme in Hindi.' I nodded and headed towards the stage. Earlier, I used to panic, resist, and be anxious. How I had changed! From being in complete denial when told to host a programme months in advance, to the moment when I was ready to do it in a heartbeat, I had come a long way.

***

After meeting Gurudev, even Navratri became a special festival for us. When I was working with Citi, it became my annual holiday. During our stay in Bangalore, it was easy, but when we moved to Mumbai, we had to plan a lot and we would reach Ashram a day before the festival started. It is also the time thousands of people from all over the world come to the Ashram.

Gurudev goes into silence for the first five days. During these days, all visitors participated in the multiple courses happening in the Ashram. At least eight to ten thousand people would be in silence. The Ashram wore an ethereal air. I did not participate in the course but kept silence for five days and helped out in the puja-related preparations. The only time we spoke was to chant the Lalita Sahasranama and other Devi chants twice a day. Gurudev came out only once for the Rudra Puja and the satsang that followed. Swami Swatantranandji, a Swamiji from Rishikesh, told us stories from Devi Bhagvatam and Shrimad Bhagvatam.

In 2005, during our first Navratri after having moved to Mumbai, we reached the Ashram and went straight to Shakti Kutir to offer our pranams to Gurudev. He was in a meeting with the Ashram administrators. Looking at me, he exclaimed, 'Oh, Rajita has come, she will do it. Isn't it?' I replied, 'Yes, Gurudev.' I had no idea what I was supposed to do! Gurudev asked me to immediately go out and discuss whatever it was with the administrators. But, I had only just arrived! And Gurudev would go into silence in a few hours. I was seeing him after a few months. I wanted to be in his presence and bask in the fragrant and scintillating energy in the Kutir. I could sense the presence of the Devi already. I went outside the Kutir and learnt in the meeting that Swami Swatantranandji had expressed his desire to keep silence that Navratri. So someone had to take over his role and narrate the customary stories from the scriptures during the festivities. This was what Gurudev had said I should do.

I was aghast. Giving general speeches was one thing, but this was on another level altogether. How would I prepare? I had to talk in front of thousands of people and the programme was being webcast live all over the world. I myself was about to go into silence in a couple of hours. Didi would be in silence too. Who was going to help me? My mind began spinning. I collected myself and ran to my best recourse–my husband. Painstakingly he worked with me through the night to read through the Devi Bhagvatam and Shrimad Bhagvatam to select stories and knowledge. Didi reviewed it in the morning in silence, and indicated a few changes.

That evening, after Rudra Puja, I sat on the stage, a few feet away from Gurudev, and began speaking. My lips were trembling, but I was sounding perfect. My mind was blank but I was speaking words that felt like pearls. My eyes were teary, but I could read perfectly. After every few sentences, the gathering would applaud loudly but my ears heard nothing. I was floating in a ball of energy, carried lovingly and lightly. Everyone praised me profusely after my talk. I did the narration on all prescribed days, and continued being the storyteller for many Navratris thereafter. I have spoken on the Nava Durgas and the

Dasha Mahavidyas and narrated stories of the various conquests of the Mother Divine. The scintillating stories of the Devi defeating mighty demons like Mahishasur, Rakta Bijasur, Madhu Kaitaba, Dhumralochan and Shumbha Nishumbha filled me with phenomenal thrill and energy. What courage and power the Devi had! If every woman remembers that she is the embodiment of this same brilliance and strength, she would know that she is empowered. With Gurudev's blessing, it was not just the literal meaning, but the subtle knowledge that we understood and shared.

Every year, many other Art of Living teachers paired up to speak during the event, in different languages. One such year, Swami Pragyanandji Maharaj, a respected saint from Rishikesh was at the Ashram. It was decided that he would speak every evening in Hindi, during the first days of Navratri and I would translate his words into English at the end of the talk. Gurudev blessed me to do this, and as is customary, went into silence the day prior to Navratri. Unfortunately, the next day, I got very high fever. It was almost 103 degree F (39.4 degree C). I felt so weak that let alone stand up in front of the huge satsang to speak knowledge, I was unable to sit. What would I do now?

Didi gave me strength, saying, 'Rest in the day, you will be fine in the evening.' True to her words, my fever did come down a bit, but I was still weak. At the satsang, I carried a book to make notes when Maharajji spoke, so that I could translate them later. Because of my weakness and also the unclear audio, I could not hear him well. So, I requested a few people sitting next to me to make some notes. At the end of his talk I turned to them, but they were so engrossed in listening to the stories, that they had written nothing! I stood up to speak. As I held the mike, my book had just a few points. Maharajji had spoken for a good half hour. What was I going to say? I looked in Gurudev's direction. He was sitting in samadhi with his eyes closed, looking serene and divine. I bowed down to him and began. I spoke eloquently and without a break for twenty minutes. When I was done, the audience broke into thunderous clapping. Rain had started pounding the metal roof of the Yagnashala Mantap. My eyes met Didi's. She smiled at me brightly and showed me a thumbs-up sign.

Later I learnt that I had translated almost every word verbatim. I continued to be ill with high fever during the day that would subside in time for me to speak during the satsang. Every evening, I translated Maharajji's wisdom spoken in chaste Hindi into English. Speaking during Navratri has become a tradition for me for many years. There is no greater blessing than to speak of the glory of the Divine. Gurudev's Grace made it possible for me to experience it.

Gurudev had once said to me, 'You just say yes, I am taking care of the rest.' This has become the integral sutra of my life. It has presented me with opportunities that were out of my reach and made me do things significantly beyond my capabilities. I have become quite fearless and my mind seems to know no boundaries. Obstacles may come my way but I get the strength to overcome them. Like a petal floating on the flowing waters of a river, I feel as if I am floating ahead on the stream of life. The petal may encounter some rocks on the way or be tossed about by currents, but the inherent force of the running water propels it ahead. It doesn't have to make any effort of its own. The river keeps flowing till it meets the ocean, in a restful, joyful union.

***

Once, during a satsang, Gurudev spoke about Grace. He said lucky and merited are those who recognise that their life is run through Grace. There is no security or safety better than this. Confidence and unshakeable joy fill your life when you realise that it is Grace that is taking care of things. Grace takes you out of sorrow. Then your consciousness starts blossoming. It becomes happy and pleasant. Your intellect wakes up and gets reformatted. However, this takes time. Like a bud takes it own time to bloom and a child first crawls, then walks and then runs, we need penance and patience to recognise this.

The Guru's presence in your life floods it with Grace. You get more than you deserve, before you deserve it. How do you attract more Grace? The more grateful and content we are, the more Grace flows through. Just as you can collect more rain water in a bigger vessel compared to a smaller one, when we increase our capacity to receive, more Grace enters our life. Gratitude and contentment expand our capacity to receive. This is life's biggest open secret.

If we want to make our intellect sharper, improve our understanding and cognition, it cannot happen if we are in a sad, miserable state. It can only happen when we feel good from inside, when we have a pleasant consciousness. To become more intelligent, we must meditate. There is a great deal of research which shows the connection between meditation and improved brain function.

On several occasions, in front of large crowds, I have spoken words I never knew and used them poetically like it was second nature. Every time I spoke, I became more and more aware of the Big Mind working through me. Normally, we see that people who have the requisite skills get the job. But Gurudev gives you responsibility first, and the skill to fulfil it follows effortlessly by itself. He can spot your talents and skills clearly and definitely, before you can see them yourself.

As Art of Living teachers, all of us have experienced this in our courses. When we take our seat, a different power, a higher intelligence, takes over. We speak in languages not familiar to us, we understand languages we don't know, we answer questions on topics we may have no knowledge about, and we speak with the beauty and grace only a higher power can ensure. The resplendence, the presence, the dignity and the humility–all shine through. The impossible becomes possible and things happen that are beyond logical understanding.

***

When we had our three-day Silver Jubilee Celebrations in Bangalore, I was supposed to be the MC for the second and the third days. This was the first of its kind event for us and the logistics were humongous.

The stage was over four acres, and more than 3,500 artistes were performing. In addition, there were more than a thousand guests, speakers and dignitaries, including religious and faith leaders, many current and former Heads of states, ministers and parliamentarians from around the world, Governors and Chief Ministers of Indian States along with Cabinet ministers. There must have been at least sixty such speakers. These speeches were interspersed with the grand cultural programme, the Indian instrumental symphony, the cultural performances from different countries, and the vocal performances by some renowned Indian artistes like K S Chitra, the late S P Balasubrahmanyam, and others.

On day two, along with me, Mr Shivram, an Indian actor, producer and director whose Kannada cinema career has spanned six decades, was also officiating as the MC. I was supposed to speak in English, and he, in Kannada. Day one of the Silver Jubilee was magnificent. I had not witnessed anything of this scale and size before. Standing on the stage, I was looking at a sea of humanity. Day one also taught me that as an MC I would be on my own. The stage was so huge and everyone was so spread out that it was impossible for anyone to carry messages or share information, which is quite typical during live stage events.

On the morning of day two, Ajay suggested that we should leave immediately after lunch, so that we would reach the venue well in advance. Almost 2.5 million people were making their way to the venue in thousands of buses and cars. Being the MC, I could not afford to be late.

I had purchased a beautiful English rose pink Banarasi sari from Prasiddhi Sarees, in Bangalore, especially for the event. After the event, the sari was seen by so many people due to the high TRP of the TV telecast, that Prasiddhi Sarees sold hundreds of similar saris as the 'Silver Jubilee Sari'.

We left for the Ashram immediately after lunch to reach the venue at about 3 pm. The programme was scheduled to start at 6 pm. People had started arriving at the venue and the grounds had begun filling up. The musicians were already on the stage, having taken their positions along with their musical instruments–veenas, mridangams, sitars, tablas, keyboards and many more small and large instruments. The four-acre stage was as big as a football field. There was a huge buzz all around. Everyone was scurrying around doing their jobs. The air was invigorating.

I found a patch of shade on the open stage and sat down to go over the programme. There were so many changes that I was quite lost about how to begin. Also, there was some difference of understanding between two of Gurudev's secretaries about some instructions that Gurudev had given that morning. It was natural. There was so much happening, so many people involved, so many activities, so many international dignitaries arriving that it was like being thrown around by a whirlwind. I requested Gurudev's secretary to clarify certain details with him again and confirm his instructions. Time was flying fast, and soon, it was 5 pm. Mr Shivram had reached the venue and was asking me many questions about the schedule for which I had no answers. Prasanna Prabhu who was overseeing the live telecast and the webcast-related coordination informed me that we would go live at 6 pm sharp and that we should be ready.

I started panicking. We were about to go live and I had no clue how to start the programme. I needed clarity from Gurudev on some key points. Gurudev had reached the venue and was in the green room meeting some of the visiting international dignitaries. I requested Gurudev's secretary to check with him and let me know his advice urgently.

It was almost 5.45 pm and I still had no reply. So I decided to go to the green room to meet Gurudev. It was a huge risk, but I had no choice.

As I proceeded, I realised I had underestimated the distance. It took me a full fifteen minutes to reach the green room. Gurudev was still in a meeting, so I had to wait for another five minutes before I was let in. Once I met Gurudev, it took us about ten more minutes of discussion. Having got my answers, I walked back the entire distance to the podium, through a large crowd. It took me more than the fifteen minutes I had taken to reach the green room.

Until I reached back, I had not had even a moment to check the time. I quickly updated Mr Shivram about Gurudev's advice, and saw Prasanna rushing over to us. He said, 'Rajita, we are going live in five minutes. All set?' I looked at my watch. It was 5.55 pm only! I looked again, incredulous, but there was no time to reflect on what had just happened. Had time stopped?

In 2019, on Guru Purnima Day, in our Montreal Ashram, in Canada, Gurudev had shared this precious knowledge.

'There are two types of knowledge: Shiksha—Shiksha means education. Information is shiksha. Diksha—Diksha means initiation. Initiating, opening the door to infinity is diksha. There's a shiksha Guru—a Guru who gives you knowledge. There is also another Guru, who with his vibrations, opens your door to another realm.

That is a diksha Guru. You have both shiksha and diksha. There are great scholars and intellectuals, but they are not all deekshik—they are not initiated into infinity, to another realm of vibration. Also, mantras take you to a level of consciousness, which is called atarkya. Atarkya means beyond logic. Not illogical, but beyond logic. Anything that is beyond logic is what you call a wonder or a miracle. Life is initiated into an arena of wonder, of beauty.

It is this level of consciousness that can even take us beyond time!'

7

Karaga Banta Karaga Banta

For the few years that we stayed in Bangalore, we led a simple, straightforward life. When Gurudev travelled, I either taught the Part One course in the evening, or we used the time to catch up on all the extra work in office. When Gurudev was in town, we drove to the Ashram every evening for satsang, and spent the weekends engaged in seva. Often, due to the worsening traffic in Bangalore, the *satsang* would be over before we reached the Ashram. On such days we felt content that we had set our feet on the Ashram soil. We would meet a few people, stay for a while and drive back home. If we were lucky, we got Gurudev's darshan.

On one such day in April, though we reached on time, the *satsang* was already over and we went for Gurudev's darshan to Shakti Kutir. Gurudev was sitting on his chair, surrounded by teachers and devotees, and on spotting Ajay, he asked, 'Did you drive here in your car?' 'Yes, Gurudev,' Ajay replied. Patting his leg, Gurudev said, 'Have dinner. Then, let's go in Ajay's car.' We had no idea where we were to go. It was enough that we were going somewhere with Gurudev!

After dinner, Gurudev announced, 'A few of you boys can also come.' 'Was I not part of this plan?' I wondered, but did not want to ask. What if I was doubting it for no reason? When Ajay brought the car close to the main gate, people were waiting to see Gurudev off. This is something beautiful–whether Gurudev steps out for a short drive or a long journey, there are always devotees to see him off! While Gurudev sat in the car, I waited tentatively, not knowing what to do. Many questions flashed through my head. Just then, Gurudev said to me jokingly, 'Are you waiting for an invitation? Get into the car.' I jumped, in and Gurudev told Ajay to drive towards Town Hall, very close to our home in Richmond Town. Gurudev informed us that it was the day of the Karaga Festival, and we were going to a temple for darshan. By the time we reached Town Hall, it was almost after 11 pm. I had thought that the streets would be deserted but a different, unexpected sight awaited us. We parked the car and followed Gurudev on foot. He was familiar with the route. The streets were crowded. It was as if two worlds existed here—one, which was awake and alive, and another, which had gone to bed. Men and women, children and elderly, all dressed in their festive finery were walking purposefully towards the temple. Makeshift stalls of sweets and savouries had come up on both sides of the road, giving it the feel of a *mela*. There was something distinctly celestial in the air.

Suddenly, a man who was walking towards the temple spotted Gurudev, and walked up to him to seek his blessings. In no time, the crowd that had been walking towards the temple was retracing its steps, to throng Gurudev.

In one of his *dohas*, Sant Kabir ji says,

Guru Gobind Dono Khade, Kake Lago Paay, Balihari Guru aapne, Jo Gobind Diyo Milaye

(When faced with one's Guru and one's Lord, whose blessing should I seek first? The Guru is truly great, for he showed me the way to God).

I have observed this on several occasions, when I have accompanied Gurudev to temples. Gurudev would be bowing down to the deity, and the devotees would be keener to catch a glimpse of him and bow down to him in reverence.

As we walked, the four of us tried to create a cordon around Gurudev, but to no avail. The crowd had become so large now that we were getting jostled. Gurudev seemed unconcerned. Even in that tiny space, he stretched out his hand above his head to accept flowers from people, and blessed everyone. When the pundits of the ancient Dharmaraya Swamy Temple got wind of Gurudev's arrival, they rushed out to escort Gurudev inside.

Dedicated to the Pandavas, the major characters from the epic Mahabharata, Dharmaraya Swamy Temple is the only temple in India which honours the Pandavas and their consort, Draupadi, who is worshipped here. Mythology has it that Draupadi created an army of soldiers, called Veerakumaras, after the Mahabharata war, to fight a demon called Timirasura. When the Pandavas were ascending to heaven, the Veerakumaras implored her to stay back. She promised them that she would return to earth once every year. The ten-day Karaga festival marks this homecoming of Draupadi.

It was a hot, humid April day. Ajay and I were sweating profusely, as we waited outside the temple with Gurudev's *padukas*. There was so much to see that my eyes were darting everywhere, trying to capture the buzz and beauty of the activities, a veritable feast of sights, smells and sounds. After about twenty minutes, the pundits escorted Gurudev out.

I was overwhelmed by the ethereal landscape. This was a world of festive radiance that I had never seen. A post-dinner drive had turned out to be a blissful surprise. Gurudev continued to walk zestfully, his hurried strides leading us to one of the small lanes by the side of the temple. We followed him eagerly, bumping into people, literally wading our way through the crowd, and reached a Krishna temple. To our surprise, this temple was relatively empty. The Krishna idol was completely smeared with white butter and adorned with jewellery. Later, I learned that it was called the 'Butter Krishna' temple.

As soon as he saw Gurudev, the lone priest in the temple rushed out to greet him respectfully. We offered our prayers. Gurudev spoke to the pundit for a few minutes and expressed his wish to linger in the temple for some time. His eyes wore a faraway look as he began sharing fond memories of his childhood. He told us about how his parents brought him and Didi to the temple to participate in this festival. How as children they would find it difficult to keep awake till so late in the night, but how the overall frenzy and din ensured that they woke up periodically, in case they fell asleep. He gestured animatedly, his eyes twinkling, as he imitated how people would chorus, 'Karaga Banta, Karaga Banta (Karaga has arrived, Karaga has arrived),' and craned their necks to catch a glimpse of the Karaga that would whizz past in a flash due to the incredible momentum of the energy. Many times, the shouts would make all eyes turn expectantly in the direction of Karaga's arrival, only to be disappointed. Yet, the vigil would continue, crammed in tiny spaces, with bated breath and unshakeable faith that the Karaga would keep its promise.

As Gurudev reminisced, the four of us and the temple pundit absorbed his every word. It was as if we were isolated on an island of our own, in reverential quietude just metres away from the crowds, the loud sounds of drums, the *nadaswarams*, the bells and the occasional blowing of the conches. This was the first time I was not only hearing about this festival commemorating Draupadi, but also partaking in it.

A unique feature of the Karaga festival is that a man chosen from the Acharya Pujari sect of the Tigala community, dresses as a woman (Draupadi), and carries the Karaga, a tall pot with ritual water decorated with flowers, on his head. Joining him are hundreds of bare-chested Veerakumaras (valiant young men). The Karaga bearer leaves the temple around midnight, with the Karaga expertly balanced on his head. In a trance, he dances along to the houses of the Veerakumaras where their families perform puja to the Karaga. At the Dharmaraya Swamy Temple itself, people continuously sing devotional hymns, chant, and wait at the temple for the Karaga's return. This festival has been celebrated uninterrupted for over 800 years.

Fascinated by this tradition, and mesmerised by Gurudev's narration, we kept waiting. Gurudev waited too, with childlike innocence and wonder. It is believed that the Karaga has to come past the Krishna temple on its way to the Dharmaraya Swamy Temple. The wait was meditative. Waiting for the world is 'tapa' and waiting for the Divine is 'tapas'. We were in the most joyful tapas.

Around 3.30 am, the noise and the excitement peaked. People had gathered in droves. It was unfathomable how in spite of residing just a few kilometres from the Krishna Temple, we had no inkling of this enchanting world. Despite not having slept a wink and having had a hectic previous day at work, I felt enlivened. The temple's precincts and its surroundings were pulsating with high *prana*, and I was experiencing its power. All of a sudden, the energy of the place became palpably indicative of something spectacular that was about to unfold. An ambrosial fragrance filled the air.

Just then, we heard loud chants of 'Karaga Banta, Karaga Banta!' There was an uproar, and a collective expectant holding of breath. Men, with small children perched on their shoulders, people squatting on the parapets of nearby buildings, some seated on the steps of ladders, women balancing themselves on the tiny perches of boundary walls, thousands occupying both sides of all the narrow alleys–everyone leapt to their feet in one sweeping motion to catch a glimpse of the Karaga. Alas, it was a hoax. Just as it had risen, the wave settled down, and the wait continued. At least four times after the first false alarm, we oscillated between joyous expectation and disappointment. I could relate so well to the story of Gurudev's childhood.

At about 4.30 am, before we could get a proper glimpse of it, in one swoosh, the Karaga, surrounded by the

Veerakumaras, zipped by. The cry had barely been raised than the Karaga arrived and sped past in a microsecond. The moment we had heard the crescendo, we had moved to the edge of the Krishna Temple, with Gurudev standing on the outermost edge, almost on the road. People had respectfully left that space empty for him. As it passed the Krishna Temple, the speed of the Karaga slowed just a tiny bit for Gurudev to shower some flowers on it, before it sped ahead almost at the speed of light.

It was like being showered and soaked in the scintillating, effulgent energy of the Divine. People stood transfixed, their heads bowed and hands folded in a namaste. Time stood still. There was only Karaga. Nothing else mattered.

What a spectacular contrast of realities. My body shivered and my heart pounded as tears started streaming down my cheeks. I felt both empty and full. My whole being reverberated and I closed my eyes, awash with the fervour. My soul was content yet yearning for more, all at the same time. Maybe this is how the experience of complete communion with the Divine feels.

Once the Karaga passed us, and the crowd had its darshan, it began to disperse. In a few minutes, it thinned substantially. Gurudev took leave of the temple pundit and led us out of the same alleys to the car park. We walked in silence, still in a state of mesmeric bliss. It was almost five in the morning. Another car had arrived from the Ashram to drive Gurudev back. When we did pranam to Gurudev, and took leave, the smile and the look he gave us is still etched in my memory like a snapshot, a good twenty years later.

The relationship of Draupadi and Krishna is often quoted as one of the epitomes of devotion. They were like brother-sister, the best of friends, a Guru and a disciple, and God and his devotee. She followed his every word with implicit trust. She lived through a life of adversity and challenges, with only one strength—her faith and devotion to Krishna.

A story goes that Rukmini and Satyabhama, the wives of Krishna, were very jealous of Draupadi. They felt that despite all the love and care they showered on Krishna, he was always thinking about Draupadi. One day, they decided to confront her. They went to her chambers and asked her why Krishna loved her so much. No matter what they did for him, why was it that it was she who was always on his mind? Draupadi answered that of course she too loved Krishna, like they loved him. But, she said, there was difference in her love for Krishna and their love. In their love for Krishna, they always said, 'Krishna is mine, Krishna is mine.' In her love for Krishna she said, 'I am Krishna's, I am Krishna's!' This story brings tears to my eyes. It is the ultimate example of surrender to the Master, of living a life of being his perfect instrument.

Draupadi had an arduous life. Yet, she had no complaints, no questions. All she said was, 'I am Krishna's! I am his instrument. My life is his, my joys are his and so are my sorrows.' Then, does he have a choice but to have her on his mind!

Gurudev asked once in a satsang, 'Why do you need to think about yourself? You just think of me, I am thinking about you.'

That night Gurudev went to a temple that venerated the Pandavas and Draupadi. He waited almost the whole night to get a glimpse of the Karaga.

It is said that not only does a devotee pray to her Lord, but even the Divine pines for the devotion of his devotees.

Gurudev says, 'God is all over. God is in the stone. God is in the flowers. God is all over. But a devotee is not all over. So God runs behind His devotees. To God, devotees are very dear, so dear.'

It's a mystery why we were part of this once-in-a lifetime, dreamlike, real experience. I can only wonder!

8

Connecting the Dots

In the year 2002, Ajay moved to New Delhi to join General Electric. I continued to live in Bangalore. Till one of us got transferred to the other city, we had to settle for this arrangement. We visited each other as often as possible, meeting once in two weeks at least. In Delhi, Ajay decided to buy a new car—the Honda City. It was a big purchase for us at our young age; a moment to celebrate. I decided to go to Delhi. On the day we were to take the delivery of the car, Ajay and I left early from our respective offices, so that we could reach in time to pick up our car from the dealer. By the time we drove through the traffic to reach the dealership in Central Delhi, it was already past 8 pm. We completed the formalities and drove in our new car to our home in East Patel Nagar.

That evening I was feeling particularly wistful and missed being in Bangalore. Had we been there, the pundit boys from our Vedic Gurukul would have performed a grand puja for the car, we would have distributed sweets to all our friends in the Ashram, enjoyed the drives through our leafy green neighbourhood and celebrated in a big way. I longed to be in the Ashram.

We reached home past 9 pm. Ma advised us to first take the car to the nearby temple so that the Punditji could perform the puja. My heart jumped with joy. Ajay felt that it was too late, but Ma was insistent, so we agreed.

When we reached the temple, Punditji was about to leave. Ajay rushed towards him. I continued to sit in the car and saw Punditji open the lock and go inside the temple. Ajay returned looking happy, and as Punditji had instructed him to buy a few things for the puja, he walked towards the market.

As I waited in the car, my mind flew to Bangalore yet again. I missed the energy of the Ashram, the cheer and the sense of celebration that defined the spirit of the place. On the empty, dark road, I remembered Gurudev and the cheer that surrounds his presence. The joy I felt about our new purchase was tinged with a trace of melancholy. I couldn't put my finger on the reason, but couldn't ignore it either. Sometimes, a sliver of sadness slips into a perfectly normal moment. Wisdom is to detach the thought of sadness from the feeling. When we treat the sad thought as one of the zillion thoughts that cross our mind, it passes on. When we hold on to the emotion that the thought carries, it overtakes us.

Our car was parked at a T intersection of the road. I saw Ajay rushing back from one side of this intersection. He was carrying a few flowers and a coconut wrapped in a newspaper. He handed over the bundle to me and walked briskly to a shop on the other side of the T intersection to buy other puja items like camphor, sacred thread, and incense sticks. I placed the newspaper bundle on my lap, and waited for Ajay to return.

The strange heartache and the longing to be at Bangalore became more intense. As I sighed, the bundle on my lap started opening up. I looked down to wrap the flowers properly, and my eye caught something familiar. It looked like a picture of the Bangalore Ashram. I was sure my mind was playing tricks on me because of my yearning. Nevertheless, expecting nothing, I smoothed the creases of the newspaper, and opened it taking care not to let the flowers fall out.

My eyes widened in surprise and unexpected joy. It couldn't be, but there it was, in black and white, a full page interview of Gurudev. The title read, 'All I want you to do.' My heart started beating faster, my lips broke into a spontaneous smile and my eyes moistened, as I started reading it. Every cell in my body burst with elatedness. It was a beautiful interview with deep wisdom. I drank in every word, but realised that the page carried just half of the interview. The other half was not in the bundle. Just as my spirit had soared, I felt deflated. I wanted to read the whole interview. A sense of incompletion dawned on me, but I could do nothing about it.

Gurudev had said, 'All I want you to do . . .' What did he want us to do? How would I get to know the rest of his words? At that moment, it was all that I wanted. The suspense was killing me. What could I do at that hour on a deserted street? As I contemplated on my options, I saw Ajay rushing back.

He had another bundle in his hand. He signalled to me to come out of the car, as Punditji had started the preparations for the puja. Taking the garland from my hand, Punditji hung it on the car. We stood next to him holding the other bundle open for him to take whatever he needed for the ritual. As Punditji picked up one thing after another, the bundle opened—and there it was, the other half of the newspaper carrying the rest of Gurudev's interview! My attention shifted instantly from the puja to the words on the page. I was euphoric.

I waited rather impatiently for Punditji to finish the puja. The moment it was done, and he was about to crumple the newspaper into a ball, I all but snatched it from him. On our way back home, I opened the newspaper and began to read. What did Gurudev want us to do? In the first part of the interview, he had said, 'All I want you to do . . .' I took a deep breath, and read, '. . . is to be Happy!' the words sprang up. How could it have been anything else?

Two halves of a newspaper picked up unintentionally and with no knowledge whatsoever of the import of doing so, from two shops situated on opposite sides of a road, from two different vendors, arrive into the hands of a nostalgic young woman just to convey to her that nothing else mattered but her happiness!

What are the chances? When you have a Guru, quite high!

***

Once, during a *satsang*, a devotee had asked Gurudev, 'You have thousands of devotees, how do you know when I am in pain?' Gurudev had answered, 'You have thousands of hair on your head, yet don't you know when even one hair gets pulled?'

Such is the love and compassion of a Guru. Nothing is hidden from him. I have been in situations where we would be in the middle of a discussion and Gurudev would instruct us to call someone on the phone. On calling we would realise that the person was facing a problem or dealing with a crisis. The supreme intelligence of the universal consciousness is guiding us, nurturing us and lifting us up when we need it, in just the way we need to be lifted—every moment, every day, in every way. But is it so really? When there are no two, who is lifting whom?

Gurudev has said, 'God is calling you every moment. He is singing through you. He is waking you up through the sounds of the birds, through little animals and creatures, through the voice that says, 'Coo, coo.' It fills the whole atmosphere. If you listen to it, your heart starts glowing. Something happens inside you. You start becoming more alive. Love flows into your life. In the morning, have you heard the birds sing? God sings in the voice of birds to you. He is waking you up every morning. But we miss Him. We have missed Him in this crowd, in our mind, our concepts, and our ideas. We want God to fit into our costumes. We say, 'You should come with such-and-such a costume.' We don't recognise God when he is right there in front of our eyes.'

It is believed that in times of ultimate helplessness and profound gratitude, when a devotee calls out to the Divine, the Divine responds in many different ways. I have heard countless stories of how people have experienced sounds, fragrances, and signs from the Divine in miraculous circumstances.

I have experienced that the more we get connected to ourselves with our spiritual practices, the more we enhance our ability to be connected to the universe. The calmer we are, the stiller is our mind, the more observant and perceptive we are. We can connect the dots. It is quite like what we experience in our relationships. When we are in tune, just a sign is enough. There is no need for words.

***

In May 2006, I had to go to Seoul on an official visit. It was the week of Buddha Purnima and Gurudev was in the Bangalore Ashram at that time. I truly wished that I could get a few days off and be in Bangalore too. In Seoul, my Citibank colleagues and I, worked for at least fourteen hours every day. But, as the weekend drew closer, I felt an inexplicable longing to be in Bangalore in the presence of Gurudev.

That morning, I was in the Citibank office in a service quality review meeting with our Quality Team. We were in the thick of the meeting when my mind and my gaze wandered beyond the window. We were on the eighth floor. Something was pulling me to look out. Right then, from nowhere, a large eagle swooped down to the windowsill facing my side of the table. It looked me straight in the eyes with the most benevolent look. Then, in a fraction of a second, it was gone. To a practical mind, it may mean nothing. If you look deeper, you cannot ignore such signs.

Gurudev says that longing itself is God. Supremely blessed are those who feel the longing for the Divine. The eagle is the *vaahan* (vehicle) of Lord Vishnu. Where there is the vehicle, the Master is not far behind.

The next day I was flying on the 9.15 am Singapore Airlines flight from Incheon, Seoul. The yearning in my heart was still strong. Gratified and mystified by the previous day's experience, my heart was full, but I was still missing something.

On landing in Singapore, I headed to the lounge. After freshening up and reading the newspapers while enjoying a hot cup of my favourite Earl Grey tea, I decided to take a walk around the airport. Every time I was there, I would dine at the Indian restaurant, Kaveri, where I would have a south Indian meal—idli/vada sambar and masala dosa, before boarding for Mumbai.

I decided to do the same that day. The system at the restaurant was self-service. As I waited for my turn, my mind drifted to what would be happening at the Bangalore Ashram, what Gurudev would be doing, what knowledge he would be sharing. When my turn came, I placed my order, paid the money and extended my hand to receive the token. My token number was 1305! The thirteenth of May. Gurudev's birthday!

***

Every year, Gurudev tours North America around April and May. One year it so happened that because of my work tour schedule of June and July, I did not get a chance to meet Gurudev in person for almost four months. When I visited the Bangalore Ashram finally, it was August and the longing was too much for me to handle. This was probably the longest time at a stretch I had not seen Gurudev. When I reached his Kutir, he welcomed me with his ever-loving and enthusiastic, 'Oh wow!' When I bowed down to offer my pranams to him, I said, 'Gurudev, I am seeing you after so long.' Looking at me lovingly, he said, 'Really, Rajita? How come? I have been seeing you every day.'

As a devotee, there is no greater joy than being in the physical presence of the Master. We all wait for it, pine for it. It is the best blessing! Reminding ourselves and knowing that the Guru is a *tattva*—an omnipresent, omnipotent, omniscient principle—not a physical body, is true wisdom. Establishing connection with this tattva, the underlying Oneness that connects all of us, is the source of the greatest strength. He is always with us, watching over us, because He is us as us and we are Him as Him. This is the Ultimate Truth. We just have to awaken to this reality.

The Guru allows you to relate to him in such a normal, matter-of-fact way, that for the devotee to never lose sight of the Guru's enlightened Self at all times is not an easy task. It has happened with Gurudev so many times.

Once we were driving on the German Autobahn from Frankfurt to the German Ashram. Ewald Poeran, one of Gurudev's strongest pillars in Europe, was driving. Gurudev was in the front seat and I was at the back with Bernt Heckman, the President of Art of Living, Germany. I was playing Meera *bhajan*s sung by Lata Mangeshkar, on my iPod. Gurudev was listening to the *bhajans*, talking about normal organisational matters with Bernt. Suddenly, Gurudev went quiet for a moment. His phone rang. We could hear him say, 'Yes I know, she is with me.' It was a call from one of our teachers whose mother had passed away a few minutes ago.

Years ago, we had had a similar experience when Paati (Gurudev's mother, Visalakshi Amma) had left her body, and we had taken her from the hospital to the Ashram in Bangalore. Only Ajay, Didi and I were in the car when Gurudev called on my phone. 'Amma is with me and very happy. She is blessing all of you. Don't be sad.' At that time, I had no idea what he had meant by saying, 'She is with me.'

A couple of years ago, Papa had to be hospitalised for water collection in his lungs. After the surgery when I met him, I told him that I had just spoken to Gurudev who had finished his speech at a big conference in Bangalore, and that he had sent his blessings to Papa. 'How can Gurudev be in Bangalore?' Papa asked incredulously. 'He was standing right next to me all through my surgery!'

One afternoon, Didi, Ajay and I were in Gurudev's Kutir when a famous head priest from the south all but ran in and fell at Gurudev's feet crying inconsolably. His wife who had accompanied him too was sobbing. She told Gurudev how her husband had woken up one day to realise that he had lost his voice. He couldn't utter a word. There was no apparent reason why it had happened. He had made the rounds of the best doctors, and tried all kinds of treatments, undergone every recommended test. The reports showed that his vocal cords had been permanently damaged. Gurudev held the priest gently by his shoulders and assured him. 'You will speak now,' he said. 'Speak,' he encouraged him, but the only sounds that emerged from the priest's mouth were 'Aaaaaaa'. 'Say Ram,' Gurudev urged. 'Aaaaaaa,' went the priest, straining his vocal cords to no avail. 'Ram, Ram, Ram, Ram,' say it now. 'Ram, Ram,' Gurudev all but commanded, looking into the priest's eyes. The Kutir reverberated with Gurudev's chant of 'Ram' and the priest's heartrending 'Aaaaaa', and as Gurudev's voice rose higher and reached a crescendo, something changed right before our eyes. We began hearing a chorus of 'Ram, Ram, Ram, Ram'. The priest was chanting. He was crying, laughing and chanting all at once. In Tamil, words of deep gratitude flowed out of his mouth, as his voice was restored right in front of our eyes. We were rendered speechless.

The five-year-old daughter of an Art of Living teacher couple from Bangalore, our close friends, underwent a serious four-hour bladder reconstruction surgery. Gurudev was touring out of India at that time. After the child regained consciousness, her parents introduced her to the doctors and nurses who had performed her surgery. The little girl quipped, 'But, none of them were there. Only Gurudev was there, holding my hand.' Two months later, when the family met Gurudev on his return to India, he lovingly said to the child, 'Wasn't I with you in the hospital? Your mother was worried for no reason.'

The daughter of a Norwegian devotee, Anjula Patel, had a seizure while swimming in the ocean. She was in the hospital for many days. Anjula had placed a photograph of Gurudev by the daughter's bedside. Every day, Anjula and her husband used to stand near the bed and chant Om Namah Shivaya. On the day of the daughter's discharge, pointing at Gurudev's photograph, the attending nurse asked the little girl, 'Do you remember him standing near your bed, every day?' Anjula was taken aback, as Gurudev was not in Norway at that time.

On July 26, 2005, when a deluge happened in Mumbai, I was in the Citi office at the Bandra Kurla Complex. Heavy rain was pelting us since morning. Papa kept calling me to return home. Gurudev was in Bad Antogast. At about 2 pm, I got a call from the German Ashram landline. It was Gurudev. He said, 'Leave for home NOW' and put the phone down. Along with a couple of colleagues, one of whom was heavily pregnant, we left at around 2.30 pm. We were the last few who left office that day. The waters kept rising and people were stuck in their offices for the next three days. Navigating through waist-deep waters, we covered the distance of forty-five minutes to our home in eight hours.

Gurudev says that our mind is like a frequency analyser and can catch any frequency at any time depending upon its strength and reach. What realms and what levels of frequencies an illuminated mind can reach is a mystery. At the level of consciousness, we are one, manifested as different beings. In the Art of Living, we say that we don't believe in miracles; we rely on them. People all over the world have experienced several such miracles, but Gurudev doesn't make a big deal about them. He makes them sound as casual and normal as the fact that the sky is blue. In fact, he wants us to transcend them. Truly enlightened beings live as normally as possible, tricking our mind to treat them so. I have done my best to keep my awareness about this high, and maintain the respect and dignity that it calls for.

Once, in the Bangalore Ashram, Gurudev was preparing for a TV interview. The crew was making last-minute arrangements of the furniture and cameras. I pointed to Gurudev that the border of his *veshti* had turned upside down. 'I am borderless,' he replied.

It's not that I understand all of Gurudev's worldly actions. Why he is compassionate to someone, why he pulls up someone, why he lets someone be despite committing mistakes, or why he does something when he does it. There is no way to fathom the depth of his decisions. He can be quite unpredictable. When you expect him to be tough on some matter, he can let it be, and sometimes, it's just the opposite.

When Gurudev was on a tour of UK in 2016, our local teachers requested him to join them for a late evening drive in London. Many of us got the chance to be in the van with Gurudev. As we passed many buildings and monuments, he recounted his memories from his visits to UK in the Eighties. He shared how once he was invited by a well-known industrialist to his home in London. But this time clashed with a satsang that was already fixed. Gurudev attended the satsang. When we all exclaimed, he said, 'What's so big about it? I want to be with my devotees above anything else.' He went on to tell us how in Chicago, he was invited to meet someone who later went on to become the President of USA. But even then the appointment clashed with the commitment Gurudev had made to a course group. He went to the course!

Once Gurudev said in a satsang, 'If you can understand your Guru, then he is not your Guru. If you can fit him in your frame of understanding, he is not your Guru.'

This one statement has freed me of all questions, doubts and debates. It has liberated me from the 'How can Gurudev do this?' 'Why is Gurudev doing this?' situations. He knows. He sees across lifetimes and beyond time, perfectly in tune with each one's individual karma. He lives in the present moment, his every action and word in perfect alignment with the cosmos.

9
The Heart of Leadership

I had a successful career in Citi, my first and only job for eighteen years at a stretch. Every few years, at regular, expected intervals, I got promoted to higher positions. I got meaningful, substantial roles where I could expand my professional capabilities, learn and contribute to strengthen Citi's global brand. Do your best and be your best became my way of life. I travelled around the world, saw some stunning places and was exposed to a new level of sophistication and style in working and living. I got the fulfilment of grooming my young juniors into brilliant professionals and watching them succeed on their own. I experienced the joy of inspiring people, taking enormous responsibility and being part of an institution that was a world leader. It was a time of excellence, pride and success.

Simultaneously, my responsibility in the Art of Living also grew. I became a Part 1 course teacher (it's now called the Happiness Programme), then the Teacher Coordinator for Bangalore, then a Karnataka State Apex Body member, and then a Trustee of the Ved Vignan

Maha Vidya Peeth—a national position. As I kept growing in seniority in Citi, my work at the Art of Living also kept increasing. Or was it the other way around? I was surprised at how effortlessly I was able to balance both. I worked hard, but over a period, even that became easier. I could feel my focus improving and intellect becoming sharper with the practice of meditation and Sudarshan Kriya. This increased my productivity manifold. Sadhana, satsang, seva, *sahaj*, chanting, and listening to knowledge became a way of life making me aware of a wonderful blossoming happening inside me. Things were working out. Life was working out. Gurudev always says, 'You do my work, I will do yours.'

***

As I started handling bigger roles, I had to deal with several leadership challenges and fight battles that are not alien to women in any part of the world. Especially in the roles that I handled for Gurudev, I had to interact with a number of external stakeholders—the Government, bureaucracy, regulators, media, local communities, partner institutions and donors. I had never done that before in any of my Citi roles. Even with respect to internal team management, at Citi, I was used to a definite structure of working, a clear line of command, and systematic reporting in a fairly predictable environment. But here, since everyone was a volunteer, everyone was their own boss! Gurudev himself had an incredibly flat organisational structure, where everyone could reach him directly. Imagine being able to reach your global CEO directly, over your local CEOs. That ensured that the organisation stayed realistically aligned to the ground at all times. Being a woman added another angle for me from the point of view of the external stakeholders. I have been challenged, opposed, obstructed and stonewalled many times, not based on my capability, but on my gender.

Once, when in Bhubaneswar, Gurudev introduced me to a senior person from the government telling him, 'Rajita looks after our university.' To my shock, the person retorted, '*Yeh ladki*? Gurudev, *isse kya hoga*? (This girl? Gurudev, what can she do?)' I was crushed and angered by the unkind remark. The person's disdain was unmistakable. No one had said something so deflating to me before; certainly not to my face.

I spent the rest of that evening feeling terribly low. Sensing my state of mind, Gurudev asked me, 'Why are you so bothered by what people say? Let them criticise. You take what you want and move ahead. They don't know what I do. You keep doing your work. I am with you.' He has trusted me more than I trusted myself, backed me up and supported me in every way. His conviction has shaped my capabilities, and given direction to my life, steering it gently and steadily on a path that can be rocky. He often says that the Art of Living is not about having a life that is a bed of roses, but to be able to navigate skilfully through the thorns on the way.

Even now, there are times I face resistance, but it bothers me less. I walk royally, armed with the faith my Guru has in me. I have walked into offices of Presidents and Prime Ministers, met sports stars and rock stars, dined with scientists and authors, all with ease and naturalness. I have chaired board meetings with Members of Parliaments and CEOs on the board, with me being the only woman. I feel no distance and have strongly developed the unique skill to relate to people in authority with a sense of equality. Not higher or lower, just equal. Not too eager, not too casual. Just the right respect blended with enough humility. In dealing with people who are in such exalted positions, I sometimes forget how high up Gurudev has elevated me. I realise that in all such situations, it is his vision, his energy and his intention that are working through me.

***

Gurudev's own leadership style is unique. He has built a global organisation spanning 156 countries of the world in just a short span of four decades. It is as local as it is global. Over ninety-five percent of all people involved are on a voluntary basis. Once the World Bank President asked Gurudev how he managed such a large organisation and still looked relaxed. 'That's because I don't manage anything. My volunteers do everything,' he had replied laughingly. At the same time, Gurudev knows every minute detail of every project and every volunteer across the world. At another level, the amount of freedom and independence we have in leading our projects is unprecedented for a global institution of our size.

How does he manage it? How does he keep the balance between control and autonomy, between trusting and taking charge, between challenging and letting go? How does he build consensus and how does he resolve conflicts? He calls himself the Chief Encouragement Officer (CEO) of our organisation. He can roll up his sleeves and work at the ground level with the volunteers. Whether it is any of our rural projects or projects at an international scale, he encourages them all. When the

Art of Living Youth Leadership team approached him to share their concerns about the dry rivers in Maharashtra, he immediately urged them to take up the project of rejuvenating and reviving the rivers. Once the work caught momentum, he personally visited Latur to oversee the progress. Today, forty-seven rivers are being rejuvenated in four States of India in less than five to six years. Rural Development, Agriculture, Education, Ayurveda, Medicine, Skill Development, Women Empowerment, Youth, Environment, Village Development, Natural Resource Conservation, indeed the range of Art of Living initiatives is so diverse and large that sometimes people cannot comprehend its magnitude. Thousands of people across the world are working on these projects. Through them we are contributing in many ways to each of the United Nations' Sustainable Development Goals.

If leadership is about having a big vision, taking the team along, trusting your people and being committed to their well being, Gurudev demonstrates all this and much more. He envisions projects and events that are humanly incomprehensible. The World Culture Festival in 2016 in New Delhi seemed impossible by all means, with 3.75 million people attending from all over the world and over 40,000 artistes performing over three days.

The cultural programmes were to be held in the evenings with the mornings hosting a Global Leadership Forum, where leaders from industry, politics, government, sports, academics and media would address a delegate audience of over 5000 people. The logistics, the coordination and the scale was unprecedented. Nothing like this had ever been done anywhere in the world before. The stage for the cultural event itself was

The day of our Engagement

The early days at our home in Bangalore

supposed to be seven acres in size. There were many doubts and questions. Gradually, over hundreds of in-person, phone and Skype meetings with people from all over the world, Gurudev built consensus and created enthusiasm for the event. Everyone felt heard and their views considered. Work picked up, thousands of people got involved and country after country came up with unique ideas and plans. To add to the logistical and organising challenges, there emerged some opposition on whether this event would destroy the banks of the Yamuna, where the programme was planned. The way the hostility was building up indicated the work of some vested interests at play. Thousands of people arrived from all over the world including many current and former Heads of State and religious leaders. On the day before the event, news arrived that the National Green Tribunal of India may stall the hosting of the event. The media went on a rampage covering the news. Every news channel was blaring its own version of the truth.

Gurudev was at a devotee's home in Vasant Vihar area of New Delhi, and we were all in the hotel near the venue about ninety minutes away. The media landed up at Gurudev's place, wanting to interview him. Everyone advised him against it. Anyone of us could take on the media. But he was resolute in his decision. It was his event and he didn't have an iota of hesitation in defending his position. I spoke to him on the phone at that time. I felt helpless. He said, 'Don't worry. You keep up as per the plan. Our event will happen.' And, it did!

The quintessence of his leadership approach and wisdom is incorporated in the Transformational Leadership for Excellence (TLEX) programmes that we teach all over the world. I have seen CEOs, Heads of States and senior leaders from diverse fields benefit from it tremendously. I have been part of the massive change management efforts of organisations, where individuals, teams and the institution as a whole, remodelled themselves with Gurudev's knowledge and techniques. With his sterling leadership qualities, Gurudev has brought about new transformations globally.

Happy!

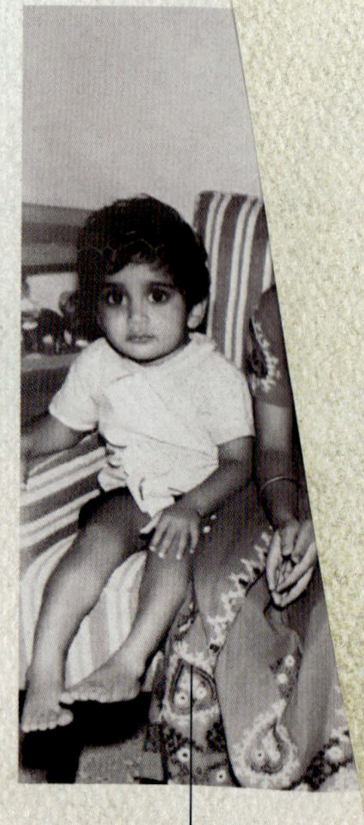

With little S

With Gurudev at Lake Tahoe

Meditation - Exploring The Unknown Edge

The Art of Living's Silver Jubilee celebrations in Bangalore, attended by 2.5 million people

Stuck inside the Lavender Room of The Taj Mahal Hotel, waiting to be rescued during 26/11 attack

Miraculous escape during the 26/11 attack. This picture was published on the front page of every major newspaper in the world

supposed to be seven acres in size. There were many doubts and questions. Gradually, over hundreds of in-person, phone and Skype meetings with people from all over the world, Gurudev built consensus and created enthusiasm for the event. Everyone felt heard and their views considered. Work picked up, thousands of people got involved and country after country came up with unique ideas and plans. To add to the logistical and organising challenges, there emerged some opposition on whether this event would destroy the banks of the Yamuna, where the programme was planned. The way the hostility was building up indicated the work of some vested interests at play. Thousands of people arrived from all over the world including many current and former Heads of State and religious leaders. On the day before the event, news arrived that the National Green Tribunal of India may stall the hosting of the event. The media went on a rampage covering the news. Every news channel was blaring its own version of the truth.

Gurudev was at a devotee's home in Vasant Vihar area of New Delhi, and we were all in the hotel near the venue about ninety minutes away. The media landed up at Gurudev's place, wanting to interview him. Everyone advised him against it. Anyone of us could take on the media. But he was resolute in his decision. It was his event and he didn't have an iota of hesitation in defending his position. I spoke to him on the phone at that time. I felt helpless. He said, 'Don't worry. You keep up as per the plan. Our event will happen.' And, it did!

The quintessence of his leadership approach and wisdom is incorporated in the Transformational Leadership for Excellence (TLEX) programmes that we teach all over the world. I have seen CEOs, Heads of States and senior leaders from diverse fields benefit from it tremendously. I have been part of the massive change management efforts of organisations, where individuals, teams and the institution as a whole, remodelled themselves with Gurudev's knowledge and techniques. With his sterling leadership qualities, Gurudev has brought about new transformations globally.

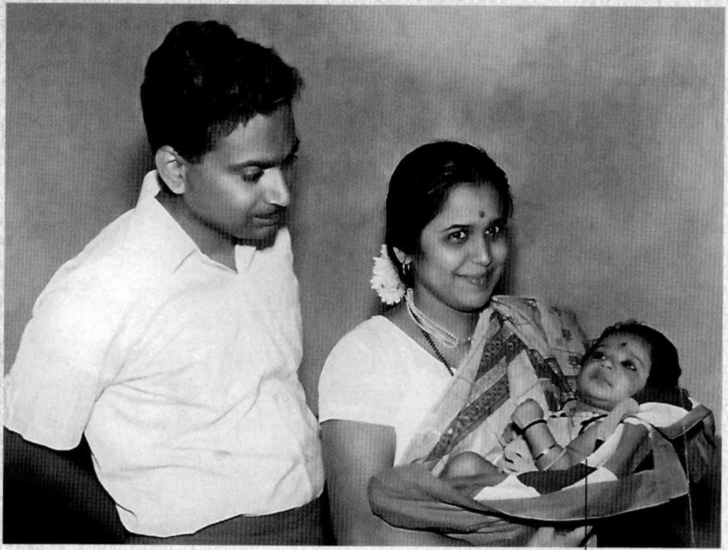

Hello World!

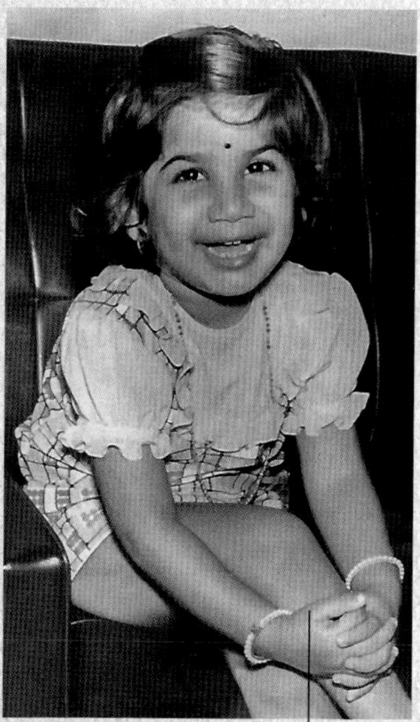

Happy!

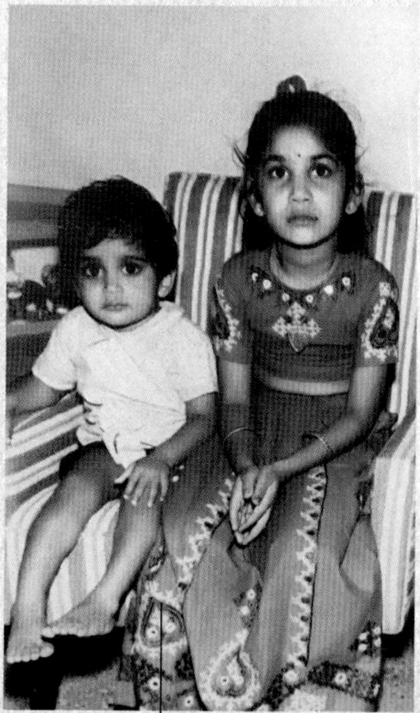

With little Shantanu

The day of our Engagement

The early days at our home in Bangalore

Speaking at the European Parliament for the WFEB Conference

With Gurudev, H E Boutros Boutros Ghali and global dignitaries at WFEB conference at United Nations, Geneva

WFEB Ethics in Sports Awards - recognising global role models

ational Leadership Sym
Mr Roland Koch

Gurudev at the Royal Albert Hall, London

European Parliament, Brussels, 2016

Penalty kick at the FIFA headquarters, Zurich

Gurudev with FARC leaders. The mediation ended a 52 year-old civil war in Colombia

The Art of Living's World Culture Festival in Delhi, attended by 3.75 million people

Shantanu's 40th birthday

First International Day of Yoga celebrations
at the Lincoln Center, New York

Teaching meditation to TLEX participants in Bahrain

Gurudev receiving the Padma Vibhushan from the former President of India Sh. Pranab Mukherjee. Gurudev has also been conferred the highest civilian awards in Mongolia, Colombia and Paraguay.

Gurudev and the Chief Minister of Odisha, Sh Naveen Patnaik at the foundation stone ceremony of Sri Sri University Ayurveda Hospital

Team Sri Sri University

Sri Sri University Convocation

Vidya - Sri Sri University Skill Training Center with Larsen and Toubro

With Gurudev and Smt. Asha Bhosle at Sri Sri University

The Guru is not a person but a Principle, a benevolent presence.

Satsang at The Art of Living
Bangalore Ashram

10
Main Hoon Na

November 2008. It was a tough month for us. A crash as bad as the one in the 1930s had brought the world markets tumbling down and taken a toll on the financial markets in a way the world was not prepared for. With both Ajay and I being in banking and financial services, every day dealt a new blow of unpleasant news. It involved friends losing jobs, customers losing businesses, and investors suffering unparalleled losses. This tragic trail started in September. One of Ajay's childhood friends was in Lehman Brothers. When we spoke to him about his job, he seemed upbeat and said there were talks of a bailout and he would be fine. A couple of days later, news broke on CNN that Lehman was shutting down, and almost everyone was losing their jobs. Ajay's friend was one of them. Many other friends in Singapore saw their net worth crashing from millions of dollars to a few thousands. A lifetime of savings wiped out in weeks. The professional lives of friends, colleagues, associates built with decades of hard work, were getting destroyed in minutes. The stock market and the housing finance market had crashed.

Ajay was the CEO of Lotus Asset Management, one of the youngest CEOs of a mutual fund company in India. Having built the company from scratch, he had taken it to ₹ 10,000 crore of Assets Under Management in a short span of two years. It was unprecedented growth by any standards. But, he was already experiencing the pressure of the crisis. Capital inflows had dried up, returns had to be made up for investors, avenues to raise capital were drying up and the prospects looked very grim. The situation was bad enough for them to consider sale of the company. Ajay was under huge pressure and I would watch from the sidelines his valiant attempts to tap every possible opportunity to stave off this sale. He would be on the phone for sixteen to eighteen hours a day, calling every person he knew, knocking on every door possible. Finally, it was decided that Temasek, the primary investor, would sell out.

Ajay would be working long days, coming home at 4 am or 5 am. Personally too, it was a busy time with Ajay's younger sister Rupa's upcoming marriage in December. She had met her fiancé, Benoit, in Vancouver, where they were to get married. The date was fixed for December 8, 2008. Our family was to travel from different parts of the world to Canada a week prior to the wedding. Our tickets were booked for November 30. I had taken on the mantle of all the wedding shopping, gifts, food, clothes—practically every little thing that is needed for a big fat Punjabi-French wedding.

While on the one hand we were dealing with having to let go of the company that Ajay so passionately built, on the other, there was the joyful excitement of the upcoming wedding. It was a month of mixed emotions and feelings. To top it all, we had to travel to Brussels in the second week of November for the World Forum for Ethics in Business (WFEB) Annual Summit at the European Parliament. It was a jet-setting trip of four days over a weekend. The summit themed 'Capitalism Quo Vadis' was extremely timely, raising the vital importance of ethics and values in pursuing profits. Considering the world had lost billions of dollars of wealth, the discussions were loud, sentiments angry, and there was a huge amount of anxiety and the fear of the future.

I was on the Board of the WFEB, and one of my colleagues on the Board was Erika Mann, a German politician and Member of the European Parliament (MEP). Erika mentioned to me that she was travelling to India along with a delegation of MEPs in the week of November 21, and would be visiting New Delhi and Mumbai, for trade and business meetings. Their first stop was New Delhi and they would arrive in Mumbai on November 26.

Erika wanted to meet me and Ajay while she was in Mumbai and enjoy a good Indian meal with us. We decided the best time to have dinner was on her arrival on November 26.

On November 21, I had to travel to Delhi for work. It was good timing. I could pick up from Ma all the last-minute shopping she had done for Rupa. It was also the day that Art of Living was hosting Brahm Naad, a one of its kind musical event where more than 1200 sitarists would play the sitar together for the first time ever. (Later, this event went on to become a part of the Guinness Book of World Records).

After finishing my meetings, I picked up all the wedding shopping from Ma and drove with Shantanu and Shubhangi to the Brahm Naad venue. It was a stunning exhibition of talent, coordination, collaboration and sheer genius. I met Erika there and we agreed to meet in the lobby of the Taj on November 26 at 9 pm, and proceed for dinner.

I flew back to Mumbai early morning on November 22, because we had to drive to Pune for my cousin Rahul's wedding. Ajay was busy finalising the sale deal of Lotus. I was travelling and shopping for Rupa's wedding. On the way back from Pune, for some reason, I decided to take a holiday on the 25th, and with Mummy's help finished all the gift-wrapping and packing in ten hours. When Erika's secretary called to fix our dinner meeting for the 26th, I felt it was better to eat at a restaurant. There was too much going on at home.

The morning of November 26 was busy. Ajay had returned from office at 4 am. A team from the Temasek Singapore office was in Mumbai to be part of all the final aspects of the Lotus sale deal. They were staying at the Trident Hotel at Nariman Point. We were getting ready for office, eating breakfast, and finishing the calls. We decided that we would go for dinner to Kandahar at The Oberoi. We always liked the food there and it was across the road from Ajay's office.

I left for office. It was a busy day full of conference calls and meetings. At about 11 am, a weird thought crossed my mind—should I indeed meet Erika for dinner? Should I go to the Taj Mahal Hotel tonight? I wondered why such questions were crossing my mind. I even tried to reach Erika's secretary in Brussels to see if I could change our appointment for that evening, but couldn't reach her. I continued working, but at about 3 pm, I felt uneasy and physically ill. There was a strange weight on my heart. I tried to ignore it, but by 4 pm, it became unbearable. I decided to call it a day, and drove back home. On reaching home, I asked my driver to leave for the day. When he was handing over the car keys to me, I told him to go home and stay home. Even as I said this, I wondered, 'What am I saying?' He looked at me quizzically, but I insisted that he should just stay at home. He nodded, but probably thought of it as a strange instruction.

That evening I changed my mind three to four times about what I was going to wear. It was uncharacteristic of me. I am a quick and firm decision-maker. I was intrigued by my own behaviour.

We decided that I would pick up Ajay from his office, drive to the Taj to pick Erika up, and go to Kandahar at The Oberoi. We didn't eat out much because with all our travel, eating at home was a luxury for us. But, we liked Kandahar. The service was fantastic and Ajay loved the Peshawari food.

Surprisingly, Ajay came home by 7.30 pm. Tired, he wanted to drop out of the dinner plan. He told me to go ahead, and offered to pick me up after the dinner. I had promised Erika that we would both be there. We had a small argument about this. Finally, he agreed to accompany me. As we were leaving from home at about 8.10 pm, I told the housekeeper to keep some light dinner ready for us. For some inexplicable reason, I felt that we may not eat out. It was a peculiar thought.

We lived on the twenty-second floor of Jupiter building in Cuffe Parade. Ajay told his driver to leave and decided to drive himself.

When we reached the parking lot, Ajay noticed that I was not carrying my purse and insisted that I carry my BlackBerry too. In Citi, the policy was to keep voice and data on two separate devices. Again, we argued, but as Ajay insisted, I took the lift up twenty-two floors to get my BlackBerry. Now, because I had two gadgets, I had to carry a small purse. Generally, I avoid carrying one.

The drive from Cuffe Parade to Taj Mahal Hotel at that time of the night takes just about fifteen to twenty minutes. With the delay in leaving, by the time we reached the Badhwar Park, Fisherman's Colony signal, it was about 8.40 pm. The nagging unease was back. I was feeling suffocated.

The more connected you are to your Self, the more connected you are to the universe. We were getting one signal after another of something being amiss, something aside of normal, something not okay. Somehow, I couldn't add it up.

At 8.55 pm, we were in the lobby of the new Taj. Ajay was getting a call, so he went and sat on the sofa. I noticed a scruffy-looking young man sitting with a backpack, on the other end of it. I caught myself thinking that people should dress up decently when they come to such a place, but chided myself on being judgmental.

I continued to walk about the lobby, waiting for Erika. I read the announcements board. Listed were a Unilever meeting, and a few weddings. Normal events in a five-star hotel. It was 9.10 pm. No sign of the punctual

Erika. At 9.15 pm, Ajay's patience began running out. He wanted to leave. He told me we could catch a bite in one of the restaurants of the Taj and he would pick me up after dinner. I could see he was tired. As he waited at the patio for our car, I ran out to ask him to stay. Anyway, he relented, and as we entered the hotel, we saw Erika walk towards us. It was 9.20 pm.

We decided to not go to Kandahar and eat at the Taj itself. I said, Chinese in Golden Dragon. Ajay said, Indian in Masala Kraft. Erika also voted for Indian. So we walked the thirty steps to Masala Kraft. Being a weekday, it was crowded with business diners. I could see a few families too. The hostess indicated a table by the door. Ajay sat with his back to the door. Erika and I were facing him. The captain handed us the menu cards. We caught about a minute of conversation, where Erika mentioned that her colleagues, the other MEPs from their visiting delegation, had gone for dinner to the suburbs, straight after landing from Delhi. She had come downtown because we had planned to meet her for this dinner. We just started deciding what to eat when we heard a loud bang. I thought it was crackers, remembering the list of weddings I had seen in the lobby. Instantly, Ajay leapt from his seat and rushed to shut the door. I was shocked and surprised at the same time. I thought, 'Why is Ajay doing this?' Even the hostess seemed taken aback by his behaviour. Another loud bang! I had never heard such a sound before; so I had no way of knowing these were gunshots. By then, an elderly Sikh gentleman joined Ajay. Both of them shut the large silver metal door and held it closed with their backs to it. There were people on the other side trying to push the door open.

Someone switched off a few lights. I was confused and concerned. What had Ajay sensed that I was not able to grasp? Erika had a serious look on her face. Many people were continuing with their dinner as though nothing had happened. I was trying to signal Ajay to come back to our table. We heard some more sounds—shrieks, loud shouting and running, outside in the passageway. In a tremulous voice, Erika said, 'We are under attack.' Her face was a pale white. Attack? In Mumbai? In Taj Mahal Hotel? Who would attack us? Why?

Soon, there was a lot of frenetic activity in the restaurant. The Captains, Chefs and the serving staff hurriedly moved some tables to secure the door shut. Ajay returned to our table. All the guests were talking on the phone, trying to find out what was happening.

'Gang war,' I heard whispers. The Head Chef announced that we were all needed to leave our tables and gather near the kitchen. It was past 10 pm now. At home, dinner is never later than 8 pm; so this was really late for me. I could feel my head start to throb. I was hungry and my throat was parched; I yearned for a glass of water, but the atmosphere had become tense and serious. That something horrid was going on outside the door was sinking in. One guest got into an argument with the staff, because he was not being served his dinner.

Ajay's phone rang. It was a friend wanting to confirm that we were safe at home. 'We are at the Taj,' Ajay whispered. 'What!' I could hear the friend almost yell. Then there was an audible silence. 'Ajay, the Taj is under attack. Terrorists have gotten inside. Are you sure you are at the Taj? Oh God, Ajay, take care'. He filled us in on more details, his voice shaking and concerned.

It was clear now that Mumbai had been attacked by terrorists. Ajay received an email from his colleagues staying in the Trident Hotel, who had been informed that their hotel had been attacked by terrorists. Someone got information that the Oberoi Hotel was under attack too. This was crazy.

It was almost 10.45 pm now. We got news that Chhatrapati Shivaji Terminus, the main train station of Mumbai had also been attacked. We heard about Leopold Café too. The appalling enormity of the situation was slowly dawning on us. Erika was getting impatient. She was asking questions I had no answers to. Where are the commandos? Where are the police? Why are we not being vacated from the Hotel?

We decided to call our family and let them know we were stuck in the Taj. I called up Gurudev when we gathered in the kitchen at around 11 pm. He was in Bali, Indonesia. I had mistakenly thought that Bali is one and a half hours ahead of India time, when it is two and a half. The phone had rung a few times without an answer, so I had hung up. I had also tried Didi's number. She was with Gurudev on this trip. Her number too was unreachable. As a last resort, I had called Bindiya, a dear friend and an ardent devotee from Delhi, who was with them. I knew she would either be sharing Didi's room or in an adjacent room. The phone had rung several times and just as I was about to hang up, Bindiya had answered with a sleepy hello. It was 1.30 am, two and a half hours ahead of India time. When I apprised her of the situation, she shrieked. She was in the same room as Didi, and woke her up. I recounted all the happenings to Didi. Her first response was exactly like Mummy's. 'Why are you eating out?' She was extremely shocked but assured me that she would immediately walk across to Gurudev's room and inform him of this happening. She told us to pray and take care.

By now, some of our friends from the Art of Living and our family had started messaging us. Everyone was astounded that a couple, who does not dine out on a normal day, should be in a place which was under a full-blown terrorist attack. What are the chances? Unfortunately, on that day, a hundred percent.

When the hotel staff informed us that they were taking us to The Chambers, Ajay, who had a membership of The Chambers, argued that going there would be like getting trapped in a cul-de-sac. As no one had any information, we had to do as instructed, and people started walking out. Erika was not confident to leave without police protection. We were in a bind. We couldn't leave without our guest and we didn't want to disobey the hotel's instructions either. Just then, Didi called. 'Are you out?' she asked. I told her of our difficulty. She asked to speak to Erika, and after she hung up, Erika decided to walk out of Masala Kraft with us. After dashing through the long-winding, narrow service passages for at least seven to eight minutes we reached The Chambers. The terrorists could have been anywhere. Luckily for us, they were not in our way.

The Chambers was packed with at least over two hundred people—CEOs, entrepreneurs, businessmen, guests from the weddings, partygoers—all looking bewildered. Ajay knew many of them.

It was particularly cold. The Taj staff was handing over white sheets to everyone to cover themselves and circulating trays of cucumber sandwiches, tea and coffee.

The celebrated Chef, Hemant Oberoi, was overseeing some of the arrangements. One of the Taj employees came over to ask me if I was comfortable and needed anything. I remember telling her, 'Don't make us comfortable, just help us get out of here.'

We could now hear louder explosions. Sanjay Bhaiya and Shantanu kept calling us. We decided to use only one of our phones at a time, so that we could conserve enough battery. We had no idea how long we would be in there. Countless messages began arriving from our Art of Living family from around the world. About four hours had passed. We were getting restless.

At about 1.15 am, my phone rang. It was Mummy. She was distraught and wanted to come over to the Taj to get us out. I had a tough time convincing her to stay safe at home.

Soon, the hotel staff arrived to usher us out to safety from The Chambers. We lined up to walk out. Some managed to rush ahead, but just as we took a few steps forward, we heard furious, indiscriminate firing dangerously close. It was obvious that the terrorists were still on the rampage. Instantly, all of us turned around and hurriedly retraced our steps, running towards safety. In the mad scamper, I stumbled and fell, and a man who was right behind me fell on my back on my left side. On my right, I saw that I was getting separated from Ajay. I pulled him to my side. I wondered what had invoked so much energy in me that instead of falling down, I ran ahead pulling the two men along. Somehow, we managed to barge into one small meeting room. We were now hostage there with the injured staff and about fifteen others. To my horror, I realised that Erika was not in the room. Where was she? Was she able to get out? Was she safe? Or?

Some men sat with their backs to the door to keep it tightly closed. They moved a small table against the door. Even as my heart pounded in my chest, I couldn't help but think of unfinished business. I thought of Rupa's wedding. I typed a question on my phone and showed it to Ajay. 'If something happens to us, how would Rupa's wedding trousseau reach her in Vancouver? Ajay smiled at me comfortingly and typed back, 'Don't worry, nothing will happen to us.' Opening my purse that I had been so reluctant to carry, he stuffed some forks and spoons inside, and hung it around my neck so that it rested on my heart like a protective shield.

I was getting impatient. Everything appeared to be escalating out of hand. The deafening sounds increased and smoke started seeping inside through the gap between the door and the floor. The way it was slowly infusing the area, soon we would choke to death. A shiver ran up my spine. All I wanted was to go home and sleep. I didn't want to be here. No one did.

True to his nature, Ajay was calmly coordinating many things–helping some elderly ladies get sheets to cover themselves, consoling others, sourcing and giving information. He had a Zen-like equanimity about him.

Cooped up inside, our breathing had become laboured. The bombardment continued. A few young boys and girls who were huddled together, started sobbing softly. I could feel a teardrop trickle down my right eye. Ajay was still on his phone, sending messages, coordinating in whatever possible way to get us out. As

I watched him, all I wanted was for us to get out alive. All the little arguments, differences of opinion, fights over small things–everything seemed immaterial. All that mattered was life. I started chanting the Guru Puja in my mind. I am a Shiv bhakt and pray to Devi too. I remember wondering who I should pray to. Who would save me? My Guru. He knows me. He knows my name. If I call out to him, he will save me. It was such a childlike thought. At that time, it was lifesaving. I held on to it, closed my eyes and silently called out to Gurudev.

Rumi has said, 'When the world pushes you to your knees, you're in the perfect position to pray.' That was our state then. 'Jai Gurudev, Jai Gurudev,' I chanted ceaselessly.

Someone interrupted my chanting by showing me a message on his BlackBerry that the dome of the Taj had caught fire. News was trickling in about the loss of life at The Oberoi, the Trident, at CST (railway station), Nariman House. My heart was gripped with both sadness and terror. Who were these people killing innocent people? Why? My exhaustion and anxiety were both at the peak. Family, friends, colleagues, and members of the Art of Living family kept calling. Ajay Tejasvi too called several times from Washington to check on us. But we couldn't speak. We had to be silent. The terrorists were right outside. Didi called again. I had to disconnect. I messaged her that we were still stuck inside and the situation was grim. We had no idea of Erika's whereabouts or wellbeing. That was adding to the pressure. I was fighting myself in the mind. Why hadn't I paid heed to all the signals and just stayed at home? Why had we come out for dinner? What if this was the end?

I started writing emails. I wrote thirty-two handover emails. The handover of life. If that is possible. I wrote to Mummy about a lot of personal things, to Gurudev about matters related to the Art of Living, and to my boss about work-related handover. Ajay looked over his shoulder asking me with his eyes what I was doing. I showed him my emails. He typed a message on his phone for me: 'Type these emails but don't send them. Sending them will mean you are not confident of getting out of here. Let them be in your BlackBerry. If something happens to us and someone gets your phone, okay. If not, also okay.' I sighed. He was right. Even in this grim situation, he was a steadfast pillar of strength.

I continued to chant the Guru Puja in my mind. I had chanted it so many times that perhaps I was getting the order of the Guru Parampara upside down. Gurudev has said that the Guru Puja is the mother of all mantras, the maha mantra. He says that you can mould your whole body in such a way that it becomes an invitation to the Divine. The way the mantra is recited, there is no choice but for these Divine energies to answer the call of the Guru Puja.

The young boys and girls in the room were now falling asleep. I did my best to keep them awake. If you are alert, you have some chances of giving a good fight. Ajay and I taught some mudras to an old couple to help them delay the urge of using the toilet. As trained healers, we gave healing to the injured technician in the room. My right hand was hurt and had started to pain.

Just then, we heard the thud of running footsteps outside our room. It was followed by head-splitting sounds, like someone was pounding a heavy weapon on the ground while walking. We knew it was the terrorists. Ajay made me lie down on my stomach, and he lay on top of me with his stomach on my back, covering me from harm.

He whispered in my ears, 'If they come in and shoot, I will take the bullet, you stay still. You have to live and do a lot of work for Gurudev.' What was Ajay saying? I hadn't ventured out to have dinner for this. Ajay had refused and later wanted to leave but he was in here, in this state, because I had insisted that he stay back. Why had I dragged him into this? I was crying inconsolably now. I resolved in my mind that either both of us would go out of there alive or both of us would die together. Either ... or ... was not an option.

Suddenly, someone started banging on the door. It was a man, yelling loudly in Hindi, '*Kholo, kholo* (Open, open)'. It was one of them. He could have pushed a little harder and the door would have broken open. I huddled closer to Ajay. He hugged me tighter. I closed my eyes and prayed. This was it. I called out to Gurudev yet again. In my mind I was saying, 'I know we all have to go one day. But I do not want to go like this. I will not go without your darshan. How I get your darshan is not my problem.' I was demanding this from my Guru. Every devotee has a unique relationship with his/her Master. Father, mother, brother, friend, guide, the relationships are many. Every devotee also speaks to his/her Guru in line with this relationship. Mine was that of reverence. I had never once crossed the line or spoken casually with Gurudev. But here I was, demanding his darshan. In this moment of a life-and-death situation, even this thought crossed my mind.

As the banging on the door got louder, our hug got tighter and my prayer stronger. Just then, Ajay clutched my hand. In the softest possible whisper, he asked, 'Can you smell it?' My eyes full of huge tears, my body trembling, I found myself getting engulfed in the fragrance of roses. It got stronger and stronger until it filled the whole room. Till then I had only smelt smoke; now I could only smell roses.

It is said that the Guru is not a physical body. He is a tattva, a principle. There are thousands of stories in the Puranas and scriptures of how Gurus made their presence felt for their devotees in many different ways.

In the Bhagavad Gita, Krishna says to Arjuna, 'I am where my devotee is.' At that moment, both of us felt like we were bathed in the security of our Guru's presence. I felt tranquil, strong and fearless. The sounds of the walking feet and the banging on the door subsided. It was as though the power of sattva and the Guru tattva stood tall between us and our end. I felt so content at that moment I was even ready to 'go'.

Just then my phone rang. It was Gurudev on the line. I wanted to speak to him, but we couldn't say a word. I heard him say, 'Jai Gurudev, Rajita.' My whole being got uplifted. Tears started rolling down my cheeks. Oh, how I wanted to live! Many times, out of sheer frustration or disappointment, we tend to complain about how bad life is. This moment, no matter how it would be, I wanted to live.

I disconnected the phone and messaged Gurudev that we were still in danger and couldn't talk. He called back and said, 'You will be fine. You will be out of there soon. I am with you,' and disconnected. These words were my lifeline, my very breath. My Guru was with me.

Soon, it was daybreak. I could hear birds chirping. Other morning sounds filled the room. The world was going through its everyday motions. The sounds were mocking us, making the ordeal even more unbearable. Our bladders were full, emotions were running high, and both hope and despair were stalking us alternately. We were exhausted. A simple thing like using the washroom meant putting our lives at risk. Some created a makeshift space behind a curtain and used it to relieve themselves. Being alive means going with the body's demands. Soon, the room was filled with the unbearable stench of urine. It made me conscious of one thing. We were alive.

Ajay received a message from Sanjay Bhaiya that he was happy to know that we were out. Ajay replied that we were still inside. Apparently, there was news on TV that the Taj had been vacated and the NSG was coming in to sanitise it (to combat the terrorists). Ajay immediately messaged Bhaiya about our exact location and requested him to message us the names of the anchors reporting on the various TV channels. One of the anchors was Shivnath Thukral. As he was regularly invited on business news channels, Ajay knew many TV anchors. He asked Bhaiya to call Shivnath and share our location with him. Later, we learnt that Shivnath informed the police of our whereabouts.

Time was ticking by. Gurudev had said, 'You will be out of there soon.' We were waiting, with our eyes on the door and hope in our hearts. Surely, someone would discover that we needed help. Then we were thrown off balance by such harrowing firing and such thunderous, ear-splitting bomb explosions that the hotel shook violently. Our bodies were now trembling uncontrollably.

Someone cried. Someone else called out God's name and began praying loudly. It was the worst part of the entire nightmare. Sound after sound pounded our ears, rendering us deaf temporarily, making our minds go numb. Gurudev had assured me, 'You will be out of there, I am with you.' It struck me that it need not mean only at the physical body level. Our scriptures say that when you have a Guru, the first person who welcomes you and meets you on the other shore is your Guru! What if Gurudev had meant that? A prayer took shape in my heart. It was our only hope.

At about 7.15 am, sunrays started streaming in through the crisscross pattern of the building's exterior. What seemed hidden in the darkness of the night was now even more unbearable in the light of the morning. We were a door away from freedom, but there was no way we could open it. There was the world outside, our world with our loved ones, and the life we had carved out for ourselves.

Gurudev called again, and asked, 'Why are you not out still?' I had no reply. Only tears of hope. He assured me, 'In two hours, someone will come to save you. When they come, you just run.' He hung up. I typed this on my phone and showed it to Ajay. Our phone batteries were almost drained out.

All of a sudden, my BlackBerry alarm went off. It was a conference call reminder for an Asia-Pacific-countries call that I was supposed to be on! I messaged my boss that I couldn't join the call because I was hostage in the hotel. In a few minutes, the news that I was in danger was all over the world and it created a huge furore in Citibank and within my team. I started getting emails from many country heads, wishing me a safe exit. I even got an email from the Head of Security in New York with dos and don'ts for escaping in such a situation. But, there still seemed to be no way out. It was past 9 am.

Suddenly, there was a loud pounding sound on the door. It seemed like hotel personnel. Somehow, it felt safer to be inside than to go out. Gurudev's words rang in my ears again, 'Someone will come to save you. Just run.' The door opened. It was a Taj employee with two NSG commandos. They signalled to us and Ajay and I started running down the staircase. There was blood on the floor, broken pieces of glass and a lot of debris. We tiptoed our way through, our bodies trembling but alert, and within minutes, we were in the lobby. The way out to safety and freedom was a few yards away, and we had spent the whole night in trauma. We dashed towards the exit.

Just as we were on the first step out, Gurudev called, '*Haan*, you are out?' I was so overtaken by the feeling of being free, I choked and couldn't speak a word. Ajay took the phone from me. Gurudev told him that we should turn left where a BEST bus was parked, and board it. We indeed saw a bus waiting. We got into it, but the conductor said that the bus was not leaving and we should get off. When we were alighting, Gurudev called again, 'Why are you getting off?' It was as if he was watching us on a camera. Ajay explained why and Gurudev asked to speak to me.

He said, '*Kyon ro rahi ho? Main hoon na. Tumhara baal bhi baka hone doonga?*' (Why are you crying? I am there. Will I let even one hair on your body be harmed?) Words that have rung in my ears again and again and again ever since. The tenderness, the confidence, the reassurance in his voice infused my whole being with strength. There was a slight trace of dejection in his voice too. Like a mother would feel if her child did not trust her to take care of him. Won't a mother go to every length to ensure that her child is safe and sound?

We got off the bus and could now hear fierce gunfire coming out of the first floor of the hotel. Inside the hotel, we had the security to hide behind a door or under a table. Now, we were out in the open. There was nowhere to go. A policeman guided us to hide behind a white barricade. The photograph of us crouching behind the barricade made it to the front pages of every major newspaper in the world.

The heat and sunlight were too much for me. I was hiding behind Ajay, and had a moment of dizziness. Gurudev called again, on Ajay's phone. He told us to find an ambulance and get into it. An ambulance did come by, but seeing that we were not injured, refused to take us in. By then, there was a mad scamper of people, running in all directions, not knowing where to go. We too started rushing towards the road leading to Regal cinema. We had no idea what the situation was, where else the terrorists would be. We were just going with our gut.

My phone rang yet again. It was Gurudev. He told us to take a taxi and go home. That was not possible. The area was cordoned off and there was no vehicular traffic. We continued walking, now chased by TV channel reporters thrusting their mikes into our faces, demanding to know how we were feeling, now that we were out. They kept asking us how we felt to be victims of terrorism. We continued walking, dodging them. Out of nowhere, a taxi arrived from behind us. There was a man seated on the front seat beside the driver. He asked us if we wanted to go to Cuffe Parade. 'Yes, yes,' we chorused, and jumped in. He dropped us to our building and drove off. From where had the taxi arrived when there were barricades all around? Who was that man? How did he know we wanted to go to Cuffe Parade? It will remain a mystery forever.

It was about 11 am on November 27, when we reached home. Our driver and housekeeper were waiting for us with bated breath. We called Ma. Suparna Didi had gone over to be with her in the morning and they were waiting impatiently for our call. Ma was strong. She said, 'You both are 'Guru *ka bandas*' (Guru's devotees). No terrorist can harm you.' One by one, we spoke to everyone in our family. Everyone was relieved and happy that we were back safe. We received thousands of emails and messages from people from all over the world, some of whom we did not even know. It was a colossal outpouring of love and warmth. We felt humbled and grateful. We may have sold our company that week, but we got our true wealth here.

We were breathing free but the ordeal was far from over. Ajay's colleagues were still stuck inside the Trident. The day was spent waiting for their safe escape and then coordinating their return to Singapore. We were happy to know that Erika had managed to escape safely at the time in the night when we were caught in the stampede. She was on her way out of the country.

Being in Cuffe Parade in close proximity to the hotel meant that every minute we were constantly aware of the happenings during the three-day siege. Sounds of the bombs going off in Taj Mahal Hotel continued till the last terrorist was neutralised, over two and half days after the attack began. We couldn't hide the sight of the smoke billowing out of The Oberoi even by drawing the curtains.

That night, India lost many of its jewels—Police Officers Hemant Karkare, Vijay Salaskar and Ashok Kamte. Courageous lives cut short. The list of people who sacrificed their lives on those three days is long. The heroes who went beyond the call of duty to save lives were many. The face of little baby Moshe whose parents were mercilessly killed, haunted the world for years.

Mumbai saw a white weekend. People were going from one funeral to another. The city was blanketed by a grief never known before. Amidst this heartbreaking scenario, we had been handed a second chance to live. We knew that life would never be the same again.

I was thinking, 'How will we go to Canada now?' But, Gurudev was firm. He said, 'This is your responsibility. You have to fulfil it.' I requested Gurudev to visit Mumbai. The wounded city needed his healing touch.

Soon, we left for Canada. Rupa's wedding was beautiful. We fulfilled our responsibility in the best way possible. In the meantime, Gurudev changed his travel plans and made a trip to Mumbai. Forty thousand people came to see him at three hours' notice. True healing for every soul. We left for Bangalore the day after we returned from Vancouver. When we saw Gurudev, I fell at his feet. I couldn't stop crying. I wept inconsolably. I kept saying only one thing, 'Please don't leave us, no matter what we do, please don't leave us. No matter how we behave, please don't leave us.' I was crying so much that Gurudev pulled me up with both his hands, and said, 'Where am

I leaving you? I am right here!' I saw a tiny tear in the corner of his eye.

He made me narrate the whole incident. Several times, he corrected me. He knew. He was there. Protecting us. Carrying us. Caring for us. How could it be otherwise?

I asked Gurudev whether we could have done more to help others that night. Done anything more heroic? He told me benevolently, 'Just the presence of a *sadhak* (devotee) casts a blanket of protection over others. Your presence saved more people than you know.' The purity and sattva of sadhana spreads its vibrations not only around us, but also to the worlds beyond. This is why our sadhana is so important. It not only purifies and uplifts us, but also everything around us.

Several people asked me later, 'How did you get caught in such a situation? You have a Guru, why didn't he prevent it?' I would tell everyone how grateful I was to have gone through that night. I experienced the Divine like never before, the love of people like never before, the value of life like never before, and the protection of a Master like never before. I wrote a lot after that. Notes to myself, journal entries and poems too. It was my way to express, to heal.

The terrorists were young boys. They must have grown up simple and innocent like all other young children. The way I grew up. Why did they turn to hatred? What did they get out of it? Would their lives have been different if they had met someone who had shown them the right path? I have great belief in the power of positive influence. What if someone like them had met someone like me?

Major Sandeep Unnikrishnan died that night. He was a bright, handsome, strong thirty-one-year-old NSG officer who sacrificed his life to protect us. The only son of an ISRO officer, he took the bullets so that we could be safe. I kept thinking of him with both deep gratitude and massive guilt. A precious life gone for saving another. It was devastating. On the Republic Day ceremony of January 26, the following year, when I saw his parents receive his Ashok Chakra posthumously, unstoppable tears streamed down my cheeks. Without having met each other, that night had connected us in a strange way. In February 2009, we invited his parents to the Ashram and honoured them during the International Women's Conference. When I met them, I couldn't say a word. But the silence between us spoke volumes.

In the Guru Gita, Lord Shiva says to Devi Parvati, 'O Parvati! The Guru protects one from malicious interference from envious ascetics, heretics, and even Gods. The Guru also safeguards one from fear at the time of death.' We experienced this that night.

Years later, a famous astrologer saw my horoscope quite by coincidence. We had never met before. His first question was, 'How come you are alive?' He meticulously explained to me how the stars foretold great danger and loss of full/partial life (permanent damage to the body) and how only a Guru could have saved me from this situation. It was clear who had saved us.

For months after the incident, Gurudev also ensured that we had a continuous stream of senior Art of Living teachers and Swamijis visit us and stay with us. I was going through a lot of trauma. The smallest sound startled me. I found it difficult to fall asleep. For a few months after that I could not travel, as that meant staying alone in a hotel room. I was besieged by nightmares.

Our friends and our families took extra care of us. All their sattva and pure presence healed us at a very subtle level. Gurudev advised me to give healing to people suffering from trauma. I visited homes and offices of many people who had either themselves been caught in these attacks or lost a dear one. Giving them healing healed me.

Only a Guru can empower you to empower others.

Gurudev says, 'You have taken birth for a bigger purpose. Not just to eat, drink and sleep.'

That night Ajay surpassed all limits of courage, steadfastness and valour, in the line of fire. Without losing his cool, and with great presence of mind, Ajay saved the lives of many when he leapt to shut the doors of the restaurant. Later that night, he put his arms around me to cover and protect me at any cost, with no consideration for his own safety. He was ready to die for me. This brave, loving gesture of Ajay's is etched deeply in my heart.

In December that year, like many years before, Gurudev was travelling to Bad Antogast for Christmas and New Year celebrations. Didi was also accompanying him. She asked me and Ajay to join them. Ajay was busy with matters post the sale of his company. We decided that only I would go. It was a very restful and recuperative time for me. I stayed with Didi in her room. Germany has a tradition of celebrating New Year's Eve by bursting firecrackers. In Bad Antogast, we had a soul-stirring and foot-tapping befitting that celebration. Everyone was dressed in their festive finery and the mood was happy and cheerful. After wishing Didi a Happy New Year, I went to bed early at around 11 pm. Her room had two big windows and we would keep them slightly ajar to let fresh air come in, even in the winter. I was a bit concerned that the sounds of the firecrackers would remind me of the night at the Taj. The scars were fresh and raw. All our friends had decided to go to the top of the hill to watch the fireworks. I stayed in the room. At the stroke of midnight, the entire area burst into a roar of firecrackers and the loud cheers of people. From the big window by my bedside, I caught a glimpse of the million stars thrown into the sky by the firecrackers. The sounds were deafening. They sent a shiver up my spine and brought back the memories of the terror attack. I chanted Om Namah Shivaya and drifted off to sleep.

The next morning, the mood was upbeat and everyone was greeting each other. Gurudev came to his meeting room at around 10 am. He was asking everyone whether they had seen the firecrackers, whether they liked the show. When I went to greet Gurudev, he asked me, 'Rajita, did you "hear" the firecrackers?'

November 26, 2008, reshaped our fate in an unimaginable way. It reinstated our faith in the Divine and the deep love of the world for us. Life has not been the same after that.

I have a completely new appreciation of relationships, a renewed respect for time, and a deep value for life itself.

At Citi, I was at the peak of my career. Though I was enjoying every bit of it, after the Taj incident, I found myself asking questions about the deeper meaning of existence. Now that I had a second chance at life, how could I make it more worthwhile? I remember telling Ajji that after I turned forty, I would devote my life to doing something different. In 2010, I decided to leave my job and devote all my time to the Art of Living. Many people asked me how I could give up such a flourishing career just like that. I was confident that a bigger and more magnificent part of my life lay ahead of me.

11
Pundit, Parliament, Peace

When our 'World Forum for Ethics in Business (WFEB)' conference on 'Shared Value' at the United Nations was held in Geneva, Michael Izza, the Chair-person of the Chartered Accountants Association of England and Wales, was one of our speakers. An exceptional professional with a dignified, silent personality, his speech was very well received by the participating delegates. In one of our follow-up discussions, he expressed his desire to partner with us to host a WFEB conference in London. The date was fixed for November 13, 2015. The venue would be the grand ballroom of the Chartered Accountants Association of England and Wales in Central London. Being one of the most important financial capitals of the world, the discussion on Ethics in this environment was most pertinent.

At the same time, we had also decided to host our own annual Leadership Symposium at the European Parliament in Brussels the following Friday. Gurudev had agreed to give a keynote speech at this conference. This was unprecedented—two international conferences within a week of each other, in two different countries, with different partners and different themes.

Our preparations started on a massive scale about four months before the conference dates. Meetings, conference calls, discussions, deep dives—the WFEB global team started getting together across countries and time zones. Working with partners means upholding and appreciating their points of view, interests and priorities. It requires great skill, coordination and collaboration, with a win-win spirit.

Gaurav Gaur, one of our senior Art of Living and TLEX teachers from UK, took the lead to anchor our preparations in London. Many other volunteers soon joined the team. We also learnt that our Prime Minister, Narendra Modiji, would be visiting London to address the largest ever gathering of overseas Indians (around 30,000 people) at the Wembley Stadium. The date? It was the same as our planned conference in London. That was a great coincidence.

We started preparing for our event. The response started building up. The interest was overwhelming and we started getting confirmations from speakers and delegates at quite a rapid pace. Our preparations for the conference in the European Parliament were proceeding alongside. We had booked one of the largest halls in the Parliament and expected it to be filled with close to six hundred people. Since Gurudev would be present personally, many global leaders from the private and public sector, Members of European Parliament, Ambassadors, press and the like were confirming their presence at the conference.

Our event in London was just two days after Diwali. I left from Mumbai on the day after Lakshmi Puja. I have promised Ajay that no matter how much I travel during the year, I shall be at home for Diwali and Lakshmi Puja. It's the time to invite family and friends home, uphold tradition and experience the abundance of life. We celebrate Lakshmi Puja grandly and spiritually. I devote about two and a half hours that day to chant Lalita Sahasranamam, Lakshmi Ashtothram, Durga Devi Suktam and other Devi chants. We meditate and listen to Gurudev's knowledge. The biggest wealth we have are love and wisdom. Celebrating and honouring them is the real puja. We invite the families of all our staff members and all former staff home for dinner on Lakshmi Puja night. Ajay and I buy gifts for them and serve them food personally. It's our way of thanking them for the comfort they bring to our lives.

It also means that there is a lot to clear up after the puja. I put away all the silver utensils, and packed all the Diwali savouries for our team members in Europe.

The Mumbai-London flight was not too packed. Being Diwali, not too many people were travelling. I enjoy my time on long-distance travel by catching up on movies, books and rest. On such flights, I get some of my most creative ideas and thoughts. Gurudev once beautifully explained that when we are at such a height, both the *surya* and *chandra naadis* are active, unleashing maximum creativity in us. This has been my experience too, a countless number of times.

At Heathrow, Neringa, who is Head of Operations, WFEB, and Gaurav Gaur, were waiting to pick me up. Cristoph Glaser, Director of WFEB, a strong pillar of

Gurudev's work internationally, and my good friend, had also arrived around the same time. They were at the arrival gate with big bright smiles and fresh flowers.

It was almost 7 pm local time when we left Heathrow to drive into town. As we got closer to Central London, the effect of Modiji's visit was visible. The Big Ben and Westminster were lit up in the colours of the Indian tricolour. There were big signboards put up to welcome him. Diwali lights glittered in many places. The city looked like a bride dressed in her most stunning finery. There was joy in the air. It was a great feeling to see our country and our Prime Minister honoured like this.

It was almost 9 pm by the time we reached the hotel. We got right away into our meeting for the last dry run before our conference. We had less than eighteen hours to go before the event. By the time we finished our meeting, it was well past midnight, and I was overcome by the jet lag.

For me, it was almost dawn. I couldn't sleep well that night, tossing about, restless, and disturbed. It was unusual, because normally, I sleep quite well. I listened to a knowledge discourse and instrumental music, and managed about three hours of sleep. After my morning sadhana, I met Gaurav and Cristoph over breakfast. The talk of the town was Modiji's address at the Wembley that afternoon. The time was 3.30 pm, the same as that of our conference. Once again, we went over some areas of the conference construct that needed attention. I wrote my inaugural speech on Leadership and Ethics.

We left for the conference venue at 1.30 pm. I could feel the tiredness seeping into me. The sleepless night, in addition to the overhang of a busy Diwali, coupled with the hectic preparations for our conference, had taken its toll. But, being tired was not an option. It was a big day for us. When we reached the venue, some of our team members were already there to support Mr Izza's team. Art of Living teachers and volunteers were also helping organise Modiji's Wembley event, so our London team was divided between these two events.

Our venue was grand. It had the dignity and depth of accounting history. It was amazing to see the names of accounting greats on the Members Wall. Our team was extremely busy wrapping up last-minute logistics and getting ready to welcome our guests. Soon, people started walking in. The registration desk became busier and busier. We were expecting about two hundred and fifty people. Almost three hundred and seventy-five arrived. CEOs, Barons and Baronesses, Members of Parliament, Chartered Accountants, Lawyers, Professors, Journalists, students and more participated.

Michael Izza and I were making the opening remarks. The atmosphere was charged, the speeches thought-provoking, insightful, informative and engaging. The questions and conversations triggered the right thoughts. How can we be consciously ethical? How can leaders find the strength to stand up against unethical practices? What is the cost of the ethical breakdown? How can individuals shape institutions that have ethics as their culture? It is the vision of WFEB to create more and more awareness about the need for ethical business and leadership. It was this goal that we had set to achieve.

By the time the conference was over and we wound up, it was almost 8.45 pm. We kept getting WhatsApp messages with updates and stories about Modiji's speech and event at Wembley. We decided to go out with the team for dinner and celebrate a great day. By now I was ready to drop and terribly jet-lagged, but went along with the team. It was important to appreciate their hard work and congratulate them. The spirit of volunteerism had brought together a great team that had worked for the conference, over and above their daily professional responsibilities.

We booked a table at a fusion style Indian restaurant. Our mood was high. Some of us workaholics were already grouping to discuss a few details about our upcoming conference, the following Friday, at the European Parliament.

As the food started arriving, the chatter at our table started subsiding. Someone in our group got a call about a terrorist attack in Paris. I got my phone out to check Twitter. News was trickling in. Three suicide bombers had struck outside the Stade de France in Saint-Denis, during an international football match, after failing to gain entry to the stadium. There must have been thousands of spectators watching it. This was horrific. Despite my hunger, I couldn't eat a morsel. Someone switched on the TV in the restaurant. We got to know that another group of attackers had fired at random on crowded cafés and restaurants in Paris, with one of them also blowing himself up. The gunmen had taken hostages at an Eagles of Death Metal concert at the Bataclan theatre. By now, there was panic at our table. Everyone was messaging and calling friends and family they had in Paris. This was a Friday evening where normal people living normal lives, doing normal fun things during the weekend were targeted in this monstrous attack. Memories of 26/11 came flooding back to me. A chill ran up my spine. My hands went cold. With effort I kept a straight face, not wanting to cause any more panic than there already was. I was a senior person in the group and now was the time to show leadership, courage and strength.

We decided to wind up fast and leave for our hotels. Just then we received a message that one of the attacks was in a café a few metres away from our Art of Living Centre in Paris. People who had come together to do the weekly Sudarshan Kriya at our centre were now trapped inside. Being on the ground floor of a busy road near the Nation train station, and with a large group of people gathered there, it was seen to be vulnerable. We were told that Deepali Patel and Serge Michenaud, the Art of Living teacher couple, who lived in and managed the Paris centre, were in touch with Gurudev, and were being guided by him.

The urgency to leave from the restaurant was now palpable. We were just a few hours away from Paris. My thought went to Wembley. There was a huge gathering of people there that day. PM Modiji was in town. The possibility of something going wrong in our neighbourhood was also high. Or so the mind thought. When you are so close to danger, the mind can become paranoid.

More and more horrific news kept pouring in. The number of dead and injured was rising. The hostage situation was live.

It was close to 10.30 pm when we got out of our restaurant to return to our hotels. The normally deserted roads had scattered patches of activity, music and people enjoying Friday night out. Every pub we crossed had crowds outside. I wondered whether they had heard about the attacks. If they had, how were they carrying on like nothing had happened? As a human race we have got reasonably desensitised to violence and loss of lives. TV channels blare out such news every day while we continue with our mundane daily chores in our offices and homes.

On reaching the hotel, I switched on the TV in my room. The situation was far more horrific than I had imagined. Inadvertently, I found tears streaming down my face. So many innocent lives lost. To what avail was this hatred and violence? I was feeling giddy and my head hurt badly. In the last forty-eight hours, I had travelled for fourteen hours, hosted a major conference for six hours, worked for eight, slept for just three and was jet-lagged by four and a half, not to mention the emotional pressures of handling an event of that magnitude. To add to it, there were these terrorist attacks.

I changed and sat down on the bed. There is something comforting about soft, clean, fragrant hotel bed sheets. Instantly, I felt a sense of relaxation taking over. I chanted a silent prayer for all the people caught in the attacks in Paris, and hoped that those at our centre were safe. We had to leave for Hamburg the next day where Gurudev was scheduled to arrive. Our flight was in the afternoon, so it could be a relaxed morning. Luckily, I slept well. After my morning sadhana, by the time I came down to the restaurant for breakfast it was about 9.30 am. The restaurant was full. The talk was only about Modiji's speech, the event at Wembley, and the horrific terror attacks in Paris.

It was a relief to know that the people at the Art of Living Centre in Paris had safely left for their homes. All other news continued to be grim. The death toll was rising and the magnitude of the operation had left everyone in shock. A pall of gloom hung in the air. As I returned to my table, my phone rang. It was Gurudev. He was checking if we were all okay. He enquired about every person in our team by name. Gurudev's ability to take care of the matters of the world, and care deeply about people, despite being ever busy never ceases to amaze me. Speaking to him was reassuring. I returned to my room and finished packing.

We reached Heathrow for our flight through rain and chilly winds. It was clear that security had been stepped up after the incidents of the previous night. The tension was palpable.

Maria, an Art of Living teacher and friend, was at the airport to pick us up at Hamburg.

We were all going to stay at the Radisson Hotel, the same as Gurudev's place of stay. This was my first visit to Hamburg. As we drove in, I took in the sights of this lovely northern city of Germany.

Gurudev was to arrive in a couple of hours. We reached the hotel where Elke and Bernt Heckman, from Art of Living Germany, and their son Lars, also a good friend, welcomed us.

Preparations were in full swing to welcome Gurudev.

There is something special about awaiting Gurudev's arrival—cheer and laughter, joy and anticipation. The purity of everyone's being shines bright. Every burden seems lighter, and every worry smaller.

Soon Gurudev arrived, smiling gently and radiantly, greeting each and every person with the same enthusiasm and love. He was to give a public talk that evening in the large convention centre of the same hotel. By the time he reached his room, there was little time left before his evening programme. As instructed by him, we went ahead to begin the event. The hall was packed, and a few people had to sit on the floor and the side alleys.

That evening, Gurudev's talk was profound. He spoke about the need for inner peace to ensure societal peace, and answered every question lovingly and patiently. He led a meditation that felt like a cool shower of fresh rose water, calming and caressing the soul.

After the event, we shared the details of the WFEB conference in London, and the upcoming conference in Brussels with Gurudev.

With less than four working days left, the preparations were peaking for us. That night I slept soundly. Knowing that Gurudev was physically present a few rooms down the corridor was very comforting and gave me a strong sense of security. The time was such.

On Monday morning, Cristoph got a call from the European Parliament informing us that our conference stood cancelled due to security reasons. A decision had been taken to cancel all non-core Parliament events to ensure safety of life and property. This created understandable panic. Dignitaries and guests were travelling from many countries to participate in this event. How could we cancel it? It was our signature annual event. We rushed to Gurudev to update him about the development. He received the news calmly as is his wont.

He said, 'If they want to cancel the conference, we should abide by their rules.' Upholding the law of the land and rules/regulations of any constitutional authority is his highest priority. He has never gone against any law.

Ewald, Cristoph and I conferred on the matter. We decided to talk to Mr Jo Leinen, Member of the European Parliament and Board Member of WFEB to take his inputs. He confirmed that the Parliament had cancelled all events that week. Ours was one of the bigger events to be called off. We discussed the options available to us. It was a great disappointment that an event that our team had worked so hard for over the last few months now stood cancelled. The cost of terrorism is high in so many ways.

Mr Leinen agreed to speak to the office of the President of the European Parliament to see if some exception was possible for our conference given its global stature.

Gurudev cautioned us to not push any authority or office to take any decision out of the way. We were in a bind. Calling off our conference meant that we had to inform our speakers and delegates right away. Some of our speakers, like the former Prime Minister of Bhutan, Hon. Mr Jigme Yoser Thinley, were scheduled to travel out the next day from their home country. At the same time, we had to wait to hear from Mr Leinen about the feedback he received from Mr Martin Schulz's office. It was a state of suspense and suspension.

Soon, we were flying from Hamburg to Saarbrucken with Gurudev. On the flight were teachers and volunteers from Germany, Switzerland, Belgium, Slovenia, India, Bulgaria, Lithuania, USA, and more. Since I had sent my luggage by car, I had a very short and quick check-in process. Swami Jyothirmayahji, a senior Art of Living teacher, had just a cabin bag. Gurudev asked him where his other luggage was. Swamiji explained that what he was carrying was all he had—three to four sets of clothes, a small bottle of coconut oil and a few toiletries. He travelled with only that much all over Europe, country after country, teaching Art of Living courses and spreading knowledge and love in people's lives. I feel humbled by people like Swamiji who live so simply, modestly and dispassionately.

Our group of about twelve people was seated together, a veritable global family travelling together. A lady from one of India's prominent business families had once come to Bangalore to meet Gurudev. Doing pranam to him she had said, 'Gurudev please bless me so that my whole family comes on this spiritual path.' 'Those who are on the path, consider them to be your family only,' Gurudev had replied.

Once, while in Bad Antogast, a big Indian industrialist family was participating in the Art of Living course. One of those evenings, during a walk in the forest, Gurudev asked the teacher how the course was going and what their experience was. The teacher shared that in one of the parts of the course, a conversation had come up where she had suggested to the wife of the industrialist to consider the other participants as her own children. 'I don't need any more children. I have two of my own,' she had snapped back. When the teacher said this to Gurudev, that family was also on the walk with us. There were Russians, Polish, Italian, German, French and many others in that group walking with Gurudev. He stopped and said to the teacher, 'Is that what she said? Does she even know how many from this group here have been her children, parents, brothers and sisters in her past lives?' Stumped, I quickly surveyed the group, many of whom I was meeting for the first time to spot my own relationships from the past!

I looked around the flight. I felt the warmth of being surrounded by my family. My spiritual family, going about reading, meditating, listening to chants, resting and chatting. We were born of different mothers, in different lands, spoke different languages and followed different religions–but we were really close-knit and united in knowledge with our Master stringing us together with his love.

We drove the distance from the small and quaint Saarbrucken airport to our hotel in twenty-five minutes. We immediately left for the meeting with the Mayor, where the discussion centred around how the Art of Living Foundation could help the city of Saarbrucken to work with refugees, and how we could use the techniques of meditation and breathing to improve mental wellbeing among the youth. The Mayor thanked Gurudev for all our ongoing projects in Germany. Later that evening a public programme of Gurudev was to be held. Gurudev doesn't waste a minute. Without taking a short break or resting a little, he went straight into the meeting room to meet with the visitors. Gurudev's work schedule can compare to any Head of State's daily itinerary.

Ewald mentioned that we had received permission from the European Parliament to go ahead with our conference on condition that we reduce our participating delegates to fewer than five hundred. While we welcomed this news, restricting the number of participants posed a new challenge. This meant that we would have to uninvite about half the people who had registered.

Our team of Cirstin, Neringa, Gordana and others did a fantastic job in this difficult time.

Soon, Gurudev wound up his meetings and it was time to leave for his public talk. Travelling with Gurudev has taught me agility, acceptance and adaptability. The inevitability of the present moment becomes a living reality, not just a sutra that we teach in our course. Over the years, I have found myself becoming considerably better at adapting to quicksilver changing circumstances. You can take nothing for granted. You plan something and something totally different happens. You want something and something else is available.

At the venue, Gurudev arrived and walked through the aisle greeting people with a broad smile, his hands folded in a Namaste, his eyes brightening up on seeing a known face. His message that day resonated with what he had said in Hamburg–inner peace for societal peace. He took questions from the audience, answering them with patience, love and profound wisdom.

After the programme, we drove back to the hotel and went into a team huddle to go over the status of the preparations for our conference. Gurudev was in his room, answering calls and taking decisions about organisational matters. He had a light Western dinner of stir-fry vegetables and soup. Whenever Gurudev travels outside India, he prefers to eat the local cuisine. When devotees want to cook traditional Indian food for him, Gurudev always discourages that and asks for local food. As long as it is vegetarian and healthy, he is adventurous about trying new cuisines. To devotees bringing food for Gurudev, it is a very auspicious opportunity. They lovingly prepare elaborate menus and a variety of dishes. But for Gurudev, these treats are an everyday matter. He watches what he eats, without disappointing the devotees. When people ask him about his favourite food, he answers, 'Anything is fine.' Once in UK, a devotee brought dhokla for him. She asked him whether he liked it. 'Yes, I liked it very much,' he replied. That was it. Word spread that Gurudev loves dhokla. So, throughout the trip, dhokla found its way on his plate for breakfast, lunch and dinner!

Often, when Gurudev retires to his room after wishing everyone good night, people think he is going to bed. That's not the case. He works till late in the night, answering emails and messages, taking calls from countries which are in another time zone. On most nights, he doesn't sleep for more than three to four hours.

The next morning we were going to drive to Brussels. After breakfast, I went to Gurudev's room. Swami Jyothirmayah let me in and after some last-minute packing, we were ready to leave. Gurudev gave me permission to travel in his car. As he sat on the front seat, Swami Jyothirmayah, Cristoph and I occupied the back seat. Lars was driving. A three-and-a-half-hour drive lay ahead of us. It was a chilly November morning. As we drove out of Saarbrucken, we passed by art deco buildings jostling for space with the upcoming modern ones. Gurudev meditated for some time. After about fifteen minutes, he opened his eyes and till we reached Brussels, for almost three hours, he was on his phone and iPad, answering calls, replying to emails and dictating notes. Intermittently, he dug into his black bag and came up with the tastiest of snacks, nuts, and crisps for us to eat.

The traffic indicated that we had entered Brussels. Being the home of the European Parliament and the European Commission, along with many other important global organisations, it is very natural to bump into parliamentarians and other famous leaders in restaurants or coffee shops here. Everyone on the streets walks with a great sense of purpose and urgency, as though they are rushing from one meeting to another, each of them having a big impact on the world.

Normally, in Brussels, we would stay at the Sheraton Hotel. On this visit, we were staying at the Renaissance Hotel, just a few metres walk from the European Parliament. Our conference speakers were to arrive soon. Many Parliamentarians, the ex-Prime Minister of Belgium, and a few Ambassadors were scheduled to have meetings with Gurudev. Devotees from Brussels, Antwerp, the Netherlands and Germany had already arrived to welcome Gurudev.

Gurudev had a packed schedule. He was scheduled to fly out of Brussels to London on Friday, November 20, in the afternoon, onward to Delhi and then to Bhopal where he was to address the Madhya Pradesh Legislative Assembly on Saturday, November 21. Only Gurudev could manage a schedule as demanding as this. Once, when someone asked him how he never got tired despite his round-the-year hectic schedule, he had in turn asked, 'Does the sun ever get tired of shining or the rivers get tired of flowing?'

Our conference titled, 'The double bottom line—How Rich We Really Are' had many exceptional speakers from the Government. The World Bank was partnering with us, and so was one of Europe's important Chambers of Commerce. The European Parliament was our host.

The logistics and coordination for a conference of this magnitude is large and complex. Having to manage it within a week of having organised one, in another country, even more so. It's the amazing WFEB team that makes this possible time after time.

Hosting a conference in another institution's venue, especially like the European Parliament, is a totally different ball game. You have to abide by their security rules and regulations, the guidelines for the usage of space, what you can and cannot do in the halls, right down to how many Wi-Fi connections you can get. It's all strictly enforced and monitored. During many conferences, event organisers get access to the venue the previous day, so the set-up of all arrangements can be done at ease, but in the European Parliament, the earliest we can reach the venue is about two hours before the conference. Imagine the incredible effort and efficiency needed to prepare everything as per world-class standards in such a short time.

After a quick breakfast, we left for the European Parliament. Many members of our team and the volunteers had begun to arrive already. The Parliament was quiet, as though just waking up. The security checks were more stringent than I remembered from my previous visits.

We made our way to the main plenary hall, one of the largest halls in the European Parliament, with a capacity of about 750 seats. We got to work immediately.

To witness the synchronised and efficient work of a committed team is such a joy. I have seen it time after time at big events and small ones, national and international ones. Other organisations I know spend thousands of dollars to make this happen. In our teams, I have seen this happen effortlessly. Referring to a large global development agency whose work is similar to ours, I had once asked Gurudev how they seemed to get much less done despite having almost unlimited resources and the most qualified and highly paid workforce, whereas in comparison, we have a much bigger impact on the ground (despite our limited resources and a largely volunteer workforce). Gurudev had replied to me, 'They do it as their profession, whereas we are on a mission.' A 'yes mind' and a 'nothing is impossible' attitude is the hallmark of any Art of Living person. When the mind is stress-free and calm, it can embrace any challenge and overcome any calamity enthusiastically.

Soon, the speakers, delegates, guests, press began to arrive. The large hall started filling up with suits and smiles. The mood, though formal and stately, was cheerful and bright. I made it a point to greet everyone. I have learnt this from Gurudev. His warmth and positivity just engulf people and disarm them of any awkwardness.

It was about 9.15 am and we were getting ready to start. I noticed Gurudev walking in escorted by Ewald. His white robes glowed like a bright light in a sea of black, blue and grey suits. H E Herman De Croo and Mr Peterle welcomed him on stage. To be on the same stage as Gurudev is a big honour and blessing for me. In the earlier years, I would get nervous and be at a loss for words. Once, after an event where I had made a few mistakes, Gurudev gently explained to me to just be myself. These words became my reality. Over time, I have become more confident and courageous. To speak in front of him is like speaking in front of a parent—you feel reassured and accepted.

We started off by observing one minute of silence in the honour of all those who had lost their lives to mindless terror in Paris. There was many a moist eye in the hall. As the President of WFEB, it was now my turn to deliver the inaugural address. Though I had made notes in line with the theme of our conference, I spontaneously kept my papers aside and spoke straight from the heart. I recounted my experience at the Taj on 26/11, and shared how I realised after that experience that my real wealth was the love I received from people and the joy of being alive. I shared how it had become my double bottom line and how rich I was, and how I had started depending mostly on this love and happiness. I urged all the leaders in the house that if we kept this in mind, our actions would be ethical and our life, one of integrity and service. When life itself was so unsure, what was the point in amassing wealth unethically?

Given the environment we were in, the message resonated with one and all. In my speech, by a slip of tongue, I said that we were hostage in the Taj Mahal Hotel for fourteen years! Seated on my left, Gurudev immediately corrected me. 'Fourteen hours,' he said. I bit my lip and corrected myself with a gasp.

The hall lightened up. When I recall the horrendous event, those fourteen hours had truly felt like fourteen long years, a *vanvaas*. I completed my speech to a thunderous applause, and Gurudev's proud smile of approval.

From the stage, I watched as the attendees nodded, made notes, wrote in their notebooks and on their iPads.

Far behind, in the last row, I thought I saw Raja seated. One of our young graduates from the Bangalore Ashram-based Veda school, Raja was travelling with Gurudev on this trip. He was supposed to return with Gurudev to India that day.

It was now Gurudev's turn to speak. He spoke eloquently and reassuringly. He exhorted everyone to take responsibility for peace, reiterating that without peace and stability, no business could flourish. He emphasised the need for multi-religious, multi-faith education so that we train our future generations to be more accepting of each other. He advised all companies to keep aside some CSR funds for peace education. It was a speech befitting the time of the week in Europe, and received a standing ovation. Many people told me later in the day how Gurudev's words brought them the much-needed solace, while also making them feel empowered to take action. Many said how their feeling of despondence and helplessness had got converted to that of hope and optimism.

After the inaugural plenary, it was the time to award H E Mr. Jigmi Yoser Thinley, former Prime Minister of Bhutan. To talk about Gross Domestic Happiness (GDH) seemed timely when everyone seemed to be looking for their own personal pockets of happiness.

I thought Gurudev would want to leave after the award ceremony, given his impending travel and some last-minute meetings. He surprised us by staying back for the next panel. We stepped down from the stage and sat in the first row. Mr Thinley sat to Gurudev's left and I sat to Mr Thinley's left.

The next panel discussion began. I took a moment to check the messages on the WhatsApp group of all of us who were travelling with Gurudev at that time. Most people from this group had to stay back in the hotel because we could not accommodate them. Only a few had joined the conference, and they were continuously posting photos and updates from the conference for the benefit of those back in the hotel.

Suddenly, the flow of messages started the other way around. Brigita posted that they had all been asked to evacuate from the Renaissance Hotel because a car in the basement parking was suspected to have explosives. My heart sank. Many others too posted the same message. Our group was in panic now. It appeared that they were being moved to the Radisson Hotel, which was just a couple of buildings away from our hotel. Gurudev's luggage was still in the Renaissance Hotel. I messaged Ewald to make sure that we got it out before the hotel shut down totally. What would happen next? The WhatsApp activity was escalating with updates, guidance, advice, and instructions criss-crossing in a maze of messages.

I looked to my right and saw Gurudev listening intently to the speeches. He looked calm and serene. Just looking at him soothed my nerves a great deal. I decided to inform Gurudev about what had just happened. I wrote a message on a piece of paper: 'Suspected explosives in our hotel car park. Our team has been vacated from our hotel and asked to move to Radisson Hotel nearby.' I folded the piece of paper and requested Mr Thinley to kindly pass it to Gurudev. It was strange to request the ex-Prime Minister of a country to do a small chore for you. When Gurudev read the note, the expression on his face changed. He turned to me, and with eyes closed a little, held his right hand up in the *abhay mudra*, as though to say, 'Don't worry, all will be fine.' I messaged to our group that Gurudev knows about the situation and everyone should take care and stay safe.

It was about 10.45 am. As I continued listening to the speeches, I also had an eye on the WhatsApp activity. All was quiet for a while. Our friends seemed to have settled into the Radisson lobby or restaurant. Suddenly I received a message that they were being asked to evacuate the Radisson too! I couldn't understand. These hotels were so close to each other, with just narrow cobbled streets meandering in between, that the thought of something untoward happening or being found here was not unnatural. I wanted to ask what had happened. Just then I saw a newsfeed that a Radisson Hotel in Mali had been attacked by terrorists and a number of lives were lost. It appeared that the Radisson Hotel in Brussels did not want to take any chances and was evacuating its premises for a thorough check-up.

I could sense the alarm in our group. I decided to inform Gurudev about the new development. Once again I requested Mr Thinley to pass the note to Gurudev. He read it and wrote back to me on the paper to ask our group to move to an open space, like a town square. I conveyed Gurudev's message to the group. I could see from the communication that our group was moving to the central square.

Walking from venue to venue inside the European Parliament means that you end up meeting many senior leaders: current and former heads of states, parliamentarians, and visiting dignitaries in the hallways. With several events being held there, people of at least ninety to hundred nationalities visit the Parliament every day. Media crews of all major international news channels as well as press and digital news reporters too are parked there on a daily basis. On my earlier visits, whenever I would walk from one meeting to another, some news channel would stop me for an impromptu byte. I often generate a fair amount of curiosity because of my bright coloured saris. Many times, people have stopped me in the corridors to examine my 'costume' as they would call it and take pictures with me.

As the second panel came to a close, there was a flutter of activity in the hall. We requested Gurudev to walk to the meeting room. We were a great sight. A small framed man in flowing white robes walking purposefully, followed by men and women of different nationalities, colours, attire, former prime ministers and current parliamentarians, CEOs and journalists. As we walked, heads turned and bowed with respect to greet Gurudev. After completing his meetings, it was time for Gurudev to leave for the airport.

By then everything had been reinstated at the Renaissance Hotel and it was declared safe for occupation. All those who had moved to the Central Square had started returning to the hotel.

We ushered Gurudev out to the main exit of the Parliament building. The young pundit, Raja, also left with him.

Saying goodbye to Gurudev is never easy. That day, it weighed even more heavily on me. In his presence, the biggest problem feels very light. Now that he was not going to be physically present with us for the rest of the conference, the responsibility of carrying everyone along for the rest of the day lay on us. The news of the evacuation of the Renaissance and Radisson Hotels, and the terrorist attack in Mali had reached everyone. Many of our speakers and participating delegates were also staying in these hotels. This had understandably created some concern amongst them.

On reaching Brussels airport, Gurudev telephoned me to check if everything was okay. He also informed me that Raja could not travel with him on the flight transiting through London as he did not have a UK visa. Gurudev advised that Raja could stay in the Brussels, Antwerp, Amsterdam area till I was there, and fly back with me to India.

Raja returned from the airport with Ewald and continued to participate in the rest of the conference. It was very endearing to see a young pundit dressed in a white *dhoti* and *shailya*, listening earnestly to all the discussions on ethics, good governance, double bottom line and the like.

Once Gurudev reached London, he called once again to check how the conference was progressing and if everyone was okay. He informed me that his

London-New Delhi flight was delayed, and he would be at London airport longer than estimated.

Our conference ended on time at 6 pm. This was a hallmark of all our events. Despite their complex composition and number of speakers, we always started and ended on time. We had planned a post conference tea and aperitif. The feedback on the conference was fantastic. People were sharing how they felt enriched by the discussions. Many commented on how Gurudev's speech had touched a chord in their hearts. It had been a long and eventful day.

At about 7 pm, Cristoph received a call from Gurudev. He asked if we had all left from the Parliament and advised us to stay indoors as much as possible. We would be doing just that, as a celebration dinner was planned in the Renaissance Hotel itself.

By the time we wound up after the conference, and walked back to the hotel, it was almost 7.45 pm. I was in the hallway on the way to my room, when my phone rang. It was Gurudev checking on me specifically, asking me where I would be staying during the weekend, and if everything was organised for me logistically. I was touched and moved by his concern, but not surprised at all. His ability to keep track of each of his devotees is unbelievable.

Everyone who has travelled with Gurudev has experienced his keen attention to arrangements and his concern to make sure that you are taken care of in the best possible way. When we receive international guests in India, he personally ensures that the food is not spicy and the rooms are organised to the level of comfort that the guests are used to.

When a group of Chinese nuns visited the Bangalore Ashram, Gurudev advised the kitchen personally on a menu of steamed dimsum, stir-fry vegetables and oriental food to suit their taste. One of our teachers from London, Puja Handa, does not eat gluten. Whenever she travels to meet Gurudev, I have seen umpteen occasions where he keeps aside gluten-free food for her. Once, a group of Swamijis, disciples of a well-known pontiff from South India, visited our ashram in the US. Gurudev saw to it that every day they got the rasam, sambhar, rice and such other food that they were used to. During the Art of Living silver jubilee celebrations in Bangalore, when the number of guest arrivals to the Ashram far exceeded the registered number, Gurudev spent night after night, personally checking if everyone had bedding, blankets and water. Whenever he travels overseas, he even cooks for all the teachers and volunteers. He is a creative and spontaneous cook. I have relished the food he has cooked in many cities around the world: Washington DC, Singapore, Amsterdam, Hamburg, Riga, Dresden, Bad Antogast and many others. He often goes to the mega kitchen in the Bangalore Ashram and can easily cook a 250-litre sambhar.

After talking to Gurudev, the little tiredness of the day just disappeared. That night, the dinner was fantastic. We were about forty of us, with many of our guests also joining us. The light-hearted banter and laughter, singing and jokes, were a perfect wind-down after a hectic day and week. I had decided to take it easy the next morning. I planned a short sightseeing tour around the town with Neringa and one of our Brussels teachers. It seemed like a good way to spend the Saturday. I went to bed that night happy and content. I must have fallen asleep immediately, but woke up to the sound of my phone ringing again. Rubbing my eyes, I looked at the time. It was 8.30 am. My phone was still ringing. It was Gurudev. I answered groggily, unprepared for this conversation. Gurudev spoke brightly and hurriedly. He had reached Bhopal and was soon leaving for his talk at the Madhya Pradesh Legislative Assembly. He asked me what I was doing. I told him briefly about my plan for the day. With a sense of urgency in his voice, he told me that my plan needed to change. In fact, that everyone's plans for the day needed to change. He told us to go back to Bad Antogast immediately. He advised us to check out of the hotel as fast as possible and leave Brussels urgently.

I was still sleepy, and couldn't understand why he was saying so. This meant changing tickets, hotel bookings, organising cars, and cancelling bookings. I got off the bed and went to the window to draw the curtains. I was completely unprepared for what I saw. The road outside the hotel had many army tanks parked where there were cars the night before. Heavily armed police and army personnel paced up and down the narrow street seemingly to guard our hotel. I couldn't understand what was happening. I checked my phone for updates. There was news that Brussels was suspected to be under the threat of a potential terror attack and the Government was planning to impose a security lockdown on the city. This meant that all shops, schools, and public transportation would be shut down. The terror alert level had been raised to the highest level in the Brussels Metropolitan area. No wonder Gurudev had advised us to leave the city immediately.

I woke up Maria and messaged everyone on our WhatsApp group. Frantic calls followed to all rooms where our team and guests were staying. Lars organised the change of transportation. Some, who had long-distance travel booked on trains, checked if the trains were still running on schedule. What followed was an hour of frenzied pack-up, checkout, loading the cars, and getting together.

We decided that as many of us as could, would drive with Lars to Bad Antogast. Gurudev had advised me to stay over at Ewald's home which was about a forty-five-minute drive out of Brussels. Ewald had already driven home the previous night with Raja. Since it was on the way, Lars would drop me there enroute to Bad Antogast.

When we drove out of the hotel, the Saturday morning in Brussels had an atmosphere of war. Army convoys passed through the streets. Armoured cars were posted at central points, outside the royal palace, and at underground railway stations. The roads wore a deserted look, with only a few people, who also seemed like they were hurrying home. Army and police officers were advising motorists to leave the city immediately. This was definitely not the cheerful Brussels I knew.

When we reached Ewald's place, it was like arriving home. In anticipation of our arrival, Lillian had already prepared some light lunch for all of us. By now, news was pouring in that Brussels would be under complete lockdown for the next few days. This meant that all offices, national and international institutions, government offices, and all commercial establishments would be shut. All our meetings for the next week stood cancelled.

My ticket back to Mumbai was on November 26, from Brussels. I would need to figure out what to do for the next few days.

Gurudev's travelling secretary called me to ask if we had all evacuated from Brussels. He was updating Gurudev as he spoke to me.

I decided to take it easy for the rest of the day. The large brown sofa in Ewald's living room looked inviting. I settled in it with a cup of peppermint tea, with Lillian. Raja came down from his room on the first floor. I was chatting him up, asking him whether he had liked the conference. A question popped up in my head. How had Raja managed to get inside the European Parliament? We had not issued an entry pass for him.

Lillian chimed in that Gurudev had advised Raja to go with her and attend the conference, and get his entry pass made ahead of time. Lillian said she had her own doubts about its possibility because the entry passes for everyone had already been issued. She decided to follow Gurudev's instructions and brought Raja to the Parliament. She told me that she was pleasantly surprised when the security team agreed to issue an entry pass for him that morning. Sattva does have an impact.

I was curious if Raja got bored at any time of the day–how would talks of worldly matters interest a pundit who loved spending time praying to his Lord. He told me that Gurudev had advised him to sit in the hall of our conference and chant a special mantra for the protection of everyone's life—which he had done for close to three hours that morning.

The next few days, Raja performed special yagnas for wellbeing, good health and long life in different cities in Belgium and Holland—exactly the same days that Brussels was shut down. The day he left for Bangalore on 26/11 after completing the yagnas, the lockdown on Brussels was lifted.

I stayed the weekend in Ewald and Lillian's home. On Sunday, Gurudev called at 5 pm and asked Ewald and me to go to Norway for two days and meet a few of our key stakeholders. It was impossible to get any meetings organised at such short notice and it wasn't polite to call anyone on a Sunday! When we rationalised with Gurudev about the impossibility of the meetings, he was cool and confident. 'People are waiting to meet you there. You just land up.'

These are the moments when faith conquers reason.

We enthusiastically decided to go with the flow. Ewald booked our tickets, and made our hotel reservations. I prepared our documents and papers for the possible meetings we might have and the people who were waiting for us! We took the Monday morning flight from Schipol to Oslo. On landing at Oslo, we decided to take the train to the city centre, the fastest way to travel. We had just got into the train, when Gurudev called. 'Why are you taking the train again? Why didn't someone come to pick you up?' How did he know! We wonder, despite knowing well that nothing is hidden from him. We reached the hotel and called our local Art of Living teachers and board members. True to Gurudev's words, meetings got organised one after the other, in a manner that may not have happened even with advanced planning. It was like seeing magic unfold, as if the work was already done and we were merely going through the motions. After two days, we returned to Belgium in time for me to take my flight to Mumbai on 26/11 from Brussels.

Luckily, there was no terror attack in Brussels, but the lockdown is estimated to have cost € 51.7 million per day, counting both the outlay on security and lost business income. The total cost of the five-day lockdown was estimated to be over €350 million. The number of tourists to Brussels also dropped in the following months.

It had been an eventful week for me—seven days, four cities, three countries and two conferences. One city pounded by a terrorist attack, while another city and all of us saved from it.

12

Through the Eyes of the Master

'Why do you need a Guru?' I am asked this question several times. I never meant to find a Guru or consciously walk on the spiritual path, but when I did meet Gurudev, it was the most natural thing in the world. It was meant to be.

The truth is that from the moment we are born we have a Guru. Our first Guru is our mother, who lovingly guides us through the very first steps we take. Our father teaches us important values of life. As we grow up, many are the teachers who shape our personality and character. If we need a teacher to learn everything in life, don't we need one to teach us about life? What is the purpose of life? Why are we born? Is life what it appears on the surface? What are the deeper truths? What we can perceive with our senses is the external world. What about the mystical world within? It is said in our scriptures, that what we see of the world, is a very tiny percentage of what there actually is. When you meet your Guru, you feel a deep connection, with yourself and with the creation. Many new dimensions of life, which were hidden earlier, begin opening up when one comes in the presence of a true Guru.

Having met Gurudev, I did not know initially what code of conduct to follow in his presence. How should I talk to him? Am I addressing him correctly? Is there a protocol to be followed? I needn't have worried. Just being in the presence of Gurudev puts you at ease. 'Be yourself. Be natural. Be spontaneous,' Gurudev says. Watching him walk, work, speak has been a never-ending master class for me. I have learnt several lessons from my simple conversations with him, as wisdom flows from these very ordinary-seeming chats. Whether it is during commutes or his addresses to a mammoth audience or while solving someone's personal crisis or mediating in an international dispute, by the very way he leads his life, Gurudev sets examples. We only need to observe carefully, listen intently and be open to learning.

Gurudev is full of compassion. The way he communicates with people who have erred in some way is unprecedented. Once, two women who were visiting the Ashram committed some thefts during their stay there. The Ashram administrators recovered several things from them and wanted to report them to the police. When Gurudev heard of the incident, he instructed the administration to arrange to send the women back to their families. He instructed that they be given a sari each, flowers, and some money. Both the women broke down at how they had been treated with respect, despite what they had done. Gurudev says, 'If you want to tell someone about their mistake, tell them with care, not with anger. Tell them firmly but with a smile and compassion.'

Once, one of our teachers brought a group of two hundred and seventy members of a gang from Hyderabad to meet Gurudev in Bangalore. They looked quite menacing. I was in the meeting hall, and was a bit perturbed by their ferocity. But, Gurudev interacted with them with ease and lightness. He spoke to them in their native language, Telugu, and cracked a few jokes, lightening the atmosphere. As they laughed, they began to relax slowly. Soon, they started opening up about their lives, the difficulties they faced, and what had led them to the path of robbery and violence. Gurudev heard every word. Not once did he interrupt or oppose them. After about an hour, it felt like they had offered their past at his feet, and emptied themselves. The place felt lighter. Gurudev advised them to stop what they were doing and surrender to the police. He gave them examples of Angulimala and sage Valmiki. They listened with rapt attention. I could see their rough edges softening right there in front of our eyes. Gurudev promised to stand by them and help rehabilitate them. He assured them that the fire of tapasya would purify their karma. They touched his feet and vowed to give up their ways. When they rose to leave, they looked years younger.

Gurudev says, 'See the world from my eyes. No one is bad. It's their tendencies and stresses that make them do wrong things.' Acknowledging the person beyond their actions, knowing the purity within them, and giving people a second chance is his very nature. Gurudev's approach to those who have digressed and slipped into anti social activities, or prison inmates, terrorists, and the like, is the same. He says, 'Every culprit is a victim crying for help.' It is with this very conviction that we can tap into the innate goodness of every human being and their true nature, that Gurudev started teaching the Art of Living courses in hundreds of prisons around the world. Prison inmates, some of them hardened criminals, have reported how their lives have been positively transformed with the practice of the breathing and meditation techniques. Many of them have been released ahead of their time for good behaviour and integrated back into society to lead productive lives.

One such inspiring story is that of Jacob from Denmark, who was involved in drugs and narcotics. He happened to do the Art of Living course, and was so blown away by the experience that he was able to give up drugs. Slowly, he started encouraging his friends from the drug trade to do the course. One by one, a few hundred of them were able to get rid of their addiction. Once, I was in Bad Antogast, when Jacob brought a group of his friends over to meet Gurudev. I watched awestruck as these burly men with tough and tattooed bodies, sat in front of Gurudev like little children. Gurudev listened to them patiently without bias. He spoke to them gently like an old friend, with an ease that comes from years of knowing each other. During this very first meeting, the men were so moved by his presence that many of them cried uncontrollably. Most of them gave up their trade and now own legitimate businesses. Jacob himself is an Art of Living teacher now, teaching in prisons all over the world.

Hundreds of other AOL teachers like Jacob are helping the prison inmates to rehabilitate themselves and be integrated into society. Gurudev pulls out all stops to guide and redirect those who have veered off the path and adopted unlawful or dishonest ways. He supports them in every way to restore their honour and dignity.

He went all the way to Cuba to meet the FARC (Revolutionary Armed Forces of Colombia—People's Army) rebels at the behest of the Colombian President to mediate in a five-decade-old conflict that had cost over eight million lives. He gave the rebels a patient hearing and made them aware of the long-term consequences of their actions. He spoke to them about the Gandhian philosophy of non-violence. He urged them to consider adopting a life free of violence and strife. After three days of meetings and meditation sessions, they called for a press conference in which they announced a unilateral ceasefire. As incredulous as it may seem, it is the truth. It is not just what was said that mattered, it was also who said it. In Gurudev they saw a person who had no vested interest of any kind and were able to trust him. He had no prejudice against them. He did not judge them. All he wanted was the greater good and for peace to prevail.

Gurudev's role in mediating and helping resolve the conflicts in Venezuela, Sri Lanka, Kashmir, Assam, Nagaland, Manipur and other places has been internationally acclaimed. He has inspired terrorists to lay down guns, encouraged Naxals to turn from bullets to ballots, and created platforms for families of Kashmiri militants to interact with the families of army men killed by them. To make this happen, he can spend hours on the phone talking to people, days travelling, meeting different groups and persistently keeping the effort on, despite obstacles and setbacks. He doesn't care for his own personal well-being or his image. In 2019, he was appointed as one of the three-member committee by the Supreme Court of India to resolve the 500-year old Ayodhya Conflict. Gurudev was already talking to all the different stakeholders of the two communities since 2003 on the request of late Shri Atal Bihari Vajpayeeji. For seventeen years, he painstakingly met diverse groups, heard their conflicting viewpoints and patiently made them see reason. No matter how much they disagreed with each other, they always agreed with him. He kept all channels of communication open over the years and continued with the dialogue. As a member of the committee, he flung himself into the work like never before, sitting through meetings for twelve to fourteen hours a day. Along with taking care of our global organisational matters, he would end up working almost twenty-hour days. We were in Germany once, when the committee was on a break. Gurudev would be on so many phone calls, that he would eat his lunch at 4 pm on most days. When we protested that this was not good for him, he scolded us, 'How can you all think of small comforts like food and rest, when it's our nation's interest at stake here?'

Not only matters of national and international mediation and resolution, Gurudev also helps individuals resolve their inner conflicts and insecurities with equal importance. Once while in the Ashram, I was in Gurudev's Kutir, when a very well known Art of Living teacher and his wife came for his darshan. Gurudev asked him how his courses were going and how things were with him. The teacher answered that he was finding it very tedious to organise his courses and felt very tired. 'That's because you are teaching out of compulsion and not compassion. Drop the doership,' Gurudev advised.

Gurudev imparts knowledge to us so that we can share it with people, because it will enrich and enhance their lives. It's not for us to glorify ourselves as great teachers in the process. The doership of 'I am doing', 'I am teaching', 'I am good' can become like a handcuff holding us back from experiencing the marvel of joyful surrender. Once, it happened to me too. I had spoken at a big conference as a keynote speaker and met Gurudev after that. I excitedly told him that I gave a really impressive speech. Pat came Gurudev's retort, 'Oh, YOU gave an impressive speech!' I have learnt that offering your good qualities and achievements to the Divine keeps you humble and offering your bad qualities and mistakes makes you free of guilt.

In a story from the Mahabharata, after Krishna leaves his body, Arjuna is escorting all the women of Dwarka to the safety of Hastinapur, when they are attacked by forest-dwelling tribes. Arjuna, who had fought such a huge battle in Kurukshetra, is now unable to even pick up his bow. It is a moment of realisation for him, that all his power was Krishna's. Knowing that our skills, knowledge and good qualities are a gift from the Divine keeps us humble and grounded. It saves us from arrogance and egotism.

Over the years, I have reached a comfort level in my interaction with Gurudev. I feel very free to discuss work-related matters with him. Showing him spreadsheets, presentations and financial forecasts came easily to me. A Guru reflects his devotee; so Gurudev would relate to me in my language, at my level. He would discuss things with me in the way I was most proficient and comfortable in—with data, precision and clarity. Often, he would ask me for information on various matters and expect me to have it ready. Once, I was travelling and Gurudev called me asking for some important particulars. I did not have them handy, so I told him that I would have to check and revert to him as soon as possible. To that, he asked, 'Why? Don't you know this? You should always be prepared.' On the other hand, I would see him deal with others in a much more lenient manner. He would praise and appreciate others with even half the preparation of my level, but for me the rule was different. Over the years, I learnt that he has a personal unique benchmark and context for every single one of us. He does not accept anything less than our very best, and he knows exactly what each one of us is capable of, whether we know it ourselves or not. There are indeed several things we have no clue about, though there is the uncanny feeling that a Divine design is unfolding.

Once, Gurudev and I were flying from Mumbai to Bangalore. We settled down and Gurudev began to meditate. Forty minutes later, he opened his eyes and gave me a big smile. I had a huge pile of reports to show him but he wasn't in the mood for work-related discussions. Turning back to me, he said. 'I am looking after you.' I could see tenderness and love in his eyes. Then, out of the blue he said, '*Ajay se tumhari shaadi kara hi di na?*' (Didn't I make sure you got married to Ajay?)

Though by now I was almost immune to these pleasant jolts, this piece of news was unanticipated. In the physical sense, Ajay met Gurudev only eight months after we got married. I had met Gurudev before my marriage to Ajay, but not intimately enough to discuss it. I was very curious, but too shy to ask him what he meant.

Later, my mind kept going back to his revelation. There was no doubt that only a very powerful Divine intervention had brought us together. Ajay has unconditionally supported me to pursue my dreams. His rock-solid backing empowers me. He has taken me deeper on my spiritual path and higher in my pursuit of knowledge. He pushes me to be a better version of myself and is the basis of my values of integrity, justice and fair play. To bring such a fine gentleman into my life required the blessings of the Divine. That day Gurudev revealed who had made it happen.

We think of our meeting with our Guru in terms of the physical dimension of time. We are unaware of how we have been cocooned in the Grace of the Master across time, across lifetimes. What karmic debts he settles and how he navigates us towards the purpose of our life by connecting us with the right people and creating the right situations, is a big mystery for a devotee.

Gurudev tells many young couples who go to him for advice on how to balance their married life, 'See how Ajay and Rajita do it.' Many have come and told us so.

What Gurudev meant on the flight that day will remain an enigma for me.

***

As I started handling senior, more responsible positions in the organisation, the gravity, intensity and importance of institutional matters that I discussed with Gurudev increased gradually. For me, Gurudev's perspective was extremely valuable. In a mere forty years, he built the Art of Living Foundation into a global organisation of remarkable internationality, diversity and complexity. If there was anyone who knew about handling rapid growth, inspiring a big vision, building teams, resolving conflict, taking risks, driving scale, managing resources and many more such leadership imperatives, it was him.

He had an amazing ability to build consensus and come up with multidimensional win-win solutions. I had seen this in diverse contexts, in different countries and cultures around the world. On most occasions, I would accept his decision on the matters we discussed. However, there would be times when I felt that there could be an alternative course of action possible to what he was suggesting. Such moments would confuse me. As I understood, his wisdom was way greater than mine. So was I being right in countering his argument or contesting his decision?

I asked Gurudev how to deal with such dilemmas. His answer was very clear, 'If you feel something else should be done, it's your dharma to say it. Having said it, have the faith to trust the decision of the big mind.' It is said that a Guru is in perfect alignment with the will of the universe. He is so hollow and empty, that what he thinks, says and does is the Ultimate Truth.

With Gurudev, I got the benefit of both–at one level, his incredible knowledge of the world from his vast global experience, and at another level, the extraordinary channelling of a higher will being exercised. This balance between upholding my dharma and living my faith has been a fundamental sutra of my life. It has helped me in innumerable situations. It has kept my mind free of feverishness and doubt. It has lifted me out of the clutches of doership. It has also saved me from guilt and sorrow.

It has happened that when I brought up something to Gurudev which he disregarded at that time, was found to be correct later. I had heard that one of our administrative staff was doing something inappropriate. I felt quite smart about finding this out and reporting it to him. Gurudev heard me out and said that I might have made a mistake in my understanding, and I should be careful about my opinion. I was quite deflated by his response. A few weeks later, it did emerge that the person had to be reprimanded for his behaviour and what I had reported was true. By giving time to that person, Gurudev had given him an opportunity to self-correct. On his not doing so, Gurudev himself counselled him to improve. He did so in my presence, teaching me how to correct a person with compassion. That person did not know that I was the one who had brought this up in the first place. This saved his face in front of us. By not acknowledging me that day, Gurudev saved me from inflating my ego with my righteousness. Maybe he also saved me from taking on the karma of that person's hurt, on being admonished due to me. With delicate skill, he disentangled the situation to its rightful conclusion. Much later, in another context, he even accepted that I was right that day. By then, my ego had got completely detached from the situation.

I feel blessed that even in such circumstances, my ego did not leap out to say, 'I told you so.' Else it can engulf you into a downward spiral of questioning and doubt, which has the danger of becoming a point of no return.

Gurudev has a razor sharp memory. He remembers names, faces, situations, who said what—practically everything. A few years ago, Gurudev was on a one-week tour of UK. The first stop was Manchester. Gurudev's public event was in a large, stately auditorium. After speaking for a short while and guiding the meditation, Gurudev stood up to take questions from the audience. From the stage he exclaimed excitedly on noticing a familiar face in the crowd. He called out the name of an elderly woman. From the far end of the hall, the lady stood up happily and waved shyly at Gurudev. 'Hello, how are you?' he beamed, overjoyed as though he was meeting a long-lost friend. He then went on to call out the names of five other elderly women, all of whom stood up, overjoyed at being recognised. What followed was an intimate reunion of old friends, reminiscing the times they had spent together thirty years ago in the Bangalore Ashram. That there were 2000 other people in the hall didn't matter at all. The women standing up in the auditorium and Gurudev on the stage, were chatting, laughing, joking and reconnecting. Gurudev spoke to them with so much care and tenderness and they were responding with so much joy, that there was not a single dry eye in the auditorium.

Often, devotees meet Gurudev and say they had met him somewhere twenty years ago or attended his programme fifteen years ago somewhere else. No matter what the situation or place, Gurudev always remembers the context and asks the person something from that time. It never ceases to shock people. How does he remember? I have often experienced this in our meetings. I was once discussing a topic with Gurudev six months apart. I had forgotten some details, but Gurudev remembered everything perfectly.

Gurudev, in his ultimate compassion, shares his knowledge easily and widely. He never holds back. He has groomed thousands of Art of Living teachers all over the world to spread the knowledge to the farthest corners.

From Tierra del Fuego in South America to the North Pole, teachers have been teaching the breathing and meditation techniques to people in over 156 countries of the world. Gurudev says that his teachers are his life. He loves us, cares for us, teaches us, guides us and even scolds us when needed. It's clear that each of us is at a different milestone of our spiritual journey. We have each reached a different level in our evolution. It's like we are in a big university, with each of us in our own grade.

Gurudev meets us at our level. He gives us the knowledge we need, when we need it. A lot depends upon our capacity to receive. When we go to the ocean, some of us just wet our feet, some go swimming, others surf and yet others dive deep. They find the corals and pearls. Each of us came to him, uncut and rough. He is polishing us with knowledge and chiselling us with Grace. From normal worldly human beings, he has elevated us to the position of devotees. By making us a part of his lineage, he has made our existence eternal. In his endeavour to uncover the deepest knowledge, Gurudev has spoken on the widest range of scriptures. He has given discourses on the Bhagavad Gita, the Ashtavakra Gita, the Upanishads, the Bhakti Sutras, the Vigyan Bhairav and the Shiv Sutras, to name a few. It is unfathomable how one person has decoded and internalised the most profound knowledge of so many deep and diverse texts. I have never seen Gurudev reading any of these books, or making any notes. Where does this knowledge come from? I keep wondering.

Once, when we were in Europe, Gurudev handed me the Spandakarika, a very ancient text, commentary on the eighth century Kashmir Shaivism. I read it in

English, but grasped very little. Gurudev told me to stop after twenty minutes and asked me what I understood. Without waiting for my reply, he laughed out loud, saying, 'These are all secrets that have to be unlocked.' He went on to explain in the most easy and lucid terms, the meaning of the passages I had read. How did he unlock these secrets? When someone comes home, you can only give them what you already have at home. Only the one who has this wisdom, who IS the wisdom can share it. Gurudev has designed many different types of courses. Scores of people have taken these and spoken about their diverse, authentic experiences. Gurudev teaches only that which he himself practices, and that which is integrated in him. That which is him. He says, 'Infinity is available but not tangible. The Guru is both infinite and tangible. The Divine is impersonal. The Guru is both personal and Divine. The impersonal personified for your benefit.'

Having had the good fortune and blessing of being associated with him closely, over the years, I have grown tremendously. There are times when I wonder how I could have completed a tough task so easily, or how I could have surmounted a challenge with surprising dexterity. I have no doubt that Gurudev's Grace is at work here. I know that I am not the doer; I'm only the instrument. When I look back and see the long way I have come, the people I have met, the large congregations I have addressed, the portfolios I have handled, the untrodden paths I have traversed, it's nothing short of a miracle. Every moment seems new, every day is an opportunity to discover and grow.

One day, Gurudev sent me to greet and wish the legendary Indian singer, Ashatai Bhosle, on her eightieth birthday. She had met him on multiple occasions before that and had deep respect for him. Over these years, Ashatai and I developed a close bond. What touched me deeply was her humility, grace and sheer stamina even after seventy-five years of illustrious singing behind her. In one of our conversations, I happened to casually mention to her that I write poetry. She insisted on listening to my poems. Though I was shy about it, since she persisted, I recited them. A few of the poems were composed to a tune by some of our Ashram singers. Ashatai heard them over and over again. I saw tears well up in her eyes. She turned to me and said, 'I have heard and sung thousands of songs in my life. Such words can only be written by someone who has experienced the Divine. I want to sing these songs.'

My joy knew no bounds. Just the fact that she said this to me was a huge reward and blessing. Thereafter, she herself composed the tune of one of the songs and recorded it. Her young granddaughter, Zanai, recorded another one of my songs. The recording happened at Yash Raj Studio. When Yashji used to bank with us in the mid-1990s, he was in the process of conceptualising this studio. He had invited me for its inauguration, but by then we had already shifted to Bangalore, so we couldn't attend it. I had promised him that I would surely visit it sometime. On the day of the recording, when I passed Yashji's statue inside the studio, I silently registered my visit, albeit fifteen years after its inauguration. Life does come full circle indeed.

With Gurudev, it's a connection of a lifetime, perhaps of previous lifetimes too. An unbreakable, eternal bond that transcends time and space. The more you trust this bond, the more you blossom from within. Who would have thought that a simple girl like me, from a middle-class family, with everyday scholastic ambitions and a common dream of a reasonably successful career would get to expand her horizons across the globe, connect with people of diverse cultures, address large international congregations, hobnob with world leaders, and look after a university? Everything seems doable, nothing impossible. This has been the reality of my life. It is also an opportunity available to anyone who is open to it.

13

Where Flowers Grow On Stones

In 2009, I was in Seoul on one of my regular official visits. It was about 4.30 pm on a Thursday, when my local Korean number rang. It was from one of Gurudev's secretaries. He informed me that Gurudev had proposed that I would now be looking after the Sri Sri University project. He asked me whether I could reach Bhubaneswar that Sunday for an important meeting with the government.

This was out of the blue. I had no idea about this project and I wasn't sure what 'looking after' meant. How could I go for an important meeting with the government when I knew nothing about it? I was travelling back to India on Saturday, which meant I would reach Mumbai around midnight after an almost eighteen-hour journey. Travelling on Sunday morning immediately would be very tiring.

I could address the first challenge by getting someone to apprise me of the latest developments. It was the second one that concerned me. I explained it to Gurudev's secretary, who promised to update Gurudev and call me back.

After the meetings for the day when I returned to my hotel at around 6.45 pm, a familiar face was waiting for me at the hotel lobby with a packed dinner for me–a special service for me from the nearby Taj restaurant in the Myongdong neighbourhood. On one of my first visits to Seoul, my Citi colleagues had taken me to an Indian restaurant for lunch. This was at the Taj. We had entered the restaurant and were waiting to be seated, when one of the young waiters rushed to me exclaiming, 'Didi' and dived straight at my feet to do pranams! My colleagues were alarmed. I reassured them, still wondering who this boy was. The waiter gave me a bright smile and asked me whether I had recognised him. I did find his face familiar, but couldn't recollect where I had seen him before. He reminded me that he was one of our YLTP graduates (Youth Leadership Training Programme) from Uttarakhand and had attended one of the team-building sessions I had conducted. He went on to tell me how he got this job opportunity, how it had helped him financially but also how much he missed home. He was delighted to see me and said that he felt as if he was meeting a family member. He offered to bring dinner for me to my hotel when I reached back from work, every time I was in Seoul. This was a fantastic proposition. Otherwise, almost always, I would end up eating pasta or pizza, the only vegetarian options available on room service. Since then, on many occasions he would bring me a simple packed meal of roti, vegetables, dal and rice. A big treat for me. I have been fortunate to have had similar wonderful arrangements in almost every country I visited the local Art of Living teachers sending me lunch and dinner too. Korea was probably the only country where they stayed too far from my location and I couldn't have this luxury. Then I met this kind soul! You are not left wanting for anything.

Back in my hotel room, I was looking forward to a quiet evening. Just then my phone rang. It was Gurudev's secretary calling to inform me that Gurudev had asked him to get the meeting with the Government of Odisha postponed. He wanted to know whether the following Sunday was convenient for me. He conveyed that Gurudev had advised me to not tire myself, and was getting the meeting postponed to suit my schedule!

Gurudev is as concerned about the individual's development as he is about institutional growth. He even named his Indian organisation Vyakti Vikas Kendra, i.e., the Centre for Development of the Individual. In many of our project meetings, if team members even mention they are tired, or finding it difficult to cope with the workload, Gurudev's first response is to ask the person to take a break and rest.

Gurudev emphasises that the organisation is like a photo frame; it's the people that are the photo and should be valued. In leadership theory, the ability to put employees first is considered fundamental to customer satisfaction and organisational success. Employee first, Customer second is a popular management mantra. Gurudev has taken this to a level of care and concern that is quite unprecedented. Sometimes, during meetings, Gurudev doesn't discuss the technical matter at hand. Instead, he spends time understanding if the people are happy and well. It's not uncommon to hear Gurudev say, 'Work will happen. Are you happy?' Even during our large global events like the Silver Jubilee Celebration in Bangalore or the World Culture Festivals in Berlin and Delhi, when the work at hand was understandably much more than normal, Gurudev's concern was more about the volunteers, their comfort and the state of their mind. Often, when I have met Gurudev for his advice on an important organisational matter, instead of discussing that, he has asked me, 'Have you eaten lunch?' This consistent unconditional care and compassion for his people is one of the biggest secrets of his inspirational leadership, attracting millions of people around the world.

Even in the case of the meeting with the Odisha government, my health was more important for Gurudev than the critical meeting that could decide the speed of passing our Sri Sri University Act. The coming week, I attended the meeting at Bhubaneswar. This is how I became a part of the Sri Sri University team—in absentia. Most of my organisational appointments for the Art of Living have happened similarly. Whether it was being appointed the Teacher Coordinator for Bangalore, a member of the State Apex Body for Karnataka or Trustee for the Ved Vignan Mahavidya Peeth. I heard about them when someone informed me that Gurudev has appointed me to do the job.

When I made my first-ever trip to Bhubaneswar as planned, I did not know that Gurudev too would be joining us for this meeting. This meant he had changed his own schedule to suit mine. I felt touched. Gurudev told me that we would visit the Sri Sri University site the next morning.

I was excited. Being a banker, I was very comfortable with data, numbers and balance sheets, but the field of education was new for me and building a university from scratch sure felt like a big adventure. I was told to carry an umbrella or a hat because it could be hot at the site.

Nothing had prepared me for what I saw! It was acres and acres of barren, arid, rocky land with humongous quarries. Apparently, this land was quarried illegally for many years and had been rendered useless.

Tall, sharp, pointed grass and thorny shrubs had grown wildly across the land. There were only two large trees across 180 acres; nothing else. One tree was very close to the point from where we entered the site from the main road. The other one was almost a thirty-five-minute walk away, towards the central part of the site. The rest of the land was uneven and unkempt. This was the site for our Sri Sri University!

Gurudev stood at the edge of one of the larger quarries and intently fixed his gaze in one direction. When I looked in the same direction, I saw nothing. But he continued looking like he could see something. It was a quiet moment. The few of us with Gurudev were trying to make sense of what we were seeing. Gurudev was now scanning the entire landscape with his eyes, almost like he was creating the architectural plan of the campus.

Turning to me, he said, 'Rajita, there will soon be thousands of trees and the most beautiful flowers in this place.' One of our local teachers remarked that scientifically it was not possible for anything to grow on rocks. Gurudev raised his hand and stopped the teacher from continuing. It was like he was taking a *sankalpa* (an intention) and he didn't want a single negative thought to sour it. He continued speaking, 'Our University will be one of a kind in the world and will revive the lost glory of the ancient Indian centres of higher learning, Nalanda and Takshashila, but first, we need to do something for the surrounding villages.'

The scorching midday sun was practically melting our bodies. As far as my gaze reached, I couldn't see anything but yellowish red rocks, sand and thorny bushes. Not even a bird in sight! Gurudev obviously saw something else. He saw trees and flowers. He saw buildings that would be architectural marvels, and happy students. I wanted to see what he saw.

Having faith in the unknown is known as *shraddha*, the ability to have faith is a big blessing. It is said that the one in whom the seed of doubt has taken root can neither be happy in this world nor hereafter. Doubt comes from low *prana*. Keeping your prana high with a regular practice of yoga, breathing techniques and meditation is vital for a happy life.

It was a surreal moment. It was as if the plans for the next thousand years were being made right there. When a Guru takes a sankalpa, consider that the work has already been completed successfully. All you have to do is be the instrument.

In the battle of Kurukshetra, when Arjuna hesitated to wage a war with his elders, Gurus and his family, Lord Krishna told him that He had already won the war for him; Arjuna just had to go through the motions.

Once, Gurudev had asked me to teach the TLEX programme to the trustees of various trusts in India. The group would be of over forty people, all very senior and seasoned office bearers of the Art of Living organisation in India. Since the TLEX course involves a lot of strategic planning and discussion, we normally teach such a course as a team of two or even three teachers. I was alone, and Gurudev kept adding more people to the group. Finally, I expressed to Gurudev that this group was too big for me to handle alone. Gurudev immediately replied, 'You just have to stand there, I am doing everything for you!'

We walked some more in different directions until we reached the other tree. It was noon and we had walked around for almost an hour. The heat was unbearable. I was soaked in sweat. The thorny bushes had scratched my legs in different places through my sari. Gurudev was taking long strides and walking purposefully, unconcerned by the heat, unmindful of thorns abrading his skin through his *veshti*. He was covering every inch of the land as if to bless it with his positive energy and intention.

By the time we reached the other tree, a huge group of villagers had gathered to take Gurudev's *darshan*. Men, women, elders and children, all flocked around him.

Meeting people is as natural to Gurudev as flowing is to the river. Except the first five days of Navratri, every year, when Gurudev maintains silence, he meets people every single day of the year. When he is in the Bangalore Ashram, three days a week are designated as days for public *darshan*. Hundreds of buses come to the Ashram on such days, loaded with devotees from different parts of India. Often, devotees farther away from Bangalore, book a full train to come for such *darshan* days. The Ashram team organises these days very meticulously. Devotees are seated in parallel lines and Gurudev walks through the rows listening to them, answering their questions and blessing them. People bring flowers, sweets, turbans, silk stoles, food they have personally cooked for him, handmade craft and many more such expressions of their love for their Guru. Gurudev accepts each of these lovingly and respectfully. Many times, during his dinner, I have heard him ask, 'Where is the butter that the elderly lady from Basvangudi brought in a steel box?' or 'Give me the Puliogare rice that the two ladies from Banashankari had brought–it was in a box with a red lid.' It's astonishing how he remembers each and every thing. Once, a devotee had carried something for Gurudev all the way from Kerala. Later, it couldn't be located. Gurudev had it searched for almost two hours until it was found. When he ate it later, he exclaimed that his devotee would now be feeling so happy!

On Ashtami day in Navratri, Gurudev meets close to a hundred thousand people in about four to five hours. It's the same on Maha Shivratri day, when he meets about a hundred thousand people from 11 pm onwards, only to go to his Kutir for a shower and return for the Rudra Puja, early next morning. Devotees can't have enough; many come back a second time and no matter how big the crowd, Gurudev smilingly points them out, and everyone breaks into peals of laughter. Often, they keep asking him the same question repeatedly, without even realising it.

Once I witnessed him telling a young boy who had a question about his further studies, 'I just answered this question when you asked me on the other side of the hall!' It's the same thing on his tours in India or different parts of the world, even in countries where people don't speak English. On a tour to Russia, Gurudev was meeting devotees and almost each one was offering him large, red, yellow, white, pink, orange big roses with long stems of over one and a half feet. He kept accepting them from each person with his right hand, and placing them on his left shoulder. In no time the bunch of piled up roses became so big, that some roses started falling down. When some volunteers went forward to take the huge bunches from him, Gurudev would not part with them. Instead he had them pick up the fallen roses and pile them back in the big bunch. Later, he said, 'My devotees bring me these flowers with so much love, gratitude and devotion, how can I just give them away?' At the same time, I have also witnessed Gurudev advise every one again and again to not bring him anything. He says, 'You blossom and smile, that is enough for me.' But, devotees have their own rules. Gurudev lovingly acknowledges that.

***

Once, while in Sri Sri University, Gurudev asked for the car to be readied because he wanted to drive around the villages near the campus. He asked me to carry fruits. On seeing how many fruits I had got along, he asked for three times more. They were mostly oranges. An Art of Living teacher sat next to me and between us sat the three huge baskets of fruits. Gurudev had the car driven from village to village, stopping at every other home to greet people and talk to them. He was particularly keen on talking to the elderly women and seemed visibly pained by their poverty and plight. He would talk to them from his window and reach for the oranges and hand them over. We must have driven for at least an hour, and three times, I had to call for a refill of the fruits. Since most of the fruits were oranges, Gurudev's hands and clothes had become stained with the juice of the fruits.

Gurudev may have met at least a thousand such women on that drive that day. He was deeply concerned with their state of penury and asked me to immediately start some vocational courses for the young girls so that they could learn a skill to become economically self-sufficient. We started five tailoring institutes in the villages around our campus, where hundreds of young girls and women have taken training in tailoring.

It is no coincidence that the nearest neighbouring village of our University is called Vidyadharpur (it literally means 'the village of the one who upholds knowledge'). One day, some villagers gathered to meet Gurudev. They told him that they felt that a part of the land marked for us by the government as the land for the University, actually belonged to their village. They wanted that small patch to be demarked again in their name. Gurudev heard them patiently and told one of the local teachers to look into the matter immediately.

There were two factions in that group; one, slightly belligerent, and the other, moderate. They spoke amongst themselves, thanked Gurudev, and left.

After we had completed the preliminary formalities for setting up the University, during a commute, Gurudev called up the late Mr T N Seshan. A name familiar to every Indian for his upright, ethical and fearless style of leadership, Mr Seshan was the President of Sri Sri University then. Gurudev introduced me to him, praising me for my capabilities and knowledge. He told him in Tamil, 'You don't have to worry now. Rajita will look after everything.' Again, I heard the words, 'look after'! I so wanted to ask Gurudev what he meant. The words would reach the tip of my tongue but not find their way out. Gurudev looked back from his seat and gave me an endearing smile, as though he had gauged the mental circus going on inside me.

In the Art of Living Happiness course, we speak a lot about how responsibility is taken, not given. I decided to stop worrying about what 'look after' meant and started doing any work that came my way.

From that moment on, Sri Sri University became my baby. Moms don't need to be told what looking after their babies means. They just know. Somehow I started figuring it out too. Along with my already hectic job and the Asia Pacific travel, I devoted every spare moment to work for the launch of the University. Expanding the team, working with architects and infrastructure companies for the campus plans, working with the regulators to understand the launch plans for various courses, academic discussions, statutory planning, branding, designing, policy drafting, procedure making, the work was endless. Mr Seshan would not get involved in the nitty gritty of matters, which were then left for me to handle. I also became the via media for people to communicate with him and for him to convey his advice. Building an institution needs ideas, individuals and inspiration. Building it from scratch or like in our case from negative infrastructure, means all this and much more.

Slowly, the meaning of 'look after' began dawning upon me. It called for doing everything for everyone at all times. It involved taking care of every aspect of work, no matter how big or how small. It entailed looking after the team, juniors, peers and seniors. It meant executing

Gurudev's grand vision for this University in every sense of the word.

Since I had a full-day job, I would start my University-related conference calls after 8 pm. Sometimes, the calls would stretch to beyond midnight. On the days I would travel out of India, I had to juggle the differences in the time zones too.

Many weeks, I would travel from Monday to Friday to some Asian country for my official work and fly to Bhubaneswar on Saturday morning for in-person meetings, to return to Mumbai on Sunday, only to fly to another country on Monday (sometimes, even late night on Sunday). There seemed to be no limits to my physical and mental capacity. No matter how much my office work increased or how much the University work increased, it was astounding how I could just go on and on.

That is what Gurudev must have meant when he said, 'You just have to stand there, I am doing everything for you!'

The work of our approvals picked up and things began moving fast. Mr Seshan requested to be relieved as the President due to his ill health. Mrs Akhila Srinivasan was appointed as the next President. Our team was expanding. Since Gurudev had said that we should first do something for the surrounding villages, we decided to set up a skill centre in the University. We signed a Memorandum of Understanding with Larsen & Toubro, one of India's largest infrastructure companies, to set up 'Vidya', a skill training centre to impart vocational training of construction skills like masonry and bar bending. The programme would last for three months, at the end of which all the students would get jobs at the

Larsen & Toubro construction sites. About sixty young boys from neighbouring and faraway villages of Odisha enrolled in our first batch. Most were school dropouts; some had studied up to class ten and very few up to class twelve. Severely malnourished, some were addicted to smoking and chewing *gutka.* It was humbling to see them enjoy their meals in our small kitchen, heartily. Many of them shared with me that they had seldom eaten two meals a day.

All the students were taught the Art of Living course where they learnt the Sudarshan Kriya. Morning *sadhana,* and evening sport and satsang became a part of their daily schedule.

The nutritious food they ate plus the daily practice of breathing techniques, and meditation along with physical sporting activity, began improving their health. They started looking and feeling much better than when they had arrived. Most of them could give up smoking and *gutka.* We witnessed the transformation right in front of our eyes.

Since it was the first batch of this programme, Gurudev had a keen eye on its progress. Every once in a while he would even inquire about what vegetables we were serving the group. I may have had no idea what was cooking in my own kitchen on some days, but I had to be very particular about what was being cooked in the campus kitchen.

Three months passed by quickly and it was time for the graduation ceremony of this first batch of our Vidya students. It was a big day for them and also for us. I had been deeply involved in every aspect of this programme.

We had been dealing with a lot of teething problems, fixing them, and moving ahead.

The discussion about the allegedly disputed patch of land was still going on with the villagers. We were in constant touch with the government to help us resolve the situation. It was taking its own time. Now and again the villagers would come over to discuss the matter. We would reassure them that it would definitely be resolved. Sometimes, they would be complaisant, at times, combative. We were as keen to work out an amicable solution to the matter.

Soon, we fixed the date of the convocation of the first batch of graduating students of Sri Sri University`s Vidya project. We invited the local Member of the Legislative Assembly as the Chief Guest for the event. Senior officials from Larsen & Toubro too were arriving from their Mumbai office. My flight from Mumbai on the day of the convocation was delayed, and by the time I reached the campus, it was almost 5 pm.

In those days, I had a ritual. As I used to stay either in our guest house in the city or a budget hotel, I would have limited time on campus. The construction of our buildings had not yet started and all the meetings would happen in our city office. So whenever I reached the campus, I would drive all around our land. It was my way of paying my respects to it. Our Vidya building complex was right at the entrance of our campus.

When I reached the campus that evening, everyone was waiting for me. I wanted to go for my customary drive around the campus, before the convocation ceremony.

Realising that there was not enough time, I decided to do so after the event.

The graduation ceremony was very poignant. It was gratifying to watch the young boys, who had arrived malnourished, unemployed, and addicted, transform into healthy, de-addicted, strong youth with jobs. (Since then, hundreds of boys have graduated from Vidya and it continues to be one of our important initiatives on the campus.) Many of them shared how the three months had changed them, their personality and their outlook towards life. Their stories of gratitude moved us. After the programme and celebratory dinner, I decided that I would go for the drive around the campus.

It was November, and darkness had set in. I knew I wouldn't be able to see much, but wanted to honour my ritual. I was planning to drive up to the small bright yellow one-storey project office we had built that stood close to the second tree on the campus (near the Vidyadharpur side), and then turn back. It was pitch dark when we reached, and the only light was that of the headlights of the car. Our car made its way through the rocky, uneven terrain. As we came close to the project office building, we noticed a long shiny horizontal line. We couldn't make out what it was, so we decided to go closer to inspect it. To our shock, it was a long horizontal line of milestone boulders placed to create a boundary line. A junior staff from the project office revealed that some villagers had come that day and forcefully built this as a claim to their patch of land. Since the matter of their claim to the land was still to be resolved, one section of the village community seemed to have taken matters into their own hands, and decided to declare their own land boundary. 'How can they do that?' I asked, adding that we should break it down. It was illegal because it was on our land. But, our team was not so keen about it. I was adamant and angry. Unethical behaviour always bothers me. I said, 'How difficult can it be to break these boulders and flatten the boundary wall?' I went closer and with the intent to check the strength of the boulder, pushed it hard. It broke and toppled over immediately.

Just then, my phone rang. My phone was in my purse, which I had left in the car. I was in no mood to answer calls and intent on flattening the boundary. But the phone kept ringing incessantly. Wondering who it could be, I walked the few steps to the car and picked up my phone. It was Swami Paramtej. I answered the phone and could instantly hear loud sounds on the other side. It seemed like a large gathering in a satsang. Swamiji said, 'Rajitaji, Gurudev will speak to you.' In a moment, Gurudev came on line and said, 'You have broken one, don't break any more!' and hung up.

Had I heard right? My phone rang again. It was Swami Paramtej again. He said, 'Gurudev has advised you to leave the campus immediately and go back to your place of stay.' He also told me to message him once I reached my hotel.

Swami Paramtej is one of the jewels of Gurudev and I am proud that he did his first Art of Living course with me. I tell everyone with great delight that it is my honour that he is my student.

Swamiji told me later, that on that evening, Gurudev was in deep meditation in a public satsang in Lucknow. He suddenly opened his eyes and asked Swamiji to call me. After speaking those few words to me, he went back into meditation. Gurudev must have sensed that it was not so safe to take the confrontational approach–after all, no matter what they did, these villagers were our neighbours.

I left the campus immediately. On reaching the hotel, I messaged Swamiji to convey to Gurudev that I had reached safely.

The breaking of that one boulder created a huge furore and the villagers thought of it as an aggressive stand from us. Gurudev called me again the next day and advised me on the steps to take and the officials to meet. He also told me to go back and tell the villagers that Gurudev would come soon to the campus and resolve the matter once and for all.

The next day was most challenging. I experienced conflict like never before; vested interests, double-faced communication and much more. Though the situations and discussions were complex and quite difficult, I was surprised at my composure.

Gurudev changed his schedule to come to Bhubaneswar within the next ten days. He met all the villagers, assuaged their concerns and advised us to build a community hall in that area, which could be used by villagers as a collection point and shelter during storms and typhoons. Since then, this hall has been used regularly by the villagers during cyclones like Hudhud, Phalin and Fani. The dispute about the patch of land has also been resolved. Our relationship with the villagers in all the villages surrounding our campus is excellent, with many of them now employed with us.

The last evening before Gurudev's departure from Bhubaneswar, there was a moment when only a few of us were with Gurudev. He looked at me straight and said, 'Situations are being created to invoke the valour in you, I am taking care of the result!'

Gurudev's comment hit me like a bolt. It would be safe to say that over the years with Gurudev, my attitude towards life has become quite valorous. It's incredible how I don't cow down to challenges and am ready to face them head-on. As a woman and in a leadership position, it is certainly not easy in India or anywhere else in the world. We have to deal with unique biases, preconceived notions, judgements and barriers. Any time I am faced with a challenge or a difficult situation, institutionally or individually, I just remember Gurudev's knowledge. I reckon he wants us to be like a lion, regal and courageous.

Gurudev's vision is getting unveiled day by day and Sri Sri University is growing into a unique, one of its kind educational institution globally. Having received multiple awards for academic proficiency, innovation, our unique approach to teaching, the foundation of spirituality and also for being a green campus, it is becoming a distinctive example of how you can combine the best philosophy of the East and the West for the benefit of students. In a short span of eight years, it is ranked sixth in the top twenty-five private universities of India (Higher Education Review 2020).

We have won several awards for being a green campus, our faculty and students are filing a number of patents, and hundreds of academic papers are being published. We are known as the University of start-ups! Over thirty-five start-ups have been incubated in our campus, and are running successfully. Starting from five programmes, we have reached over fifty programmes now. We are launching unique niche programmes that are becoming trendsetters in their respective fields. We are the first university in the world to launch a Department of Contemplative and Behavioural Sciences, the first university in Asia to start a Faculty of Osteopathy and the first university in India to start an undergraduate programme in Agri-Business. We will be the first university in eastern India, if not the whole country, to have a one of its kind integrated hospital of Ayurveda, Allopathy, Osteopathy and Naturopathy.

Being an NGO, we don't have the financial luxuries enjoyed by other private institutions. When we were discussing the financial outlay for the hospital, that worry showed on our faces. Gurudev said, 'If you stay with Narayan, Lakshmi will follow.' We just need to stay with knowledge and truth, be ethical and integral and abundance is bound to flood our lives.

Our campus is called one of the happiest campuses and we are proud that it is a drug-free, alcohol-free and smoke-free, vegetarian campus—a huge security for students in today's world.

As visualised by Gurudev, we have almost a hundred thousand trees on the campus already, with a multitude of fruits and flowers growing in abundance. They attract beautiful birds and butterflies of all types, making our campus a must-visit place for visitors to this area. Our infrastructure of hostels, academic blocks, ISO 22000 certified kitchen, clinics, labs, yoga and dance studios, sports facilities with what may be the world's first underground badminton and tennis courts, cafeteria, bank, convenience stores and even a beauty salon, has turned our campus into a mini city. We are building it brick by brick, bench by bench and book by book.

Every word Gurudev said is becoming a living reality. The Sri Sri University team is expanding, students are growing, new courses are being launched and the campus is a bustling, bubbling, dynamic centre of academic excellence! Many people are investing their time, energy and passion to build this great institution. Many of our senior leadership team members are part of national and international education bodies, councils and associations. We are definitely emerging as the thought leader in higher education, for following a holistic, value-based approach. No surprise really, considering it is Gurudev's sankalpa and has his attention every moment. In such an environment, where even flowers have grown on stones, it's only natural that the human spirit too would blossom to its full and fragrant self.

Education is the foundation of any civilisation. The classrooms of today shape the world of tomorrow. It is both a responsibility and an honour to play a part in shaping the future of the world. For me personally, it has been an enormous learning experience. Every day, I have to give speeches on subjects that are not my core expertise, interact with hundreds if not thousands of people, be up the curve on every regulatory and statutory development, build and maintain external stakeholder relationships and keep up the brand of Sri Sri University. Every day is a new challenge. Keeping together an ever-growing team of academicians and administrators, who have all joined us from different walks of life, different States of India, and many countries of the world, is a monumental task. A leader in such cases has to play a number of roles–parent, sibling, friend and even a child at times. She has to be an escalator, a shock absorber, a coach, a counsellor, a cheerleader and the conscience keeper. The optimism, the courage, the compassion and the excellence quotient of the leader cascades to the team. In these years I got the chance to experience all this and more.

That in such a short time, everyone is aligned to a common vision and works collaboratively in a mutually supportive and trustworthy environment, is a testament to the hard work and effort each one of us is putting in. Organisations grow every single day and organisational culture gets shaped every single minute. We know and can see the human effort, but what we can't see is the intention and Grace of the Master, which is making it happen. During our annual strategy meet last year, Gurudev joined us for a short while virtually from St Petersburg, Russia. We shared with him our goals for the next six months, one year and three years. 'Have you made a 3000-year goal Rajita?' he asked. He looks ahead and looks far. Being part of a vision as unfathomable as this, we rise above ourselves into a realm unknown and unseen.

Epilogue

In February 2020, Papa was hospitalised and in the ICU due to a build-up of water in his lungs. He recovered soon, and returned home after four days in the hospital, looking cheerful and fresh.

In the first week of March, Ajay and I went to Sri Sri University, because Gurudev surprised us with a long-awaited visit. On the third day of our stay, Gurudev decided to visit the Jagannath Puri temple. We were on our way, when Shantanu called to inform us that Papa had to be hospitalised again. I hadn't expected this sudden downturn in Papa's health. I could sense the panic and concern in Shantanu's voice. All was not well. I wanted to return to Mumbai immediately to be with Papa and my family, but it was already 4 pm, and there were no flights from Bhubaneswar to Mumbai until the next morning. At the same time, I felt compelled to be in SSU, because with Gurudev on the campus, we had organised meetings to take several important decisions. I was torn.

That evening I prayed to Lord Jagannath to bless Papa and take care of him. We decided to fly back to Mumbai the next day. Gurudev blessed us and told us not to worry. When you are in a responsible position, to have a leader who allows you to prioritise your family during a crisis, is a big gift. All my SSU colleagues assured me that they would take care of things in my absence. To have colleagues and a team that you can trust implicitly and that will have your back in such times is a boon.

Returning home was the right thing to do. Papa was in the ICU for six days. He had to be on continuous support of oxygen and BiPAP machines. When he was discharged, one of our bedrooms was converted into a mini home ICU. Shantanu moved in with Mummy-Papa, and with Shubhangi's rock-like support, they felt reassured. Their son, little Ishaan, showed maturity beyond his seven years. Papa's slow journey to recovery began.

After staying for a week in SSU, Gurudev returned to the Bangalore Ashram. By then, Covid-19 cases were on the rise in India. Many offices began switching over to the work-from-home mode. Things were changing rapidly. The ever-bustling Mumbai had begun wearing a deserted look.

On the morning of March 13, after my sadhana, I had a feeling that we should prepare ourselves for the eventuality of a shutdown of SSU. I called up the Vice Chancellor and suggested that we start planning for it. Though it seemed a trifle far-fetched at that point, he respected my judgement. We chalked out a detailed plan of how to send students home safely, how we would take care of the remaining curriculum, how to adapt to teaching online, organise our work, and so on. Our meeting was over at 2.30 pm, and at 3 pm, the Odisha government announced the shutdown of all educational institutions. In a matter of three days, we arranged to send all two thousand students to their homes all over India. Many resident faculty members too returned to their home towns. With intense planning, 24-hour workdays involving massive training, backend arrangements, bandwidth strengthening and HR planning, Sri Sri University went hundred percent online for all classroom teaching. It was no mean achievement. Google Meet cells and Zoom grids replaced physical benches. For the first time ever, students and teachers visited each other's homes through their virtual screens. This transformation was suffused with a different sense of adventure and a positive spirit in the whole team. No one had expected or experienced such an unusual situation. The already strong culture of collaboration and trust reached an incredible level of mutual support and understanding. I would be on conference calls for almost eight to ten hours a day. At the same time, Shantanu and I were meeting many doctors to get opinions for the next course of action for Papa. One school of doctors suggested a high-risk surgery called TAVR, while another was totally opposed to it. It was confusing. On March 20, I spent the day with Papa. He was in pain, but his high threshold to bear it made him resolute. That evening when I took his leave, he was taking a short nap. He looked peaceful and contented.On March 22, Prime Minister, Narendra Modiji announced a national curfew. It was the first of its kind for the country. He extended it to a twenty-one-day national lockdown from March 24 onwards. As I watched his speech that evening, I wondered how we could go through what looked like an ordeal. We would all have to adjust to a new way of life that was going to distance us from our neighbours, family, friends and colleagues. The only contact with the outside world was to be through technology and telecom.

Our family conferred and decided that we would revisit the pending decision on Papa's surgery, after the lockdown was lifted. Unfortunately, it got extended. Luckily, Papa's health seemed to improve. The lowering levels of pollution were helping him significantly. He was breathing cleaner air.

From all over the world though, only bad news kept pouring in. For the first time, an unseen enemy had attacked every corner of the world, rendering human beings helpless. Nobody had a clue about how to tackle it. Humanity was humbled and brought to its knees by a tiny virulent organism. Sensing the effect of the new 'normal' on the collective human psyche, Gurudev started conducting live meditation sessions twice a day. It was our lifeline. Millions of people from all over the world began participating in it.

Every day, there was news of rising stress levels, new mental challenges, suicides, strife inside homes, loss of jobs, woes of the migrants, poverty, hunger and deaths. Cases of depression were escalating. Loneliness stemming out of social isolation was engulfing the world. In such a time, Gurudev's words of wisdom and assurance were like a soothing balm on a sore wound. It gave us confidence, faith and hope. Meanwhile, at SSU, we were progressing well to complete the 2019-20 academic year curriculum. At home, Ajay and I settled into a daily rhythm of sadhana, work and some leisure-time activities like reading, writing and listening to music and chants. We stayed in touch with family and friends via FaceTime and WhatsApp video calls. Everyone was dealing with their unique challenges and battles.

The pandemic showed no signs of retreat and the lockdown in India was extended again. The quiet streets, the empty offices, malls and restaurants gave Mumbai the feel of a ghost town. Mumbai's lifeline, the local train service, was shut. Police patrolling increased. Civic authorities drove through the city making announcements on loudspeakers, urging people to stay indoors, creating an eerie feeling of fear and anxiety.

On the morning of May 6, Shantanu called to inform us that Papa was feeling extreme tiredness and fatigue. He looked pale and could barely whisper on the phone. The doctor prescribed new medicines. The next day was full of calls and meetings. The online exams at SSU had commenced. Since this was the first time we were doing this, it needed extra preparations and precautions. After dinner that night, I called to speak to Papa. He sounded weak, and in a feeble tone said that he was feeling very exhausted. I assured him that he would be fine soon with the new medicines prescribed. We had an inordinately long chat, considering his condition, and I hung up feeling fulfilled. I retired to bed after my usual ritual of reading and writing, but sleep eluded me. Ajay was working in the study. At midnight, he barged into our room, his face ashen. 'Shantanu called. Papa is not responding,' he said. I leapt out of bed. Deep down, I knew something was amiss. I packed a small bag in a rush, and soon we were on our way to Papa's.

We were stepping out of the house after forty-eight days. We passed through seven police check posts. Surprisingly, no one stopped us. We drove in silence. Hoping for the best but knowing in our hearts what the reality could be. When we reached, I dashed up the flight of stairs to our apartment on the first floor. Shantanu opened the door, his eyes red, face puffy, and body shaking. I hugged him. I couldn't bring myself to enter Papa's room. With my heart thudding wildly, I peeked in through the door. There was my beloved father lying on his bed, his face peaceful and radiant. The dam burst. I collapsed. In the fraction of a second, Papa's heart had given up on him and he had left us. He has chosen the night of Buddha Purnima to say his final goodbye.

My father was a man for all seasons: loving, caring and dependable. He was a pillar of support to every member of our family and all his friends. He gave without expectations, touching the hearts and lives of those who sought him. He attended all functions, from naming ceremonies to death ceremonies. Ironically, during his final moment, no one could be present because of the lockdown. As the news of his demise spread, the family and friends around the world started calling, wanting to have his last darshan on video call. In normal circumstances, hundreds of people would have gathered to bid him adieu. Now, it was just us, his immediate family.

Soon we had to get down to making the preparations for the funeral. We called for the ambulance and were stunned when the driver told us that the average waiting time for ambulance responses was twenty-four to thirty hours. By some benediction, we got one in half an hour. Shantanu went from one crematorium to another to look for one which had no Covid-19 cases arriving. Finally, we found one in Shivaji Park, which cremated bodies of those who had died of causes other than Covid-19, till noon. Body. The word struck me hard. This was Papa, my beloved father. Now, a body!

While we managed to find a crematorium to perform Papa's last rites, no pundit was willing or able to come to perform them. Anna guided us on what to do on the phone. When circumstances change, however trying they may be, it's best to accept the situation. As we followed Anna's instructions, the power of sentiment and intention over ritual dawned on me.

Ajay, Shantanu and I carried Papa in the ambulance. I was broken. Amidst uncontrollable sobs, I called as many of my aunts, uncles and family members on video call, so they could see him one last time. As I helped carry Papa lying peacefully on the stretcher, I thought of the innumerable times he must have carried me as a child. Love is a debt that one can never repay. In our family, women do not go to the crematorium or become pallbearers. I did both. There was no question of not accompanying Papa on his last journey.

The crematorium was empty and clean. Papa was the first 'case' of the day, the manager said. First, a 'body'. Now, Papa was a 'case'. A living-breathing flesh-and-blood human being metamorphoses into non-existence in a trice. Soon the electric facility was ready. We placed Papa on the chamber that would carry him into the blazing furnace. I could sense the white heat. How could Papa withstand it? I cried out aloud in agony, trying to pull Papa out. Ajay pulled me aside gently. I let go. In one swoosh, Papa was sucked inside the furnace.

Nothing—no knowledge, no words—prepares you for the death of a loved one. We know that all of us will die. It's inevitable, this truth. Yet, we live without its conscious awareness. Till our parents are alive, we feel that we are immortal. In fact, we assume that our parents will always be around, and that life will continue the way it is forever. No matter how old we may be, we feel young. Losing a parent shakes us up, upends the world as we know it. It rips apart the roof over our heads. It leaves one unanchored and uprooted from the very foundation of life as one knows it. After spending fifty-two years of her married life with him, Mummy would now have to find a way to live without him. How would she do it?

Papa—he was so contented, disciplined and dispassionate–moored me. On the day of his online prayer service, family and friends shared their unique memories of him. From a seven-year-old to a ninety-year-old, everyone had something special to say about him. He had touched the lives of many. Though he had merged with the Divine, his presence was palpable. It would be with us forever.

After ten days, when I spoke to Gurudev, I shared my anguish about not being able to complete the customary rituals due to the lockdown. Pat came his reply, 'He is with me, why are you worried about rituals?' It is believed that when you have a Guru, seven generations preceding you and seven generations succeeding you get liberated. It is rightly said, Guru *bina gati nahin* (you cannot traverse the ocean of *samsara* without a Guru).

Grief adds depth to life. It made me think hard. Questions besieged me. What is life about? How much time do I have left? What more can I do for others? How useful has my life been?

Most of us live on auto pilot. The day begins, and we go through the motions, consumed by activity and work. How do these days add up? We don't realise it, but every second makes up our life. Every single day matters. What else is life but a wonderful accumulation of these moments? Papa's passing away left an indelible impact, and heightened my awareness of this truth.

On Gurudev's birthday, May 13, my song 'Main Hoon', sung by Ashatai Bhosle was released. Everyone loved it. Even those who didn't understand Hindi were moved by the sentiment. '*Tumhare hone se hi, main hoon*,' I wrote. 'I am, only because you are.' This is the Ultimate Truth of every devotee. Gurudev had once said, 'The greatest fortune in this world is to be a disciple or a devotee.' I have been blessed with this good fortune in abundance. Papa used to love this song. He had forwarded its music video to all his friends. Unfortunately, he missed its actual launch by five days.

By the time this book goes into print, we would be almost a year into the Covid-19 pandemic in India. Except for the two days that I stepped out to go along with Papa on his final journey, I have been mostly confined to my home. For years, my life teemed with packing, unpacking, checking in, checking out, flight schedules and flight delays, arrivals and departures for almost two to three weeks a month. The pandemic forced me to take an extra-long breather. Though I was not filling or removing the contents of my suitcase, in this downtime, I was unpacking a lot.

'How are you managing?' everyone asked me. To be honest, quite well. Meditation twice a day with Gurudev kept us highly energised and rejuvenated. Along with my daily chanting of Guru Puja, I also started chanting my favourite Ganesha, Shiva and Devi chants. I made a ritual of calling up one friend or family member a day just to check on them. It felt wonderful. Old colleagues, current professional peers and industry leaders reached out to me to learn meditation. For the first time in years, I found time to admire the gorgeous sunsets and the stunning views of the Arabian Sea, from our thirty-second-floor apartment. All through, Gurudev interacted with thousands of people on a day-to-day basis, advising them on how to handle the challenges that the pandemic was creating for businesses, academics, youth, women, industry, sports and all aspects of life. Not one soul was left untouched.

Without doubt, the pandemic has reshaped the world forever. It has recalibrated the way we live, work and communicate. It has changed us physically, emotionally and mentally. While there were sporadic incidents of indifference and apathy, largely, the world seemed more accommodating and compassionate. Life mattered above everything else.

Knowledge and my *sadhana* have kept me upbeat and equipped me to reach out and help others. When everything external falls apart, it is our internal strength that bolsters us. For all things material are impermanent and finite; only our spirit, the infinite and eternal Self is permanent, unblemished and luminous. With Gurudev's presence in my life, I had begun this journey a long time ago. During the pandemic, it caught speed, and yet, slowed me down. Without moving an inch, it took me on a tour of truth and joy.

Eventually, things will return to normal. There are bound to be fallouts, good and bad. As we move ahead, the lessons we have learned should be our guiding light, and they are many.

Can we create a world that truly lives like a big global family? That is Gurudev's dream for humanity. A world where we respect our differences, celebrate our diversity and embrace coexistence—Vasudhaiva Kutumbakam. As it happens, there will be seasonal changes, and challenging weather. The waters will become turbulent from time to time. Yet, can wisdom, not war, anchor us at such times? When I look back, there have been unpleasant and unhappy moments too, times I have felt betrayed and let down. At times, I felt I did not get what I deserved. Instead of fretting over these, I choose to feel grateful for the good that came my way. I have been guided till now and I know I shall be guided further down the path of life.

In the appraisal of our life, we give ourselves too much importance. In the context of time and space we are but a dot of existence. And yet our life matters. It is a reminder to stay driven and inspired, and to contribute. I do have some tangible goals to achieve–make Sri Sri University the best in the world, make sure our schools become the best there are, help leaders unleash their true potential, pursue the cause of ethics, education and empowerment, and teach meditation and breathing techniques across the globe. I want to be open to the new opportunities that life brings my way. I want to give my hundred percent to what I do. That is the way to attract hundred percent Grace. I long to be one of the thousand hands of my Master that helps achieve his vision for the world. I wish for everyone to walk on the path of wisdom, and experience the bounty of joy, love and peace. For, 'A city without streets, a king without a treasury, a merchant without a business, a face without a nose, life without wisdom and a Guru is all considered the same.'

I hope to move from 'doing' to 'being'. Being a better human. Being better than the day before. Being light, and being the light.

Knowledge is embedded in our consciousness and as I grow older, I hope that more of it gets revealed to me. The more I dig, the more I realise how little I know. We live in our cocoons believing that what we perceive is all there is. It's a finite, limited view of the universe which is vast and unlimited, a space that holds more mysteries than we have been able to solve.

The sun rises and sets every day. An unseen force makes the flowers bloom, the stars light up the sky at night, and the breeze bring tidings from all over the world. It glues human beings together with love, prods them to rise above their differences, pushes them to break boundaries and discover their highest, purest self. Even in the most trying times, it makes one feel looked after, protected and cared for. It is that which we turn to when we are brought to our knees, or pushed against a wall or about to drown. What we forget is that this seemingly unknown power is always at hand for us to wield. It is ours for the asking. Once you connect to its frequency, there is no turning back. It has been my bankable truth.

It has charged me with deep gratitude, boundless joy and abundance. It has given me a second life: one more chance. I stand humbled. The Unknown Edge guides each one of us. All it needs is our willingness to transcend the known and open our eyes to it. Or better still, close our eyes and let go.

The Art of Living
&
The International Association for Human Values

Transforming Lives

The Founder

Gurudev Sri Sri Ravi Shankar

Gurudev Sri Sri Ravi Shankar is a universally revered spiritual and humanitarian leader. His vision of a violence-free, stress-free society through the reawakening of human values has inspired millions to broaden their spheres of responsibility and work towards the betterment of the world. Born in 1956 in southern India, Gurudev was often found deep in meditation as a child. At the age of four, he astonished his teachers by reciting the Bhagwad Gita, an ancient Sanskrit scripture. He has always had the unique gift of presenting the deepest truths in the simplest of words.

Gurudev established The Art of Living, an educational and humanitarian Non-Governmental Organisation that works in special consultative status with the Economic and Social Council (ECOSOC) of the United Nations in 1981. Present in over 156 countries, it formulates and implements lasting solutions to conflicts and issues faced by individuals, communities and nations. In 1997, he founded the International Association for Human Values (IAHV) to foster human values and lead sustainable development projects. Gurudev has reached out to more than 450 million people worldwide through personal interactions, public events, teachings, The Art of Living workshops and humanitarian initiatives. He has brought to the masses ancient practices which were traditionally kept exclusive, and has designed many self development techniques which can easily be integrated into daily life to calm the mind and instill confidence and enthusiasm. One of Gurudev's most unique offerings to the world is the Sudarshan Kriya, a powerful breathing technique that facilitates physical, mental, emotional and social well-being.

Numerous awards have been bestowed upon Gurudev Sri Sri Ravi Shankar which includes Padma Vibhushan (India's second highest civilian award) and the highest civilian awards from Paraguay, Mongolia and Colombia. Gurudev has addressed several international forums, including the United Nations Millennium World Peace Summit (2000), World Economic Forum (2001, 2003), World Summit On Ethics In Sports at FIFA Headquarters, Zurich (2014, 2016), UNESCO (2015), Parliaments of France, Britain, Norway (2016) and others.

Gurudev has played a key role in conflict resolution across the world including Colombia, Kashmir, Iraq, Ivory Coast, Naxal inhabited regions of India, and many other places.

Follow Gurudev on:

Twitter - @srisri

Facebook - www.facebook.com/gurudev

Website - www.srisriravishankar.org

YouTube - www.youtube.com/srisri

Instagram - www.instagram.com/srisriravishankar

LinkedIn - www.linkedin.com/in/srisriravishankar

The Art of Living

In Service Around The World

Founded in 1981 by Gurudev Sri Sri Ravi Shankar, The Art of Living is engaged in stress-elimination programs and service initiatives. The organization operates globally in 156 countries with one of the largest volunteer bases in the world and has touched the lives of over 450 million people.

The organisation works in special consultative status with the Economic and Social Council (ECOSOC) of the United Nations, participating in a variety of committees and activities related to health and conflict resolution.

In 1997, Gurudev Sri Sri Ravi Shankar also founded the International Association for Human Values (IAHV) to coordinate sustainable development projects, nurture human values and coordinate conflict resolution in association with The Art of Living. In India, Africa and South America, the two sister organizations' volunteers are spearheading sustainable growth in rural communities, and have already reached out to 40,212 villages.

The Art of Living movement has spread peace and transformation across communities through diverse humanitarian projects.

- Conflict Resolution
- Alleviating pain in War Zones
- Relieving trauma in Post Terror Attacks
- Disaster Relief
- Environment
- Education
- Empowerment of Women
- Prisoner Rehabilitation
- Rural Transformation

The Art of Living Programs

The Art of Living programs are guided by Gurudev Sri Sri Ravi Shankar's philosophy of peace: "Unless we have a stress-free mind and a violence-free society, we cannot achieve world peace." To help individuals get rid of stress and experience inner peace, The Art of Living offers stress-elimination programs which include breathing techniques, meditation and yoga. They cater to every age group - children, youth, adults and every section of society – rural communities, governments, corporate houses, etc. These programs have helped millions around the world to overcome stress, depression and violent tendencies. Emphasizing holistic living and personal self-development, the programs facilitate the complete blossoming of an individual's full potential. The cornerstone of all our workshops is the Sudarshan Kriya, a unique and potent breathing practice.

Introductory Programs:

- **The Happiness Program (Age 18+):** The 3-day program equips participants with practical knowledge and techniques to unlock their deepest potential and bring fullness to life.
- **Sahaj Samadhi Meditation (Age 18+):** Meditation technique that deeply relaxes the mind and rejuvenates the system.
- **Utkarsh Yoga (Age 8-13):** Introduce your children to spirituality, nurture human values, inculcate self-discipline, and develop their personality to be healthy and well-rounded.
- **Medha Yoga (Age 14-18):** Dynamic and innovative educational program for both high school and college students.
- **Prajñā Yoga (Age 5-18):**

  Helps children tap into the inherent intuitive abilities of the mind.

For more information please visit: www.artofliving.org

Sri Sri University

Envisioned by Sri Sri Ravi Shankar Ji, Sri Sri University was established in 2009 as a centre for world-class education in India. The University offers a range of pivotal, unique and cutting-edge undergraduate, postgraduate degree programmes, short-term, diploma and certificate courses, Doctoral studies (PhD), that seek to preserve the ancient wisdom of the East and offer the best of Western innovation.

For more information, please visit srisriuniversity.edu.in.

TLEX Institute

Starting with the individual, TLEX® offers participants a range of tools for greater personal calm and clarity, so they feel more connected to teams and the organisation, resulting in intrinsic motivation, creativity, and enthusiasm at work. We believe that when transformation stems from self mastery and authentic social connection, it allows leaders to more clearly observe risks, opportunities, and dynamics as they are. Imagination, intuition, and creativity arise naturally from a relaxed, calm, and clear state of mind.

For more information, please visit tlexinstitute.com.

World Forum for Ethics in Business

The World Forum for Ethics in Business (WFEB) is a registered public interest foundation based in Belgium. The mandate of the Forum includes all manners of pursuing and establishing the indispensable ethical foundations of business in a globalised world through building awareness, creating ethical leaders and changing the rule of the game by pushing for collective action for transparency. WFEB works towards a just society and inclusive growth. It aims to support and showcase organisations which are profitable yet focus on sustainability and values and create shared value.

For more information, please visit wfeb.org.

The Art of Living International Centres

INDIA
21st km, Kanakapura Road, Udayapura,
Bangalore - 560 082, Karnataka
Telephone: +91 - 80-67262626/27/28
Email: info@srisripublications.com

GERMANY
Bad Antogast 1, 77728 Oppenau,
Baden-Württemberg
Telephone: +49 - 7804-973-90
Email: info@artofliving.de

CANADA
13 Infinity Road, St. Mathieu du Parc,
Quebec G0X 1N0
Telephone: +1 - 819-532-3328
Email: artdevivre@artofliving.org

USA
639 Whispering Hills Rd,
Boone, NC 28607
Telephone: +1 - 828-263-4910
Email: info@artoflivingretreatcenter.org

www.srisriravishankar.org
www.artofliving.org
www.iahv.org